D.A.R.K PLANET

CHARLES W. SASSER

Gold Imprint
Medallion Press, Inc.
Florida, USA

Dedication:

For Donna Sue.

Published 2005 by Medallion Press, Inc.
225 Seabreeze Ave.
Palm Beach, FL 33480

The MEDALLION PRESS LOGO
is a registered tradmark of Medallion Press, Inc.

Printed in the United States of America

Library of Congress Cataloging-in-Publication Data

Sasser, Charles W.
 Dark planet / Charles W. Sasser.
    p. cm.
 ISBN 1-932815-13-9
 1. Life on other planets--Fiction. I. Title.
 PS3569.A76D37 2004
 813'.54--dc22

                        2004027451

D·A·R·K P·L·A·N·E·T

CHARLES W. SASSER

CHAPTER ONE

It was my first time operating with Humans. Not that I had anything, much, against Humans. I was half-Human myself, a misfortune of birth I might have disavowed were it not for certain unmistakable physical characteristics which identified me with that contentious tribe. The simple fact was that I had been assigned to DRT-213 — a Deep Reconnaissance Team. I accompanied only because the Humans required my special talents as a Sen to follow the Blobs' telepathic spoor in the galaxy, to sniff them out like a trained sensor before they built up sufficient forces to launch their campaigns of destruction and death. While Humans were starting to make strides in extrasensory perception, telepathy, and all the other mind-bending and mind-stretching disciplines, no Human was as accomplished at it as we Zentadon who possessed the Talent.

Humans placed most of their faith in technology, as the Indowy once had before their fall. They replaced their God with it. They ventured into space to see and what they saw instead of the face of God was merely a larger and grander mechanical molecule. I sometimes pondered how my own genes were influenced by the presence of Human DNA.

It was a sobering thought.

The insertion began with the Stealth undocking from the mother ship and being whipped around Aldenia's two moons, using their weak gravity to place it — and us — into an elliptical orbit around the Dark Planet. The craft depended upon the accuracy of the mother ship's computer calculations until orbit was established. Space flight had long ago relegated most vital matters to computers and artificial intelligence.

The Stealth automatically hard-braked beyond the two moons and slung back toward the planet's far side, decelerating by about sixty gravities. Deceleration forces were offset by the crew's snugging ourselves into the form-fitting couches with their padding and pressure controls. As G-forces rapidly bled off and the Stealth settled into orbit, all external electronic systems shut down and the crew resumed control of the ship to some limited extent. Hopefully, if the Blobs were scanning, they would mistake us for merely another piece of space debris.

"Locking in for final maneuvers and microgravity," Captain Amalfi said through the craft's intercom.

"Piece of cake," Atlas said.

"Another old, old Earth expression?" I asked Gun Maid. She laughed, but the men ignored me.

We dismounted the time-couches and assumed our stations. The control bridge was crowded and busy for awhile in the pale red panel lights of gauges and dials and the blue glow of computer screens running systems checks. Communications among the crew of eight — seven Humans and one Zentadon — were minimal and had to do with technical adjustments and duties. Air whispered through ducts. The hull vibrated reassuringly through our feet. We felt the comforting thrust of the powerful wind engines.

Real-time graphics on the view screen were excellent in wraparound techno-vision. We seemed to be watching from a detached third point of view because of a system of refractory camera angles that revealed the Stealth, us, in orbit around the planet. Everyone gathered for a first hushed look at Aldenia.

I had seen Earth once from a similar perspective. I had not landed, but I saw it and marveled. Even after all the wars Humans engaged in among themselves, all but destroying their own sources of life, the planet remained a translucent blue-and-silver-and-green pearl, more beautiful than anyone could imagine.

There was little about this planet, however, that might be called beautiful. I experienced an indefinite sense of foreboding. Surely its sinister appearance had more to do with my people's collective remembrance of it in the time of the Indowy ascendance than to any inherent quality it possessed.

The sun star Ceti, around which the Tau Ceti Cluster revolved, and the bright sun star of an adjoining cluster, worked at cross angles to provide almost constant light shining on Aldenia. There were two separate nights within a day's cycle, one lasting about two hours and the other four. Even with almost continuous illumination, however, little sunlight penetrated the dark condensation of clouds that crusted the planet. Lightning storms snapped and glowed at various points, like painful inflamed boils about to burst. Noah in the Human Earth Bible built an ark to float out forty days and nights of rainfall. On Aldenia, forty days of rain was a mere sprinkle. Rain fell virtually all the time, cycled by a system that wasn't quite understood. Water covered two thirds of the globe. Where water could be seen through the clouds, it was black, and the land masses were even darker. It made an ideal setting for the VRs young Human prolies savored.

I shuddered looking at it on the view screen. My ears twitched. Two separate DRTs had previously attempted to recon the planet. None of the members had returned. Blobs were blamed for their disappearances. DRT-213's sniper, Sergeant Darman "Blade" Kilmer, was the only known recent explorer to survive Aldenia. That was before the Blobs were spotted here and before the disappearing DRTs, when

Blade had been a low-ranking member of an explorer mapping team. He was the sole survivor.

"The rain will drive you mad," he explained. "If that's not bad enough, lightning bolts fill the air with enough electricity to power Galaxia for a century. Bolts strike trees constantly and will make a crispy critter out of you when they can. Everything has teeth or thorns or both. The fauna has switched places, so that bugs are the size of land rovers and houses, and mammals are no bigger than mice and shrews. Lord knows what other monsters might inhabit that dreadful place. Fu-uck. Higher-higher might as well take us out and shoot us now and save us all the misery of dying there."

"You were the only survivor of a mission," Captain Amalfi pointed out. "Why don't you apply for hardship transfer and stay behind?"

"Fu-uck," Blade scorned. "I have my reasons."

The planet's hostile appearance, sinister ambience and foreboding reputation were all reasons why it had remained uncolonized except for a brief period during the taa camps of nearly eight centuries previous. Although the Indowy managed to exist here long enough to build their great slave camps, laboratories, and war factories, its discoverer and explorer, the Indowy Xctplm, nonetheless called it a parasite on the galaxy, a malignant place where, if evil had a source, evil must dwell.

C·H·A·P·T·E·R
TWO

All races, all species, are possessed of a certain amount of selfishness and self-interest. Certainly that was as true of we Zentadon as of the Indowy, the Terrans, the Kutarans, the Tslek or the Humans. So far as we knew, among all the fantastic forms of life that occupied the universe — two heads and six eyes; eight legs and antenna; blobbish chunks; shadow forms; intelligent insects and civilized amphibians — we Zentadon and the Humans were the most genetically alike, notwithstanding that most Zentadon had tails and Humans didn't. Origins of both peoples could be traced back through DNA to a common pair of ancestors the Humans looked upon as their Alphas, whom the spiritual called Adam and Eve. It was more than probable, however, that Adam and Eve came to Earth from space and had tails. Humans were undoubtedly a genetic offshoot of Zentadon, not the other way around. The universe, as the Humans liked to say, turned out not only to be stranger than they imagined, it was stranger than they *could* imagine.

They had been sailing the vast, dark seas of space for only a millennium. Less, actually. Humans were of a contentious and warlike nature. They fought over race, ethnicity, religion, sex, land, and simple greed. They would likely still have been swarming over the crust of their home planet, further defiling it and fighting among themselves, had not the nuclear-proton Earth wars of the twenty-second century Earth-time made the planet such an unpleasant and polluted place that it drove them to seek new unspoiled worlds. Among the Humans were those who truly believed extraterrestrials, if we existed out here, were above all Human vices.

It turned out their God had a dark and ironic sense of humor. The universe was full of beings of a contentious and warlike nature, who fought over race, ethnicity, religion, sex, land, simple greed, and specieism. In fact, Earthlings had to play a lot of catch up. They proved to be quick understudies. After barely three hundred years of subjugation by the Indowy and we Zentadon, they revolted and ultimately controlled space. At least this part of the galaxy in the Tau Ceti Cluster neighboring their own Earth Cluster.

The Tslek, or the Blobs, as the Humans called them for obvious reasons of appearance, were the most threatening invaders to penetrate the system since the victorious Humans established the Galaxia Republic to govern the Tau Ceti Cluster. If the Humans were to the Zentadon the most genetically similar form of life, then the intruders were the most dissimilar.

Rumors about the strangers nosing in through the Posleen Blight had been circulating for nearly a half-century, but it was not until the nomadic Tchpt discovered the recent remains of a ship crashed on a barren Magya satellite that their presence was confirmed. The ship contained dried, featureless "puddles" of what was unquestionably a form of intelligent life. The Tchpt called the dead trespassers Tslek; humans called them Blobs.

Blob aggression intensified into open hostilities. Galaxia survey and commercial ships flying the edges of the Blight began vanishing. Blob kinetic strikes obliterated entire colonies, Human and otherwise, on planets out toward the Tau Ceti tail. Blob fleets probed the perimeter of the galaxy, sniffing around for prey and advantage. After a Republic Battlestar ship survived an ambush by a squadron of gigantic meteor-like craft, President Carl Oboma dispatched a Galaxia combat fleet from IV Corps Sector Command to engage the invaders. Although the fleet defeated the Tslek in a major month-long battle, it had not been a victory without significant losses.

Since then, the "war" had ebbed into a cat-and-mouse game of probe and counter- probe, with frantic frontier colonists suffering most in the fledgling conflict. Ready Reserves were activated and thrown into up-training mode. DRT scouting teams were dispatched into enemy space to dig for every scrap of intelligence they could find on what kind of beings these Blobs were, what their ultimate intentions were, and what strategic, tactical, and technical capabilities they possessed. Several DRTs had already turned up "missing, presumed lost."

President Oboma declared a galaxy emergency and placed the support superstructure on the capital planet of Galaxia on a war footing. Manufacturing of battle material — "beans and bullets," as the Humans quaintly put it — went into overdrive thirty-two hours a day. The threat of invasion generated a renewed interest in the superior Indowy war technology which the Indowy had destroyed after their civilization imploded and the survivors turned pacifists. Shifts of scientists labored continuously in hopes of unraveling Indowy secrets of antimatter, molecular displacement, and time-mass travel. Enterprising entrepreneurs could literally earn millions of credits and become unbelievably wealthy by successfully mining Indowy arms and battle technology.

It was amidst this feverish atmosphere of War! War! War! that Commander Mott chopped me from my instructor position at the 4156th Interstellar School to assign me to DRT-213. The reason I was selected, as it turned out, was because I was the only Sen available on short notice, and because I was half-Human and therefore could be at least half-trusted.

"Kadar San," he said, "the Humans say that when you have only seven — now eight, counting you — on a DRT team, you get close working asshole-to-belly button for months at a time out there, way out there where their God does not go without per diem."

"Zentadon do not get that close to Humans," I said.

As a minority of one with seven Humans, I faced the prospect of a long and perilous mission with beings who distrusted me, and whom I distrusted, from centuries past. We harbored suspicions of each other that were almost as much a part of our genetic makeup as the coloring of our hair and eyes and, well, the length and fullness of our tails, for those of us who still possessed them.

Trust between Humans and Zentadon was certainly not enhanced by the Zentadon Homeland Movement, a rapidly growing organization of separatists agitating for the dissolution of Human hegemony over the Zentadon home planet of Ganesh. Cells of young Homelanders conducted underground war against the Human power structure. While I sympathized with the goals of the Homelanders to some extent, mine was a voice against their methods. For the first time since the Indowy days of infamy, Zentadon were utilizing taa against Humans. Taa used in this manner usually meant suicide missions.

Commander Mott regarded me with his enormous

cat-pupiled eyes. Zentadon had two basic eye colors; purple or green. His were purple. Mine were emerald green. Commander Mott was among our most sensitive Sens; he actually read thoughts and communicated via the mind alone with others of equal achievement in the science. I envied him. Like most rank-and-filers, I sensed emotion, sentiment, passion in other beings, especially if such feelings were strongly represented, but rarely could I catch and hold onto another's well-formed thoughts.

I suspected the part of me that was Human limited my abilities. I assumed Commander Mott suspected the same thing about me. He sat behind his great gnarlwood desk and studied me with his penetrating purple eyes. He stroked the thick fur of his tail resting across the creased tan uniform of his lap. He had injured the tail in his youth while under the influence of taa, it was said, so that it now hung lifeless from the opening in his trousers. It was a habit of his to pull it out of his way when he sat down, lay it across his lap, and absently stroke it.

"The Tslek penetrations have provided a sterling opportunity to prove that we can work together in a mutual purpose," he said. "The Zentadon, the Humans, and . . ."

He hesitated. You didn't have to be a Sen to finish the thought.

"And we who are both and are neither?" I said.

Although it was against the law of both peoples to cross-mate, I was proof that some Zentadon would screw anything when the breeding heat came upon them.

"You are of both worlds, Sergeant Kadar San," agreed Commander Mott. "That is why you and others like you, rare that you are, have been selected to work with the Humans in their first major joint effort between our peoples. As you are half-Human — your mother was Human, I understand —?"

"She died when I was born. From the shock of seeing me, I suspect."

I was a Zentadon of a different sort, as Commander Mott was pointing out. While some of the younger Zentadon had their tails surgically removed in order to suck up to Humans, because Humans believed tails were remnants of beast ancestry, I had never had one. I was born with a mere tiny button at the end of my spine.

My teeth were also less sharp, less predatory than full-bloods. I had the Zentadon hair, however, just much less of it. Zentadon hair came in either black, silver, or gold. Commander Mott's was silver — not gray, *silver* — and flowed thick back off an intelligent forehead and down his neck and spine underneath his Republic uniform to reappear with his invalided tail. I naturally preferred gold, as my own hair was of that hue. I possessed relatively little of it on my body, certainly no more than the average human prolie stevedore working the space docks.

It was said that in first encounters between Humans and Zentadon, some of the Humans slew Zentadon for our fine and woven hair because they thought it really *was* gold.

"I see," Commander Mott resumed, then finished his previous thought. "Being half-Human, you are anticipated to have a better genetic understanding of them. It is to our mutual benefit that we cooperate against the Tslek. For, if the Tslek prevail, they will ultimately destroy all within the galaxy."

"I am being sent out to save the galaxy!"

"No, Kadar San. You are being dispatched to do your job as a Zentadon Sen."

C·H·A·P·T·E·R
THREE

In DRT-213's team room, music throbbed contrapuntal and over scored, synthesized, jagged, and loud the way it was in the VR clubs off-post. Life-sized holographic cartoons populated the room like squads of ghosts, producing a dark military humor involving smashed hovercraft, bent rocket howitzers, crushed bots with mechanical, near-life-like heads, and other battle-damaged robots that resembled rusted hydrogen cans still used in the smoky high-rise prolie tenements occupied by the lower levels of human and Zentadon society. One of two Human holos in a VR bar filled with every form of fantastic life to occupy the edges of the Posleen Blight was saying to another, "Have you ever seen so many foreigners in your life?"

Captain Shinkichi Amalfi, team commander, entered the room with me close on his heels like a loyal pet grafette and clapped away the music and holograms, leaving only a translucent gray light emanating in soothing tones from sources in walls, floor, and ceiling. The mission warning order had already been issued, accounting for the tension I felt among the assembled team members, but the hostility and resentment could only derive from my addition to the operation.

"They issuing elves now, sir?" growled a stocky man whose eyes in his fair skin were black like twin holes in space.

We Zentadon, especially one half-Human like myself, did in fact bear resemblance to the mythical fairies and elves of Earth lore. It amused me sometimes to think that Zentadon visiting Earth may even have been the source of that Human whimsy.

There was some muffled laughter, which seemed to please the stocky man. The team had apparently spent much of the day at the rifle range, firing Gravs. The M-91 Grav, the Galaxia Republic's main battle rifle, was a real bitch to clean. Due to its incredible muzzle velocity, 30,000 kilometers per second, carbon and uranium sublimed and coated the breach and bore with a substance so hard to remove that it was like chipping off glazed nickel. While the Humans had stolen enough Indowy technology to construct certain weapons systems such as chameleon-camouflage combat uniforms, protection force fields, ordnance, and energy transference, they lacked facilities and know-how to perfect them. As a result, munitions and other sophisticated items gummed up barrels, overrode each other, or failed at inopportune moments. The present Indowy were no help in correcting problems, as they no longer practiced war and depended upon their former serfs, both Human and Zentadon, to protect their limited sovereignty in the Tau Ceti Cluster.

The stocky man must be the team's sniper; he cleaned an M-235 Gauss while the others worked with Gravs. He had the eyes of a sniper and handled his weapon in a sensuous way that suggested sufficient arousement to breed with it at any time. He was not a tall man compared to the others, but he was solid and muscular from body enhancements. He stared in an unblinking, indecipherable way that was like the stab of a dagger's blade, which, I assumed, accounted for why he was called "Blade." Sergeant Darman Kilmer was undoubtedly a dangerous Human to have as an enemy, and perhaps even as a friend.

"Sir," he sneered, "couldn't you have at least got an elf with a tail?"

"At ease, DRT-bags."

Captain Amalfi was tall, but then all Humans, or at least most of them, were tall compared to Zentadon. He was gaunt, a Nordic greyhound that appeared built for speed and stamina. A victim of that easy familiarity among Humans that bred nicknames and malapropisms, he was known as "Captain Bell Toll." As from the Human literary phrase, "Never ask for whom the bell tolls, it tolls for thee." "It tolls for thee," he would say whenever he had to pick one of his soldiers for a particularly unpleasant detail. Unlike the others, however, all of whom had nicknames, never was he referred to as "Bell Toll" to his face.

"This man . . ." Captain Amalfi began.

"Man?"

Blade the sniper made it difficult to ignore him. If I were Human, if I were more Human, my pointed ears would not twitch and give me away as they did whenever I was nervous or excited, uncertain or uncomfortable, or even sexually whetted during the annual Zentadon breeding season. The Captain fixed Blade with a level gaze. Blade shrugged, opened the breech of his Gauss and sneered into the bore.

"This man is Sergeant Kadar San," Captain Amalfi continued. "He has been assigned as Sen to DRT-213 for the duration of the Mission. As a member of the team, he will be treated as such."

I wore the Sen badge on the chest of my new Republic khakis. Our Zentadon's cat's eyes made Humans anxious, especially if we were Sens and they thought we were reading their minds. It was to my advantage to let them think I could do exactly that.

Tentatively, I mind-tested the mood in the room, reaching out for a collective sampling first and then testing individuals one at a time. Reaction to my presence ranged from mild suspicion on the part of the female to almost a blow in the face from the hulking sniper.

"Clear, DRT-bags?" Captain Amalfi barked.

"Do you trust him?" asked a wiry soldier with short-cropped black hair, a dark olive complexion, and a face like the rusted edge of a hatchet.

"He's a Sen, Ferret."

"That's not what I asked, sir," Ferret said. "I was thinking about the Homelanders."

Sergeant Taraneh Ferreira, called Ferret, the team's scout and point man, seemed as small and quick and inquisitive as the Earth creature from which he acquired his name. I was to learn that implanted battlefield sensors made him supersensitive. He could smell game from a hundred meters away and feel with the soles of his bare feet the heat from the tracks of whatever entity passed ahead of him.

"The only DRT to make it back from any Blob recon mission had a Sen along," Captain Amalfi pointed out.

Humans were a superstitious lot.

"What about this . . . this drug?" asked a fit-looking Viking-type with cropped yellow hair. Staff Sergeant Florian Ronnland, "Atlas," a designated hitter, a grunt in the crude military parlance of the Humans, glanced at me, then glanced away. He sat so near the female that I assumed they must be a breeding pair.

Captain Amalfi looked to me to answer the question. Humans who had had little association with Zentadon always asked about taa. Zentadon with the same ignorance of Humans inquired about how it was that Humans could have sex all the time.

"The drug, as you refer to it," I replied, my left ear twitching, "is called taa. Strictly speaking, it is not a drug at all. It is a hormone manufactured involuntarily, or voluntarily within our bodies during stress."

"You aren't stressed out now, are you?" Atlas asked, and they all laughed again.

"The Zentadon are dangerous when you do this . . . this taa thing, aren't you?" Ferret accused. "Two Zentadon Homelanders on drugs blew up themselves and a munitions plant two weeks ago."

The Captain had obviously considered the same question. I felt his misgivings.

"Taa is similar to adrenalin manufactured by your own endocrine system," I explained. "Adrenalin is your Human reaction to stress."

"Yes," Ferret admitted, "but when I have an adrenalin attack, I can't leap over tall buildings, run faster than a speeding bullet, and get stronger than a Battlestar. And I don't eat raw flesh."

My ears twitched harder.

"Such stories come from centuries ago when the Indowy developed a technology to turn taa in our bodies on and off against our will," I said, "and to induce us to use it for their will."

"Against us," put in a giant fully six-eight in stature

and so black his skin shone over huge muscular implants in his bare arms. Staff Sergeant Grgur Parkpoon, "Gorilla," was the team's technical support and Intel specialist. Beneath that shaved bowling-ball head and mass of muscle, I sensed a being normally quiet and introspective with a keen intelligence.

"What's to prevent it happening again — You Zentadon coming under someone else's control?" Gorilla asked. "Such as, for example, the Homelanders?"

"Nothing more than what prevents you Humans from coming under another's control," I said, attempting to project patience. "The Indowy technology that used taa against us was just as capable of using your adrenalin to control you — on a much less destructive scale, of course. We shall never permit that kind of domination over us again."

The sniper snorted contemptuously. "Fu-uck."

The vulgarity, the way he used it in two syllables, made it sound twice as obscene.

"That's all in the past," Captain Amalfi interrupted, to my gratitude. "The Indowy are today the most peaceful species in the Tau Ceti Galaxy . . ."

"Pusses," Blade muttered.

"And the Zentadon are our . . . allies."

I knew from the hesitation and the uncertainty of his emotional pattern that he started to say "trusted allies," but couldn't quite bring it off.

"They're incorporated into the Federation Army of The Republic of Galaxia," he concluded. "We need their skills against the Blobs."

"So, this elf is our token," quipped the Viking with a grin that blunted the sharpness of his observation.

"I am your token," I admitted.

The female sitting on the couch next to Atlas, the pieces of a dismantled Grav across her lap, studied me out of large blue eyes in a pleasant brown face. Her thick mop of thatched black hair rippled and sprang back into place whenever she passed her hand through it. Sergeant Pia Gunduli, "Gun Maid," was DRT-213's communications specialist. I marveled that Humans sent their females into combat. Good breeders must be protected and maintained. Commander Mott said any civilization that used its females in such a manner was not worth defending.

"You speak excellent English, Kadar San," Gun Maid observed, sounding my name in a way I liked.

"The Human tongue you call English is currently the diplomatic and commercial language in this galaxy and Earth's," I said lamely. I did, in fact, speak it well, with only a little clip at the beginning of some words and an occasional hanging diphthong because of my sharper Zentadon teeth.

"And he's such a cute elf." She laughed, and that made the others laugh with her.

All except the sniper.

"Good," Captain Amalfi said. "We receive the Ops

Order at 0900 tomorrow. We could be gone up to six months this time."

"Or longer," Gorilla added darkly.

"By the time we get back, Ferret," Atlas gibed, "that little prolie slut of yours will be bedding down with the home guard.'"

"She already is," Gorilla said.

Sometimes I envied the Humans their easy bantering.

"Sergeant Shiva," Captain Amalfi said, "make sure our Sen is issued his team gear." He turned to the others. "Whatever personal affairs you have, take care of them today and tonight. Isolation lockdown begins at 0500. OPSEC, operational security, is in effect. The bell tolls for thee."

Master Sergeant Chital "Shiva" Huang was the final member of the team and its NCOIC, second in command to Captain Bell Toll. Next to Gorilla, he was the biggest and meanest-looking human being I had ever encountered. He was easily six-and-a-half feet tall, a grizzled old bird of the Human Polynesian wrestler race, with a long jagged scar torn down the right side of his face, and nails rather than whiskers growing out of his cheeks. He didn't shave his whiskers; he chiseled them. There was no exaggeration in the phrase "one tough hard-core old sonofabitch" when it was applied to him.

"Come with me, fresh meat," Sergeant Shiva rumbled.

Blade's cycling the bolt of his Gauss stopped us. I felt the sniper hard and cold inside my head. I turned to find him aiming his rifle directly at me.

"There's no problem while we're out there as long as the tailless elf does his job," he said. "But if he fucks up, he becomes my problem."

C·H·A·P·T·E·R
FOUR

Officers and senior NCOs of the Federation Army of The Republic were allowed to live off-post if they desired. Zentadon were excluded from the ranks of commissioned officers, but I was a senior NCO and I desired a cubicle of my own in the city rather than the regimented and sterile environment of living in barracks. After my unsettling introduction to the DRT-bags, appropriately so-called, I thought, I needed a drink before I went home to get my affairs in order prior to the beginning of isolation. Cocktails were something Human to which I had become accustomed. They were delicious and cold, mildly intoxicating and wonderful.

I caught a hovercraft outside the post gates and had the bot controller drop me off at the Starside, a watering hole for upwardly-mobile young professional non-Humans like myself who had acquired certain Human tastes. I took a false tail of golden hair out of my briefcase and attached it to my uniform trousers so that it looked like I possessed the Zentadon's total number of appendages. Never mind that it lacked prehensile abilities and I couldn't use it to cop a feel up a female's kilt if the breeding season suddenly began. Like Commander Mott, I claimed it had been crushed — an old war wound — and therefore dragged out my tracks when I walked. There were some places you didn't go if you were Human, half-Human, or overly associated with Humans.

A warty Kutaran breeding pair of indistinguishable sexual characteristics occupied a dark booth at this early hour and a convention of four-armed Zutu merchants in on a flight from the planet Nesshoue were whooping it up with squeals and shrieks under the colored lights. It was cool and relatively clean inside the lounge, especially when compared to the hot dry winds that blew down the streets of the Capital, rattling discarded food containers and whipping other trash about like missiles. My eyes still burned from the smog. The barkeep, a Zentadon, stirred up a potato gin cocktail and, after a contemptuous glance at my wilted member hanging off the back of the stool, delivered the drink with his own adroit appurtenance. He grinned his full-blood Zentadon sharp-toothed grin.

Show off.

I was half through the cocktail and already feeling

somewhat assuaged toward my unasked-for and unwanted assignment with the Humans of DRT-213 when Mina Li popped through the door. She gave my fake tail a look but kept any untoward comments to herself. Like me, she was golden-haired. Her hair was finely-woven and hung in a snatch down her back. Females had much less hair on their bodies than males. Her face was full with full lips and full green eyes. The end of her tail darted suggestively to her left shoulder and reached out to caress my cheek as she occupied the stool next to me. She assumed I would be available to her when breeding season arrived and urges started roaring.

I assumed nothing.

"I buzzed your locater," she chirped brightly. "It told me you were here."

"Lucky me," I grumped.

"Are you not happy to see me, Kadar? The time is almost near."

"Time?"

She batted her long lashes and gave me a coy smile.

"Oh." I snapped my fingers. "*That* time."

"I have our conjoining bed already prepared. There is a lock on the door that will not open again for nine days once we are inside. The pantry is stocked. I have your cocktail materials ready. Are you ready, Kadar?"

"That is me — Ready Freddy."

"Ready Freddy? Is that a term you borrow from the

Humans with whom you associate?"

"I do not associate with Humans."

"You are in their military."

"It is our military as well as theirs."

"Then why are you not an officer? Answer me that."

"I do not want to quarrel with you, Mina Li."

"Yes. Politics is not for lovers. Politics will work themselves out."

She ordered a Coca Cola from the barkeep. "Coke says it best," she said.

Humans didn't need weapons to conquer the universe. Not when they had Coca Cola, Wrangler jeans, Chevrolet hovercraft and Ford Fanger Sky Rovers. *Coke Says It Best.* The slogan was emblazoned on the cloud cover so that when the smog cleared out and you looked up, that was what you saw. *Coke Says It Best.*

What did it say best?

"You are ear-flicking," Mina Li noticed. "You are excited about our conjoining?"

"Excited."

She looked disappointed, sipping on her Coke. Her tail waved above her head, then caressed the back of my neck in a sensuous manner.

"I have an appointment next week to remove my tail," she blurted out.

"Why would you do that?"

"So you will not be ashamed of me. I will look very

good in tight jeans."

"Mina Li, I am not ashamed of you. It is just that . . ."

"Just what?"

I didn't understand what it was just.

"Just that you are more Human than Zentadon," she accused. "I have seen you look at the Human females with their tight little no-tail asses and their round no-ears that they have to move with their fingers."

Here we went again. I tuned her out. All I wanted was a bracing cocktail and a good mope before I had to prepare for the mission.

"I will conjoin with Mishal," she threatened finally. "Would you like that?"

"That would be fine."

"You would let me?"

"How could I stop you if that is what you want?"

"Mishal has a tail and he is proud of it," she scolded. "He is very brave."

"He is a terrorist and will likely die before breeding season."

"He is a Homelander patriot," she flared. "He has learned to use taa so that it will not destroy him."

She turned her back to me and sulkily sipped on her Coca Cola. The tip of her tail lashed reprovingly against the back of my head.

"He has dedicated tonight's mission in my honor," she added, intending to make me jealous. "He would be exclusive with me if I say yes."

I snatched her tail away from my head and held it. "What mission are you talking about?"

"It is none of your affair, Kadar. You have turned your back on your people. When the dreadnought explodes at its docking . . ."

She caught herself, realizing in the middle of the sentence that she had said too much. Mina Lee was never the brightest coin in the fountain. The USS *Admiral Tsutsumi* had arrived earlier in the day. Although not yet official, it was assumed in SpecOps that it arrived in order to transport a DRT to a reconnaissance of a potential or actual Blob base site. DRT-213 was the next intended activation unit.

I looped Mina Li's tail around in front of her and gave it a yank to spin her face to my face. I gripped her shoulders.

"Mina Li, you are going to tell me about this mission. Understand?"

C·H·A·P·T·E·R
FIVE

The Zentadon Homeland Movement enjoyed at least the passive support of many Zentadon both on our home planet of Ganesh, now garrisoned by the Humans instead of the Indowy who once occupied us, and here on Galaxia where we flourished as a considerable minority settlement. I thought of going to Commander Mott with the intelligence garnered from my would-be lover, for whom I had little special ardor — I simply found her unappealing as a mate, even a temporary one — but quickly dismissed that idea. Commander Mott would have no other recourse except to take action, which placed me in the unenviable, even dangerous, position of being fingered as an informant. If Mina Li couldn't keep her mouth shut to me, what made me think she could keep it shut to others? As a half-breed, I was only nominally accepted by the Zentadon to begin with.

Besides, the Homelanders had no way of getting past security to sabotage the *Tsutsumi*. Unless . . .

I decided to have another cocktail. I liked "Happy Hour," which is what the Humans called this time of day. While my drink was being mixed and presented to me by the smartass barkeep and his tail, another party of Kutaran joined the mating couple and a stag Ztura stuck his square yellow head inside while the rest of him remained outside on the end of a slender two-meter-long neck. The Market District of the Galaxia Capital, which was all the city was every called, was a port district where anything or anybody could show up and be accorded only a passing glance.

"Kadar, you will not tell Mishal I informed . . ."

"I will not if you will not. Now hush and let me think."

I went back to *unless*. The Homelanders couldn't get past security *unless*, and I had to consider this, unless the Homelanders had a plant, a contact, a sleeper inside military security to provide them with the codes to bypass the various electronic and robotic defenses that shielded the military space port.

I took a sip of my drink, then sat up straight as though jolted by the potency of the alcohol. My ears flicked.

Rumors about a Blob threat had circulated for so long that official statements were now often looked upon as so much government propaganda to keep the populace of restless Zentadon, and even more restless Human prolies pacified and controllable. Menace outside the gates and all that.

Homelanders were not concerned with Blobs. Crazies like Mishal were so myopic, so intent on the one issue of Zentadon autonomy that they failed to see the Big Picture, as Human army officers were fond of saying. The Big Picture was, the Blobs would kick our Zentadon tail-dragging butts without the support of the Galaxia Republic military. If the Blobs made serious incursions into the Tau Ceti Cluster, Ganesh would be one of the first worlds to fall under the on-slaught. Most Zentadon, like our former Indowy masters of today, were no longer warriors. Zentadon were incapable of killing other sentients without committing suicide in the process. You couldn't fight a war if you died in the same numbers as your enemy — and there were far fewer of you to begin with.

But Zentadon could make war against objects. Blow up and destroy things. I had to assume, therefore, that Homelanders possessed the intel, the planning, and the contacts to blow up the targeted dreadnought. What dis-turbed me was the realization that if they sabotaged the *Tsutsumi*, higher-higher in the Galaxia military would sus-pect another Zentadon as the insider informant. Current-ly, I was the only Zentadon working on a pending mission, one that involved use of the *Tsutsumi*. Who could be a more likely suspect?

I had to put a stop to the action, tonight, and I couldn't go to higher authority for help without presenting myself as a future Homelander target.

My ears were going involuntarily crazy. I was no hero. I was merely a Sen, and not an exceptionally good one at that. I looked at my fresh cocktail, then downed courage in a single gulp.

"Mina Li, go to my cubicle," I ordered.

She brightened. "You want me to prepare it instead of my place for our future conjoining?"

"Mina Li, conjoin yourself. I want you to wait there until I tell you to leave. I will order my SecLocks to provide you entry. You should not be hanging around these old bars and taverns anyhow."

"Oh, oh!" she swooned. "You wish to protect me!"

"Go!"

I saw her off in a hovercraft. I had no idea of how to stop Mishal and his saboteurs from carrying out their midnight mission, but I had about six hours to find them and make the attempt. Thanks to Mina Li, I knew the location of what they called their "safe house." She thought that was where they intended assembling for the start of tonight's deed. Mishal was a fool in confiding plans to a female like Mina Li in an attempt to impress her. Mina Li and Mishal probably deserved each other.

Zentadon in our natural state were heavy-grav plains walkers. I shed the phony tail and started walking rapidly toward the address, 76471 GPT, and very soon left the Market District to traverse the Human prolie slums in a shortcut to the Zentadon slums. I always found it disconcerting how peoples congregated into hives when they had plenty of otherwise open spaces to live in.

Galaxia was a small planet compared to the one the Humans called Earth; in barely a score or so of their generations, Humans had spread out over the entire dry crust of Galaxia and built their colonies like mold or lichen over the oceans of underground water that permitted animal husbandry and the growth of plant foods. What they created after the Great Revolution that freed them from Indowy subjugation, the way I understood it, were replicas of Earth's social structures. They came among the stars with high ideals of building a New Society and a New Man; they couldn't even build a New Dog, packs of which roamed the nighttime streets. The New Society, I assumed, was much like the old.

Socially, the Humans comprised three layers, four if you counted the military. On the top were the small groupings of professionals, the wealthy, the elites. Leaders, politicians, industrialists, traders, educators, planners. Movers and shakers. That was how the state-controlled media described them. Indeed, they moved things and shook things and got things done. They were in control.

If the uppers were the movers and shakers, the heads and brains, the middle layers might be called sweaters and toilers. They were the hands and muscles that kept the machinery organized, regimented, oiled and working.

At the bottom of the heap were the prolies. Assholes

and mouths who mostly consumed and contributed little other than fodder for wars and menial labor to sweep streets and empty garbage, neither of which they did very well judging from the seedy and rundown appearance of much of the city. The media constantly agonized over the "poor among us, God assures they will always be among us," and over the high crime rate. Being poor, slothful, dirty, and stealing from your neighbor apparently constituted "Human nature."

I shuddered at the thought that I must be afflicted with at least some Human nature.

I stopped at an automatic vendor and selected a sports cap two sizes too large and punched in ten credits for it. I pulled it down over my head to hide the golden glint of my hair and my pointed ears. Without a tail, in the dark, and out of uniform, I might hopefully pass for a Human prolie long enough to pass through the territory. I stayed out of the light and kept my head lowered. A gang of ratty-looking prolies strung out on artificial black market taa gave me the evil eye as I passed a sports stadium where muscle-enhanced prize fighters were holding an Ultimate Championship to their deaths. I looked small enough to be a mugging victim. Fortunately, about that time some Humans came out a side door carrying the body of a dead gladiator. That attracted the prolies' attention away from me. A squadron of Security hovercraft with emergency lights blinking flew overhead on its way to a mini-riot or a mass murder.

Humans!

Zentadon had mostly been assimilated into the upper middle classes following our own liberation from the Indowy taa camps. We owed the Humans that. We were the sweaters and toilers, the administrators and supervisors in civilian life, the sergeants and NCOs in the military. Very few of us were commissioned officers. No movers and shakers, because the Humans didn't trust us to move and shake. Most Zentadon were satisfied with that and had relocated in large migrations to the Human colonies to partake of the security offered by Galaxia armed forces. Increasing numbers, however, such as those in the Zentadon Homeland Movement, were not satisfied.

The Zentadon slums were much smaller in area and population, and somewhat better maintained, than the prolie Human districts. I soon came to 76471 GPT, an octagonal, windowless dwelling that peaked in typical Zentadon style into three floors, the uppermost of which consisted of a single small worship room. The house was made of plascrete. It needed virtually no maintenance and therefore remained like new for generations. Still unsure about how to terminate tonight's mission, naïve as I was in such matters, I stood in the dark outside among the street-milling crowds and mind-probed the building.

It was occupied, I could tell that much. I felt a subdued excitement generated by the occupants, of the sort I associated with plotters and schemers. I drew in a deep breath and approached the two-way viewscreen at the door. I was an academic at the military Interstellar School; academics placed a great deal of faith in the capability of pure reason to resolve conflict.

I showed myself to the screen and introduced myself. Those inside chose to keep their side of the screen dark to me.

"Leave," said a voice speaking Zentadon through the intercom. "This dwelling is not receiving."

"I am Kadar San," I repeated.

"I know you, Kadar San," said the same voice. I now recognized it as belonging to Mishal. "This dwelling is especially not receiving you."

"You must not sabotage the *Tsutsumi*," I said, coming right out with the purpose of my visit.

The dwelling received me after all. The heavy door slid open and I was hustled inside by Mishal and two of his confederates. A third hunkered in a catatonic state in one corner of a room so dimly lighted that only conspiracies could be conducted inside its walls. This Zentadon had undoubtedly been experimenting with taa as a recreational drug and gone into a state of lintatai. He had no mind left of his own and would follow orders zombie-like until he eventually withered and died.

"Cauri Tan," Mishal said, indicating the zombie. Mishal was a silver Zentadon with a magnificent full tail that stuck up straight behind his back at attention, reflecting the tension in the room. The other two were golds with green eyes.

One had a stub of a tail that looked like he had caught it in an automatic door and snapped half of it off. They stared at me in a way that made me acutely uncomfortable.

"You are a fool, Kadar San," Mishal snapped, carefully regulating his taa output to keep it at a manageable level. "How did you find out?"

"I am a Sen," I said, controlling my own taa level, and left it at that. Sens were held in awe among the general Zentadon populace. It was assumed that we could read all thought, whether it emanated from individuals or from collectives. Naturally, we who possessed the Talent played upon that general assumption. Mishal was none too bright. His thoughts reflected themselves in his facial expression so that even a limited Sen could read him to some large degree. I received the impression that his mind was darting about seeking someone to blame for the leak. It would never occur to him, self-centered that he was, to blame himself and his own loose lips.

"Your insider contact has been discovered," I warned, playing upon his weaknesses. "You cannot hide anything from me, Mishal. All your thoughts are coming through like a VR."

I detected a strong surge in him that centered on a female. I couldn't read who the female was, but it was not Mina Li. Another female, a sleeper feeding out intelligence to the Homelanders? There were no Zentadon females in the Republic military. Zentadon females were not warriors.

Did that mean a Human female contact sympathetic to the Homeland Movement?

"Do you wish to talk about her, Mishal?" I asked. "If I know, then the military must also know and have moved to intercept you."

A cunning look came over his face. His purple eyes narrowed. I might have made a mistake.

"Never mind who she is," he hissed, cat-like.

The contact *was* a Human female. I felt it.

"I will not think her name," he said, "because, as you can read, I only know her as a code name. And she has no knowledge of the mission. So, if you know, it is only by reading minds of those inside this dwelling. You will not have the opportunity to pass it on. You must understand how much I dislike you, Kadar San."

"I do, Mishal. You have no cause. I do not intend conjoining with Mina Li. She is all yours."

"I am the better one, Kadar San. I am a full-blood and not a mongrel, such as yourself."

"Yes, Mishal. You are a full-blood."

The verbal duel was carried out in low-key, in a civil tone. Within Zentadon, especially the males, emotions must always be kept under control to prevent the generating of taa, the effects of which could be fatal under extreme circumstances.

"But even a full-blood with half-an-intelligence must see," I continued, "that it is foolish to attack the military when it is the only thing standing between us and a Blob invasion."

"Huh!" Mishal snorted. "There are no Blobs. It is an invention of the Humans to keep us subjugated. Kadar San, in spite of our differences, you could be an asset to the Homeland. Come over to us. You have valuable information about the Human military."

"It is our military," I countered. "You will understand the threat, Mishal, when Blobs put us once more, Zentadon and Human alike, into concentration camps as slave laborers."

"My threat is the Humans," Mishal insisted. "If you are not with us, Kadar San, you are against us. Mina Li will mourn your passing, but only for a brief time."

"You cannot kill me, Mishal, without killing yourself."

"Do not be too sure of that."

"I will depart now," I said, starting for the door.

"Cauri Tan!" Mishal barked. "Guard the door."

The taa zombie obediently scrambled to his feet and blocked the doorway.

"He can kill you, Kadar San, for he is dead anyhow. He just does not know it yet." Mishal laughed the sharp-toothed Zentadon laugh. He turned to Cauri Tan. "This half-breed is Kadar San. Kill him if he attempts to escape from this room."

He laughed again. "He will destroy himself too from taa overburn," he said, "but it makes no difference to him.

One order cannot be countermanded by another, which you must know if you have ever seen lintatai. Few in this soft generation have seen it, of course. Make yourself comfortable, Kadar San. We will discuss more once we return from our successful mission."

Mishal and the others loaded their waist packs with small, but extremely potent amounts of demolitions. They pulled on light tunics to hide their loads and started out the door. Last out, Mishal turned back and grinned. Cauri Tan stood next to the door, as motionless and emotionless as a statue.

C·H·A·P·T·E·R
SIX

DRT-213 had not yet received our mission briefing, but I assumed the operation was against the Blobs and vital to the survival of the Republic. Sabotaging the *Tsutsumi* would delay the mission for weeks, even months. I sat on cushions in a corner of the safe house room while Cauri Tan kept mindless guard over me at the door. I would have to use taa myself to even think of being a match for his taa-induced strength and powers. I had experimented with taa at times, as all young Zentadon did, and had even been frightened nearly senseless once or twice when intense feelings produced surges of it into my system. I little understood how to use it; the science of employing taa had been outlawed during the generations after the taa camps and the Great Revolution of the Humans. Zentadon were no longer predators and warriors. We were vegetarians.

Know what a vegetarian is? It's a Zentadon word for an unsuccessful hunter.

But I was a Sen, wasn't I? Didn't that mean I had superior intellectual capability and senses more finely honed? Then why was I sitting here helplessly while fanatics went to blow up my ship and a near-vegetable kept me captive?

I probed the vegetable's mind. Instead of the vacuum I expected, I encountered confusion and chaos. The poor fellow's thought processes were so disorganized that the only thing he could understand was a clear and precise order. His mind would latch onto it like a drowning man seized a piece of flotsam and held on no matter what.

But what if I replaced the floating piece of driftwood?

I concentrated on the turbulence inside Cauri Tan's head. In place of the order to guard me and kill me if necessary, I substituted commands for him to sit down and go to sleep. I implemented the command in hypnotic steps. *You are tired, so weary that you cannot possible stand up. Sit. Sit. Sit.*

Good, now . . .

You are sleepy . . . Concentrate on how good it will feel to sleep, to close your eyes and drift away into slumber land. That is right. Close your eyes. You are so sleepy . . .

It was remarkably easy, considering all I had heard about taa and how the Indowy had used it to exert total control over our Zentadon ancestors. Within fifteen minutes I was back in the nighttime streets with my cap pulled low. I caught a hovercraft and had it drop me at the military base. My ID permitted me immediate entry. Rows and rows of block-like buildings stretched across the landscape, barracks for the soldiers. There were gigantic hangars for armored hovercraft, space scouters, land tracks, maintenance buildings and arms industries plants, meal facilities, headquarters buildings . . . Beyond all this were the military space docks where the *Tsutsumi* had arrived last evening, withdrawn from fleet support out by the Posleen Blight. Civilians off post would not have witnessed its approach and landing, as it was accomplished in light warp time. In fact, very few on the military base knew it was presently hangared in one of several enormous buildings nearly a kilometer in height and more than eight kilometers long. I knew of it only because Commander Mott informed me of it when he assigned me to DRT-213.

I wondered who else on post knew about it, which human female soldier had passed on intel to Mishal and the terrorists. I mind-probed and found the Homelanders. They were already surreptitiously nearing the target, were only minutes away from it. It was virtually impossible for non-military intruders to penetrate base security and move about on post undetected and invisible to electronic surveillance — unless they were accompanied and covered by proper authority.

It was not an impossible thing to bribe soldiers. In recent years, a series of corrupt politicians had rotted out the heart of the Republic.

I took a long breath and eased in a little taa. I had to try it. To my amazement, I felt like I had been suddenly supercharged. I ran from the gate to the *Tsutsumi* hangar, a distance of four kilometers, in thirty seconds flat. Talk about busting the Human one-minute mile!

I came down off the taa high so quickly that it left me prone with exhaustion and near shock. I lay for a minute in the shadows of a building near the hangar while I regained strength and courage. I was amazed at what I could do physically with just a little shot of the powerful drug manufactured within my own body. There wasn't time now to consider all the ramifications of its use. All I knew at the moment was that it allowed me to overtake and pass the bombers.

Now what? If I were a full-blown Human, perhaps, and armed . . .

I rolled onto my stomach and crawled to where I could see a vast expanse of sheeting that surrounded the gigantic hangar. A land security robot patrolled the open plascrete, accompanied by a rover ball that snooped and bounced and hovered as it fed data back to a centralized location. The robot so nearly resembled a combat-equipped soldier that it was easy to mistake it for a Human had I not known that bots had replaced live sentries. They were far more reliable and effective walking posts.

Without an authorization pass for this restricted area, I dared no closer approach. The rover ball would set off an alarm and the bot would stitch my scrawny tailless Zentadon ass with 7mm Hornet rounds quicker than I could twitch an ear.

I waited, watching as my strength returned. I didn't have long to wait. Presently, I saw shadows within shadows. Four of them separated themselves to cut across the open sheeting. I recognized Mishal by the wide set of his shoulders and the great tail gliding in the ambient light from stars and moons. The other two also had tails, but the fourth did not. It was a small female figure. A fifth shadow attracted my attention. It remained behind, almost cancelled by the dark. Perhaps there were others hiding whom I couldn't see at all.

The female turned back as the bot walked out to confront the saboteurs. She looked vaguely familiar, but I couldn't make out her facial features from this distance. The band apparently had proper authorization passes, either genuine ones obtained fraudulently by an inside traitor, or ones skillfully forged. The lighted ball zipped around each intruding individual to record and authenticate him. I had to admire Mishal's ingenuity and planning. Virtually no previous infiltrators had made it past the sophisticated devices that guarded the outer perimeter, and here these Homelanders were within meters and minutes of blowing up a Republic dreadnought. There was no way this could have been done without help from within the ranks.

The bots were programmed to sound alarms at anything

remotely suspicious. Most soldiers assumed the bots were infallible, but they were actually nothing but machines incapable of actual thinking, as these bold Homelanders were proving. A live sentry would most certainly have been suspicious of four Zentadon in the middle of the night accessing a restricted area.

So much for Human technology.

I looked around. I had to stop Mishal. Nothing came to mind. Mishal and his gang were already sauntering past the unsuspecting robots.

A pile of construction gravel used in the manufacture of armor and plascrete caught my eye. As a youngling, I had been adept in the orphanage at competitive stone throwing. The distance between the robots and me was at least two hundred meters, but I dared venture no nearer. I darted to the gravel pile and quickly selected several heavier round stones suitable for target throwing.

I missed the robot with my first cast. The stone struck behind it, between the machines and the saboteurs. Both camps turned toward the sound.

I whipped a second missile through the air. A robot getting konked on the head with a stone certainly qualified as remotely suspicious, if nothing else. The rover ball lit up the entire area with a blinding light. It tore back and forth across the sheeting at about waist high, emitting a shrill continuous scream with enough volume to crack windows in Prolie Town. Weapons ejected their muzzles from the

Human-like robot's hands and shoulders. It immediately morphed into an armored land combat vehicle. Magnified voices roared out of nowhere.

"Freeze! Do not move! Anything that moves within the restricted area will be neutralized. Do not move!"

Mishal yelled something. One of his henchmen kicked in taa and streaked for the hangar. The overload to his system spontaneously detonated just as he hurled a packet of explosives. The wet-sounding thump of the Zentadon rupturing merged with a blast and a brilliant flash of light.

The armored robot flickered and chattered as his armaments opened up. Mishal and his surviving comrade resorted to taa in order to run between the bullets, as it were. One of them — I couldn't tell which — erupted into a blooming flower of blood and flesh. He wasn't quite quick enough. The second form disappeared as armored hovercraft, floodlights blazing, suddenly darted overhead, back and forth, searching. The entire base went on immediate Def Con One, full alert.

It wouldn't do for me to be caught at the scene. Even if I survived, no one would believe my story. I would be convicted of espionage and sabotage. Even Commander Mott would have no choice except to believe I was the insider conspiring with the Homeland Movement.

If witnessing the implosion of the Zentadon wasn't enough to kick in my taa generator, then the resulting violence and excitement were. I knew, simply knew, I would go into lintatai and either blow up or lapse into a fugue state like Cauri Tan. But I had no choice.

Anyone watching might have thought I vanished from the gravel pile. I recovered five kilometers away, off the base again and back in the Capital. I looked back and saw the post lit up in bright incandescent floods. Craft darted about in the light like insects. I took a deep breath to restore equilibrium, astonished that twice tonight I had utilized taa and survived both times. It must have something to do with my being half-Human.

I felt exhausted but otherwise fit. I stumbled to my little apartment cubicle in the segregated Zentadon district. Mina Li was already in my bed, sleeping. I built a bed on the floor.

It hadn't been a bad night's work. Although no one would ever know about it, I had saved the *Tsutsumi* and preserved DRT-213's mission. I chuckled. I was a hero in my own mind.

I could use a cocktail. I went to sleep instead.

C·H·A·P·T·E·R
SEVEN

Commander Mott summoned me to his office early the next morning. He sat sternly behind his desk wearing his khakis and caressing his broken tail. With him were two silent Criminal Division investigators, both Humans, and Mina Li. The CDs regarded me with something of the eye of a fangar stalking his prey. I gave Mina Li an uneasy look. She had still been sleeping in my bed when I left.

"You look like hell, if the Humans will forgive my using the term," Commander Mott greeted, speaking Human for the benefit of the CDs. "Did you have a bad night?"

The after effects of taa left me feeling hung over. And apparently looking it. I glanced at Mina Li. "Pre-mission jitters, I suppose, sir."

I couldn't use sex and sleeplessness as an excuse. The breeding season was still three months off.

"We had a bit of excitement on post last evening," Commander Mott said. "I presume you have heard about it?"

"Yes, sir. When I arrived for duty this morning."

"These gentlemen have a few questions to ask you. I assured them that you have been a soldier with the Galaxia Republic for nearly ten years and that you are completely loyal."

"Thank you, sir."

Commander Mott made a gesture and one of the CD's stood up. He towered a foot above me and had undoubtedly been muscularly enhanced, except for his brow which seemed to have been reduced so that the single line of his eyebrows and the thorny leading edge of his hairline were only an inch apart.

"Sit down, Sergeant Kadar," he ordered. I sat down.

"Do you know a Zentadon by the name of Mishal Co Tan?"

"I know Mishal."

"How do you know him?"

"We were in the military academy together as cadets. I stayed in the military. He resigned."

"And became a leader with the Zentadon Homeland Movement," the CD added.

"I have heard such."

The CD clasped his hands behind his back and paced across the room while Commander Mott, Mina Li, the other CD and I looked on. He wore a frown that connected his brow and his hairline.

"When was the last time you saw Mishal?" he asked, obviously attempting to trap me into an admission. "I would advise you that Mishal is in custody from last night. He has made a statement."

I felt my heart pounding and concentrated on settling it. Damned if you do, damned if you don't came to mind. Then it occurred to me that if Mishal were apprehended, he must assume that I was still being held captive by Cauri Tan in the safe house. He would have told the CD nothing about me.

"I see him occasionally when we run into each other. We are not friends," I said.

The CD nodded, apparently satisfied. "Where were you last night, Sergeant Kadar?"

That one was a bit more ticklish. I glanced at Mina Li. She sat stiffly in her chair, staring at me. I probed her mind and to my surprise her thoughts were so intense that I read them clearly. *With me. With me all night.*

I sighed to give the impression that I was bored with the questioning. "I left post and went to the Starside Lounge," I said. "Mina Li met me there. We had cocktails together and then went to my cubicle where we remained for the rest of the night."

Mina Lee relaxed in her chair. "See? Is that not what I told you?" she gloated. "Kadar and I are preparing to conjoin. We will be exclusives."

I said nothing. I owed her something.

The CD seemed satisfied again. He looked questioningly at the other investigator, a smaller man with a wider brow, who shrugged and looked away.

"I think that'll do it for now, Sergeant," Low Brow concluded. "We are routinely questioning all the Zentadons on post. Homelanders attempted to blow up a dreadnought last night. One OD'd on taa. The bot killed one. We captured the leader when he ran out of taa and collapsed at the outer perimeter. We're surprised that he didn't blow himself up too. The only way this bunch could have gotten as close to success as they did was to have had someone on post helping them. If you hear anything, we need to know about it immediately."

"Immediately," I repeated.

They left, taking Mina Li with them to return her to the Capital. Before she left, she embraced me and whispered, "Please be safe. I will be waiting for you."

"I can hardly wait," I replied, trying to dilute the sarcasm.

She tapped my cheek with her tail. I flicked my ear. Commander Mott cleared his throat as the door closed behind her and the CD's.

"Where were you last night, Sergeant Kadar?" he asked bluntly. I had forgotten that he was also a Sen and could read both Mina Li's and my thoughts and emotions. It would do no good to lie to him, even if I could. I told him the entire story from beginning to end.

"You did well, Sergeant Kadar," he said when I finished. "But you should have come to me with it."

"There was not time, sir. You were with your family."

He got up and walked over to me, holding his crippled tail underneath his arm. He dropped a hand on my shoulder. His purple eyes looked troubled.

"Kadar, there is one other thing. I have my contacts also. It is suspected that the Homelander sleeper on post is a Human, not a Zentadon. He — or she, as you describe — somehow escaped last night. But the suspect has been narrowed down to the Deep Reconnaissance Teams, either a present or a former member."

"She is a DRT-bag?" I blurted out in astonishment, thinking of the female I had observed at the hangar last night.

"One female of whom is the communications specialist on DRT-213," the Commander said.

"Sergeant Pia Gunduli," I murmured. "Is she a suspect?"

"All the female DRTs are suspects, as are all Zentadon. There is not sufficient time to make team substitutions at this point. Sergeant Kadar, keep very alert on this upcoming mission. The Blobs may not be the only danger."

C·H·A·P·T·E·R
EIGHT

The Republic considered the mission so vital that the Group Commander himself, ol' General Numb Nuts, personally delivered the operations order. If Blade were the exception to the rule that Humans had humor and liked to laugh, General Numb Nuts was the exception to the rule that Humans bred all the time. It was whispered he had voluntarily surrendered his breeding certificate. It had soured him and made him nasty and petty.

"What he needs is his ashes hauled," Ferret whispered obscenely to Gun Maid.

I must have looked puzzled.

"It's an old, old Earth expression," Maid explained. "It means he needs to have sex."

"At ease!" bawled a staff colonel who followed the General in. He was short and bald. The rod stuck up his ass made him look unpleasant. "Don't interrupt again," he ordered.

He regarded the team with his unpleasant expression. "Undoubtedly, you have all heard by now that a gang of ruffian terrorists attempted to sabotage the mission last night by blowing up the dreadnought *Tsutsumi*. They failed. One was captured. They were Homelanders whom we suspect of collaborating with the Blobs. Does that give you an indication of how crucial this mission is to the security of the Republic?"

I watched Gun Maid's expression. It remained interested, concerned, but otherwise unchanged. I sampled her emotions and found no undue excitability, no particular feelings of guilt. If she were the sleeper, she was very good at hiding it.

I locked into the others one at a time as the staff colonel continued with how someone on post had been bribed to cooperate with the Homelanders. I found nothing particularly incriminating.

"We will uncover the traitors and punish them to the full extent and power of the law," the colonel roared, growing red-faced. "We will not be despoiled by a Fifth Column within, and we will not succumb to forces outside. Now, listen up to the mission briefing."

He stepped back. The General took over. The OpOrder consisted of five paragraphs: Situation, Mission, Execution, Service and Support, and Command and Signal.

"We don't know where the Tslek originate," General Numb Nuts said, rocking back and forth on the balls of his feet with his hands clasped behind his back. All he needed was a riding crop. "Certainly they must hail from outside the galaxies of Tau Ceti and Earth. We know they apparently have no need for clothing, as they seem to shape and re-shape their bodies for environmental protection. They practice a form of mitosis — splitting and dividing themselves like giant cells to duplicate additional forms. However, they appear to have biological needs similar to other life forms with which we are familiar — food, water, oxygen, fuel for their ships, raw materials, perhaps other things.

"From Napoleon and Hitler in the old Earth histories to Chien-Li and Dama-San of the Hadathranal and Ramaedan Empires in modern interstellar histories, there is truth that would-be conquerors have often been defeated by their supply lines. By the inadequacy of their resupply lines. While small units of Blobs might scrounge along the way, an actual invasion force will have to shorten its supply lines by occupying a forward base, an uninhabited M-Class planet with a carbon-nitrogen life support system capable of growing food and providing other resources, a biospheric atmosphere to cloak their activities, and ready access to transit lanes. Once the Blobs establish a forward base of operations and solve their supply challenge, Galaxia and her neighbors may well face the same fate Earth suffered during the Proton-Nuclear Wars of a thousand years ago."

He paused. He looked as though he might be standing on his nuts.

"Our Intel believes the Blobs are constructing such an advance base. The last two Deep Recon Teams sent to the area to investigate never came back. It is vital to the security of the Galaxia Republic that this Blob advance base be located and neutralized before the enemy builds itself into a power impervious to attack."

DRT-213's mission: blast off for this planet, recon the suspected Blob base without making contact or being detected, return with the information to the recovery ship. Sensor bots, previously inserted, had sniffed out faint energy emissions and hyper tracks. They performed a cursory biosphere sweep and managed to localize the emissions to a range of mountains before they inexplicably went silent.

The same thing — inexplicable silence and presumed destruction — befell the two previous DRTs sent in to recon. It was now DRT-213's turn.

I clearly read Blade's single simple thought: *Fu-uck.*

By a fortunate twist of luck, considering the immense distances in the Tau Ceti Tail corner of the cluster, a survey ship had discovered a heretofore unknown open transport tunnel to the planet which should enable an undetected approach. DRT-213 would depart in two days aboard a small Stealth craft piggybacked to a dreadnought. Once the huge warship reached destination, it would hurl the Stealth into orbit, where it would remain while the team inserted in a landing pod, conducted the mission and returned.

The dreadnought and a Republic Starship would cruise the region to provide cover support, while a battle fleet waited, prepared to annihilate the Blob base as soon as it was pinpointed.

"It's up to you to find it, fix it, and report back," General Numb Nuts said. "We think Blobs use extrasensory perception, telepathy, as a normal means of communication. That's why you have a Sen assigned to your team. Your Zentadon should be able to detect and intercept their thought waves."

My ears twitched.

General Numb Nuts turned the briefing back over to the staff colonel.

"With the exception of Zentadon Sens," the colonel said, "it appears we Humans are in this fight alone. The Indowy have gone soft. They are attempting to establish commo with the invaders and plead for peace in our time."

He shifted around the rod up his ass and made a painful sound. "Peace in our time!" he scoffed. "The Blobs appear to utilize the same general logic as Humans . . . and some Zentadon. We should therefore assume that they will expect a reconnaissance, especially after the vanishing of the two previous teams. You should remain on a heightened state of alert and expect the unexpected."

Assistants began handing out supplemental material:

target folders, area studies, maps, CEOIs, videos and photos. An aide activated a holographic display of maps and charts and globes. I experienced a short burst of taa directly to my brain. I reacted the way any Zentadon would have, even one with Human blood, when confronted with that planet, the way survivors of what in Human history was called the Jewish Holocaust recoiled at the mention of Auschwitz or Dachau.

I recognized the image of Aldenia instantly, its two moons, one large and pale with a second orbiting it; the darkness of the planet, two-thirds of the surface covered with seas, lakes and oceans. Although it was the farthest planet from the galaxy's primary sun, Ceti, it was near enough to a second sun-star that revolved with it around the outer edges of the galaxy that the climate remained predominately tropical. The two suns in opposing refractory were said to cause the eerie otherworldly lighting that had branded itself into the Zentadon collective memory.

"Aldenia," exclaimed Team Sergeant Shiva, also recognizing it.

"Exactly, Sergeant," said General Numb Nuts, delighted at the shock effect. "The Dark Planet."

"Sir?" said Captain Amalfi. "Why do we think the Blobs can colonize Aldenia when all other efforts for centuries, since the time of the Indowy Federation, have ended in disaster and failure?"

"Apparently," scoffed General Numb Nuts, "the Blobs

have not heard or do not invest credence in superstitions manufactured by the Zentadon after the taa camps. I myself do not place stock in these Old Elf Tales." He chuckled. "Contrary to popular dogma, there is nothing inherently evil about the planet of Aldenia. Would you agree with that, Zentadon?"

I snapped to attention, arms folded respectfully across my chest. "It was a dark time in Zentadon history, sir . . . and a dark place."

I thought to leave it at that.

"There is nothing inherently evil about Aldenia," the General persisted, scowling.

Blade rose to his feet. "General, sir. I have been to Aldenia. I came back."

"Not all return," I countered.

"Not all return from the toilet."

C·H·A·P·T·E·R
NINE

The dreadnought *Admiral Tsutsumi* was a powerful ship and looked it. Its hull was nearly five kilometers long and covered by a maze of heat exchangers, tractor beam projectors, com pods, heavy-duty weapons blisters and other installations common to Starship class warships. In contrast, the Stealth attached piggyback to it was a stubby, black, windowless lump, like a malignant mole on a giant's backside.

I was primarily an academic, having taught at the Interstellar School for much of my productive adult life, so could not help but be astonished at my first close-up experience with the reality of space warfare. Humans were amazing creatures, I had to hand them that. Although the Proton-Nuclear Wars wiped out three-quarters of Earth's population and made at least that same proportion of the planet uninhabitable, there were survivors whose restless energies and nimble minds continued to long for adventure and knowledge and, perhaps, even a kind of salvation. It was they who developed eph-proton fuel and cultivated the Mini-Magnetic Plasma Propulsion (M2P2) System, an "energy wind sail" capable of inconceivable light speeds. Humankind was on its way to colonizing the universe, and no other civilization would be safe again. Beings in the galaxies were soon wearing Wrangler jeans, even those individuals with three or four or five legs, shouting, "Hey, Dude!" to each other, and forming sex clubs.

Because we were piggybacking on the *Tsutsumi*, it would not be necessary to crew the Stealth until we arrived within Aldenia's gravity field. Captain Amalfi chose hibernation for the crew in the time couches. These were molded individual recliners with glass-sealed hoods. They were tiered one above the other in an available space on the Stealth, with a ladder leading to each.

"I had rather us hibernate and come out peaked fresh than to get fat and flabby for six weeks on a damned cruise ship," Captain Amalfi explained.

Due to the threat of sabotage and internal subversion surrounding the launching of the mission, HazMat teams swept both the mother ship and the Stealth for unauthorized explosives before crews were allowed aboard.

We entered the Stealth in the reduced gravity by merely stepping out of the lock and drifting down one by one, getting out of each other's way in the confined areas. As all this was new to me, having only traveled as a passenger in space liners, I paid particular attention to everything. The interior of the ship was a bit disconcerting in its clutter and chaos of arrangement and utility; hydraulics and valves, instrument panels and pipes and hoses and knobs and other gear, the function of which left me guessing. It was like an old Human submarine I had once seen in a museum. It smelled musty and oily.

"Your first time aboard a Stealth?" Gun Maid guessed. She was the only one of the team who deigned to speak to me, if you discounted Captain Amalfi and Sergeant Shiva issuing orders and Blade muttering Fu-uck every time he looked my way.

"Not exactly," I said. "I have had nightmares."

She laughed. "It isn't really as threatening as it appears. It's crowded, but entirely functional and actually quite simple in its structure. We're in the crew compartment. Aft is the M2 reactor. Forward is the control deck. The landing pod is in the nose. That's all there is to it."

"Maybe I'll take it for a test drive."

She looked at me and, after a moment, chided in that voice of hers that was both pleasing and pleasant, "You're a real puzzle, Kadar San. You're always wearing an expression that makes me want to offer you a penny for your thoughts."

I gave her a dumb, uncomprehending look. She giggled

delightfully.

"It's an old, old Earth expression," she explained. "You look a little smug."

Zentadon are not real good at repartee with the opposite sex out of breeding season. The Human part of me couldn't help noticing that Gun Maid might make an excellent breeder.

"I will work on it," I said. "A lowly Zentadon must never look . . . a little smug."

"A Zentadon, Sergeant, would get along better if he hadn't such a chip on his shoulder."

There was nothing on either of my shoulders. Gun Maid giggled again.

"Another old, old Earth expression?" I guessed.

"Can't you read my mind? You're a telepath."

I thought she looked worried that I might.

"Sens have an etiquette," I said, not completely truthfully. "It would be like rape if I read your thoughts without permission."

"Oh? But you'll rape the Blobs and other assorteds?"

"When necessary. But with much less pleasure," I replied, enjoying the exchange in spite of my suspicions.

A female medic came from the *Tsutsumi* to assist the team with hooking into the time-couch life support systems. "How do you stand those things?" she asked, shuddering. "They're like . . . coffins."

She administered hiberzine. The team began stripping

off their uniforms and climbing one by one into their "coffins." The medic came to me.

"I will pass," I declined. "The hiberzine drug does not work on the Zentadon. I'm afraid your ship has an unexpected tourist for the next six weeks."

Captain Amalfi blinked. "I always assumed hiberzine was created by the Zentadon."

"It was invented by the Indowy to be used on humans and employed by Zentadon."

"Uh . . .?"

"About four thousand years ago."

"I thought we encountered the Zentadon less than a thousand years ago."

"Elves," I said mysteriously, "have always been around."

Captain Amalfi frowned as the glass hood closed over him.

Most of the crew opted for VR — virtual reality — entertainment hookups which allowed experiencing all kinds of true-to-life adventures while they slept. Rather like dreaming, I assumed, only closer to real life. I wondered what program Gun Maid selected.

She stripped down to bikini underwear for the time-couch. No brassiere. Her near-naked body was slender and hard and brown as she settled in for the ride. I stood next to her couch as the medic attached her to IV's, electric muscle exercisers, and vital organ stimulator feeds. Atlas, from his coffin, stared at me disapprovingly. Warm, soft padding flowed around her body, supported by hard memory plastic.

"Penny for my thoughts?" I asked.

She smiled. "Okay."

"I was wondering how you'd look with a beautiful furry tail."

She was still giggling when she went under.

Suspicion and mistrust blocked all doors wherever I went on the dreadnought during the long flight. I felt like a virus, isolated and impugned. I encountered walls of fear and apprehension whenever I released my Sen powers to explore. How could I really blame the Humans after the way we Zentadon had been used against them by the Indowy? And after the Homelander incident prior to departure? I felt the same kind of mistrust toward the Indowy. My own anxiety grew the closer we came to the dreaded Dark Planet and its latent social memories of the taa camps. Had I a choice, which Commander Mott assured me I hadn't, I would have stayed on Galaxia and waited for the breeding season.

Sometimes, out of loneliness, I entered the Stealth, while Captain Amalfi and the team slept on. I stood by

Gun Maid's time-couch and watched as the VR she was experiencing animated her features. She must be having a delightful time. I experienced a surge of unfamiliar jealousy. I wondered what it would be like to have cocktails with this little brown female, then go to my cubicle afterwards together and watch her undress again. It surprised me to have such desire and it not even breeding season. And for a Human female, no less.

I tried to recall the female I had seen with Mishal at the hangar that night. She was small, like Gun Maid, built well. But I had only seen her in silhouette and, concentrate as I might, I could not correlate Gun Maid in my mind with Mishal and the Zentadon Homeland Movement. Fact was, I didn't want her to be a traitor to her people. Hers was virtually the only friendly face aboard.

Foolish Zentadon. Part Zentadon, part Human, and neither one nor the other completely.

Instead of six weeks, as planned, the journey took three months because of a chance near-Blob encounter. I attempted to report the cause of the delay when the team revived out of cocooning. However, the Stealth turned into such a feverish hive of pre-mission activity that the Captain had only half an ear for me, figuratively. Everybody jumped out of the time-couches like oversleeping commuters late for work. Nervous energy and excitement flooded the Stealth. Chameleon uniforms were donned but not activated, weapons and equipment checked, then re-checked. Sergeant Shiva supervised the inventory and storage of rations and other gear aboard the tiny drop pod in the Stealth's nose. Gun Maid had her radios and commo to prove out. As DRT-213's ops and intel specialist, Gorilla downloaded mission updates, standard news summaries and EEI requirements from the mother ship's computers, which he condensed on his palm comp for the Captain. It was he who discovered the time discrepancy. He scowled at the miniature screen.

"Captain Amalfi? Have you checked the date?"

The Captain consulted his internal chronometer. His body automatically adjusted it for time, temperature and OpPlan schedule.

"Three months! What the hell happened?"

"Captain, that is what I have been trying to . . ."

"Right, Sergeant Kadar. Save it."

He ducked angrily out the connecting hatch into the dreadnought and rushed down the steel corridor toward the mother ship's bridge and ops center, on his way to confront Lieutenant (advanced grade) Snork, the liaison officer. Ferret tagged along with him, casting back a look of reproval at me. Hey, what did a lowly Zentadon know?

I had already stowed my gear and weapons in the drop pod and donned patterned chameleons. I looked around to make sure I wasn't noticed, then followed the commander and Ferret. They were already out of sight, but to a Sen, Captain Amalfi's anger left a spoor as easy to follow as a blood trail for the giant predator fish in Galaxia's oceans. I didn't trust Lieutenant Snork, who had constantly gone out of his way during the three months to confront me on small matters. He as much as accused me of communicating telepathically with the enemy, of being the Blob plant who attempted to sabotage the *Tsutsumi*.

"Wherever you go as long as you're aboard the *Tsutsumi*," he promised, "you're going to have a tail. Well . . ." He glared at where my appendage should be. "Well, you know what I mean. You're going to have company watching you to make sure you follow the straight and narrow."

"You are straight and narrow?" I asked innocently.

"Don't be insolent, Sergeant. Need I remind you that I am a lieutenant, your superior, and that we do not trust you Zentadon?"

"I am half-Human. Do you half-trust me?"

Had my Talent for mind-reading been more refined, I would not have been compelled to sneak up to the door off the liaison office to hear what was being said. It was a distasteful scene inside between the Captain and Lieutenant Snork while Ferret watched. I sampled their emotions. Snork's deceit and disingenuousness made me nauseous.

"The creature is weird," he was saying. "He hardly said a word to anyone on the ship for three months. He just went around reading everyone's mind. One of the sailors called him out on it. The Zentadon sneered the way he does, turned his back on the sailor and walked off. Later, in full view of everybody, he went down to the gym and started bench-pressing nearly five hundred kilos. Like it was nothing.

"I don't think we realize how powerful the Zentadon are, being no bigger than that female of yours. But he bench-presses half a ton! He regularly worked out in two or three gravities. That's eerie. But it's not half as eerie as reading people's minds."

"What does all this have to do with the delay, Snork? Get to the point. I'm in a hurry. We're preparing for an insertion."

"I'm getting to it, Captain. There was another big clash in the sector between Blob fighters and some of our armed scouters. We had to break out of the trough and do a non-tunnel jump."

"Why didn't you get back in the trough after the threat was over?"

"Because that's what I've been trying to tell you . . . I went to the commander about it and he agreed with me that it would be safer not to. Let me ask you this, Captain Amalfi: How did the Blobs know we were coming through this sector? The obvious reason is . . . your Zentadon."

Captain Amalfi started to protest, but Snork cut him off. "Hear me out, sir. Your Zentadon is a Sen, right? We watched him. He would go out on the enclosed observation platform and meditate for hours. We know the Blobs communicate by telepathy. So . . . Who was the Zentadon mind-talking to all the time? You figure it out, Captain."

"That's no proof that Sergeant Kadar . . ."

"Sir, I'm just reporting the facts."

"These are assumptions, not facts," Captain Amalfi snapped, to his credit.

"Sir, this is not a formal caution and no record will be made of it. However, the commander and I felt your team should be made aware of it. I know one thing — and I'm no superstitious coward, sir — but I wouldn't insert on that planet with the Zentadon. Mark my word, Captain, if you take him you won't be coming back. If he makes one false move, I'd get rid of him. That's what I'd so, sir. Get rid of that elf."

Through Ferret, the entire team would soon be apprised of the gist of the conversation. Suspicions, once nurtured and attended, grew like strangler vines. I would have to watch my back and keep my senses tuned to the changing moods of my own teammates.

C·H·A·P·T·E·R
ELEVEN

DAY ONE

Once slung past the two moons and into orbit around Aldenia, we had two Galaxia days aboard the Stealth before we established the correct angle and transferred to the pod for entry. Entertainment packages aboard the ship provided diversion, as there was little actual flying to do and duties were minimal. Gun Maid and Gorilla read books, real paper books with covers, while Atlas and Ferret were partial to holographic games involving miniature soldiers and bots, ground armor and space ships engaged in bloody battle with lots of shooting and screaming. Captain Amalfi and Sergeant Shiva, the team's leadership, had more to do and kept themselves occupied with planning and cross-planning. Blade made me nervous, his suspicious nature further fed by the relayed warning from the wretched Lieutenant Snork. Every time I attempted to read his emotions, to sample his thought patterns and thus forearm myself, it was like he felt me probing and slammed the door shut so hard in my face that it left me feeling bruised inside my head.

He would look up in a glare and growl, "Fu-uck."

The others said Blade was too mean to breed, so the next best thing for him were his weapons. He spent hours with the sniper rifle, caressing it, ministering to this high point of infantry technology. With the M-235 Gauss he could punch ten rounds into the X-ring at one thousand meters as fast as he could squeeze the trigger, using the iron sights, too, instead of the weapon's holographic. Then he would back off two thousand meters and do it again. On the day I was introduced to the team, Blade had just won a hundred credits in a bet with Atlas on the firing range. Ferret had gone to Blade's target and, in amazement, placed a single thumb over the entire pattern; the rounds had struck that close together to tear out the man-target's tiny heart.

Sergeant Gunduli — it seemed ludicrous to call such a pleasing creature Gun Maid — maintained vigilance in front of a bank of radio and crypto equipment while she read her books.

"Apparently, the Blobs are either under tactical radio silence, they have systems I can't penetrate, or they use telepathy for even long range and intergalactic communications," she reported to Captain Amalfi.

"There's one further option," Gorilla noted.

"What's that?" Captain Amalfi asked.

"There's nothing there."

Captain Amalfi shook his head. "Energy emissions picked up by sensor bots before they vanished during the previous recon may or may not have originated from Blobs," he cautioned, "but this we do know: there is something there, whether it be free colonizers, pirates, or even another unknown species. The Republic leadership is betting on Blobs and that's good enough for me. Sergeant Kadar?"

"Yes, sir?"

"Are you receiving anything from the planet?"

"Am I receiving any 'vibes?' " I could get into this Human lingo with practice. "Negative," I amended quickly when I saw the Captain unimpressed. "I don't do intergalactic telepathy. I have to at least be on the same planet with a source."

"Humph! Keep trying, Sergeant Gunduli."

"Yes, sir. There's . . . I don't know . . ."

"What?" Captain Amalfi prompted impatiently.

She looked puzzled. "I . . . it's a feeling . . ."

"Leave the feeling to Sergeant Kadar. Stick with the commo."

"I'll keep running the bands, even in alternate time bands."

The crew became edgy, a condition that grew with the passage of relatively idle hours. It was like edginess recycled through the ship's rebreather system. My ears twitched. I sensed general hostility, like one detected noxious gas issuing from a contaminated spring. I noticed it first in Gun Maid when I thought to ask if she and Atlas were a breeding pair. I stumbled and pawed around the words, trying to get the question out, until sudden ice blocked all mental contact with her.

"Let sleeping dogs lie," she flared, which I took to be an old, old Earth expression meaning shut up, it's none of your business.

Curiosity was a common Zentadon trait that, I understood, could sometimes kill the cat.

Next, it was Captain Amalfi and Sergeant Shiva.

"Team Sergeant?" The Captain's voice rose uncharacteristically. "Team Sergeant?"

The scarred old NCO battle horse slowly came to attention. The snap was gone. "What do you want?"

"In two days, Sergeant Shiva, in less than two days, this team may be in battle with the Blobs."

"We're the Blobs' worst nightmare."

"Shiva, these DRT-bags are slow, they're sloppy, their breath stinks and they don't love Jesus. Do you catch my drift?"

"No, sir."

"I want these soldiers whipped into shape, Team Sergeant. Now, do you catch my drift?"

"What do you suggest, Captain? Double-time them around the bridge?"

"Your sarcasm is unappreciated, Team Sergeant."

"I'll whip them into shape, Captain."

"Very well." That seemed to satisfy him.

I tried to pass the atmosphere off as pre-insertion jitters. DRTs were, after all, superb soldiers, the elite Special Forces of the Galaxia Republic. They were focused and ready, like gladiators about to enter the coliseum. They were, well, edged.

But there was more to it than that. I cautiously explored my team members' brains and emotions, using my special Talent, and found aggression and suspicion, much more than before, along with little black worms of fear and unspecified anxieties. Since they had not been that way pre-orbit, I assumed it had something to do with Aldenia. While I ate, I studied the Dark Planet on the view screen, trying to figure out what there was about it that could cause such a sudden transformation. Lightning boils in the dark crust popped and flickered.

I picked at my food, since I utilized very little energy while inactive in orbit. Special rations had been prepared and packed for me: water vine, a type of lichen, and other plants. Zentadon were once exceptional predators, but that was in the distant past. I now found it disgusting the way Blade and Gorilla, and even Sergeant Shiva gorged themselves on the near-raw flesh of the mammoth Galaxia quadropod. Indowy and Zentadon had reformed basic aggressive traits in our genetic signatures. Because of taa, the killing and eating of meat could even be dangerous to us.

"Are you occupied?" Sergeant Shiva asked gruffly. "You aren't meditating again or something?"

I set aside my plate, the nuked plants half-eaten. Children in China, wherever that was, were probably starving. "I am listening for Blobs," I said.

"You can hear them?"

"Mostly I hear inside myself."

"With myself" was the best conversation I could expect while attached to DRT-213.

Grumpy and out of sorts like everyone else, Sergeant Shiva took the seat next to me in front of the viewscreen. He was a huge man, even sitting. The scar jagging down his cheek appeared etched in relief. He apparently had something to say.

"That is one ugly ball of dung," he said, indicating Aldenia.

I couldn't quarrel with that. I waited.

"Shit!" he said. He got up in exasperation, walked around the seat and sat down again. "Okay, let's get it over with. Call this your leadership briefing, although you ain't ever going to need it if there's anything the Captain and I can do about it. This is just in case he and I and Sergeant Gunduli all get it. If that happens, you're fourth in the chain of command, behind Gun Maid and before Gorilla. The chain of command goes like this: the Captain, me, Gun Maid, you, Gorilla, Blade, Ferret and Atlas, in that order."

"I am a specialist, Team Sergeant, and a Zentadon. Zentadon specialists normally do not assume leadership positions. Besides, I know I'm not trusted."

"Maybe specialists ain't leaders in that pissy-pansy school you came from," he growled, "but that don't apply in the teams. It is your rank that counts here, and that makes you fourth. You will be in charge and damned well better act like it, else Blade and the others will chew you up and spit out your heart."

"Is that a warning or an order?"

"Both. There's a couple of reasons you need to know this. This pod is programmed to return to the Stealth in exactly nine days, starting from today, whether any of us return with it or not. Nine days is what we have to recon the Blobs and get back. We'll make reports to the pod's computers every day so higher-higher gets the intel whether we get chewed up or what."

"And the other reason is?"

"The chain of command is also programmed into the pod's memory system. Its combat tacs keep track of the living and the dead. The pod will take off *before* the nine days are up only upon orders from the senior living team member. As long as the senior man is alive, no subordinate can even enter the pod. Understand?"

"But the senior man can take off without his subordinates?"

"Any leader who would do that is a lowdown dirty

sonofabitch. If you are in charge, you will leave no one alive behind. Understand?"

"Not even Blade?"

He glared at me. That was supposed to be a joke.

"The others will also be informed of the procedure," he said.

"So they can keep an eye on me?"

"That's my job. If you fuck up, I'll make sure you never have a chance to take command. Blade won't have to do anything. Don't even think of mind-talking to the Blobs."

"Why would I do that, Team Sergeant, when we have such stimulating conversations among ourselves?"

As for Blade, his unblinking, indecipherable stare dogged my every movement. His hostility toward me became palpable. You didn't have to be a Sen to feel it.

"Elf?" he said, cornering me.

"My name is Kadar San."

"Elf, is it true that taa camps weren't the only Indowy construction on Aldenia?"

"Don't you know? You were there."

"Don't be a wise ass, elf." He sneered at me. "This is going to be a long mission. Anything can happen."

I sighed and said, to keep peace in the family, "It was centuries ago that the Indowy were here."

"True, but always something remains. For example, the spawn of human whores and tailed monkey-elves, like yourself. If I were a woman, I would rather screw a dog or an ape as a Zentadon."

"I am sure you would."

He wasn't listening.

"The Indowy built experimental research and development laboratories on Aldenia," he stated. "A man could get rich if he stumbled onto some of that stuff."

"Greed precedes the fall."

He looked like he wanted to twist off my head.

"It is an old, old Earth expression," I said.

Maid, who overheard, later found the opportunity to caution me. "Blade can be a dangerous man. Don't deliberately provoke him, Kadar San."

"It does not have to be deliberate."

Atlas, wearing a disapproving look, snatched her out of my presence and piloted her into the ship's bay where I saw them in heated argument. Whatever was happening on the ship was affecting everyone. I felt like I might chew off my own arm but for the Zentadon control I exercised over myself.

I targeted the planet through the viewscreen with the full force of my concentration, which was considerable, and scrubbed the atmosphere telepathically. As far as I could tell, there was simply nothing there. Except, I still experienced a feeling of menace, of . . .

"Evil," Maid said over my shoulder. I gave a start. I had been so focused that I hadn't felt her approach.

"You did not give me a penny for my thoughts," I

scolded mildly.

"But that was what you were thinking, Sergeant Kadar."

"I thought Humans abandoned concepts of good and evil once they discovered the vastness of space and found no God living there."

"Not all Humans."

She watched the viewscreen with me. Lightning storms popped and erupted on the forbidding surface.

"Have you picked up something?" I asked her presently, sensing how troubled she was. "A signal?"

She frowned. She sat down next to me in front of the screen and lowered her voice.

"I don't get anything from it except silence." Her voice cracked with strain. "What does it mean? Our listening devices can hear the footfalls of an ant crawling across the surface of a moon. We should be able to comb something from the planet — atmospheric disturbances, electrical energies, force fields, something. We should be listening to all that lightning, if nothing else. Our gear is designed to sniff out any disturbances. Yet, it's as though we are flying through a tunnel . . ."

"We are being jammed. Is that the term?"

She nodded, still focusing on the screen. I felt her shudder where her shoulder touched mine.

"You've surely noticed how everyone's started to change since we went into orbit," she said. "It's almost like the atmosphere from Aldenia is permeating the screen into the ship, isn't it? The feeling I get is of something dark and . . ." She couldn't think of a more appropriate word. ". . . and evil."

That was, I agreed, the right word for the Dark Planet.

"Sergeant Kadar, why did your people and the Indowy abandon Aldenia after you had colonized it?"

"We did not colonize it," I corrected. "The Indowy colonized it and brought Zentadon here."

"I stand corrected," she snapped, then caught herself. "The Group Commander during mission briefing said something about taa camps. What was he talking about, Kadar San?"

I hesitated. The mere mention of taa frightened Humans.

"Surges of taa produced by the Zentadon endocrine system can bring about a physical and mental transformation," I said, speaking from personal experience after the night of the attempted sabotage. "In this stage, Zentadon are capable of what you Humans call super strength and abilities."

"I remember when I was a little girl and my great-great grandfather was more than a hundred years old," Maid interrupted, reflecting. "He told stories about the early years of colonization and exploration. He told one of the stories as a warning whenever the children were unruly and needed straightening out. Sort of like, the boogie man will get you if you don't behave. It was about how his great-great grandfather fought in the Revolution. He saw Zentadon soldiers wipe out one of our colonies. He described them as looking like devils with their green or purple eyes and their tails. They moved with such incredible speed that they were like flitting shadows, unable to be seen except the way you see a bird out of the corner of your eye before it disappears. They actually exploded buildings with only the collective energy of their minds. They shredded flesh off Humans and ate it. I . . ."

She looked pale beneath her brown skin.

"It is little wonder that Humans are suspicious of Zentadon," I commiserated.

"The story is true?"

It was suddenly important to me that I make her understand.

"The Indowy through their technology developed means of inducing taa in Zentadon at their will and thus controlling us by it," I said. "Zentadon are inherently peaceful people. We were captured in large numbers and interned in camps under the most horrid conditions. The camps were run like animal breeding and experimental stations. Hundreds of thousands of us died — as many as twenty million. All to satisfy the Indowy quest for super soldiers to be used to conquer the galaxy and enslave the Humans and other sentients to a cartel of madmen who ruled the Indowy at that period."

"The camps were here, on Aldenia?"

"Hundreds of them, all over the planet, along with various war research laboratories and factories. There was one unforeseen consequence of the taa scheme, however. Taa in sufficient quantities released into our systems may produce a condition known as lintatai, which can destroy us very quickly. Lintatai may occur in two ways. A Zentadon goes into a fugue state of mind during which he will neither eat nor sleep. He will not do anything unless ordered, and then only as a zombie reaction. He burns out on the inside and slowly withers, useless to himself and everyone else until he dies."

Maid shivered. "How awful. And the other way?"

"The Indowy wanted to build super soldiers based on the control of taa. And they did. The downside was that we literally burn up from the inside out with all that energy. Prolonged overdoses cause us to go into acute lintatai and explode from the inside, to spontaneously combust into flames."

"Like one of the saboteurs did?"

I shot a glance at her.

"I was told about it," she quickly explained. "Is that why the Zentadon are so comparatively few today?"

"The Indowy had to keep replacing Zentadon with fresh captives, running us through the camps by the millions. If we survived the camps, not many of us survived the taa rushes imposed upon us in combat. Soon, so few of us remained that you Humans were able to . . . Well, the Great Revolution succeeded. Humans have recorded it in your histories, from your point of view."

Maid looked horrified. She stared at Aldenia with new intensity.

"It is an evil place," she whispered. "Is that why it was abandoned."

"It is said that the malevolent spirits of the Indowy butchers and the Zentadon who collaborated with them are trapped and isolated in the darkness of the planet. That no one who goes there survives it."

"DRT-418 and DRT-420 did not return," Maid pointed out, turning toward me. "But Blade went and returned several years ago."

I shrugged.

"Do you believe there are evil spirits, Kadar San?"

"Are there not stranger things on Earth and in Heaven, to coin an old, old Earth expression?"

"I believe that in everything there are opposites," she said. "For your right hand, there is a left. For the darkness, there is light. For every evil there is goodness."

I nodded. "The universe is kept in balance through opposites."

"How do you explain the Blobs? Are they somehow immune to the planet? Are they stronger than evil? They can't be the counterbalance to it."

"More evil than evil?" I mused.

Before we could explore the topic further, a disturbance broke out on the bridge. Atlas' voice rose angrily.

"You damned ape!"

He sprang to his feet and rushed Gorilla, knocking the black man's book from his hands. Gorilla charged back with a primordial roar. The two big men grappled like giants, locked together in combat. They crashed to the deck, grunting and yelling, kneeing, elbowing and gouging. Fortunately, they were unable to do much damage to each other in the confined space and in the ship's reduced gravity field.

Captain Amalfi and little Ferret rushed to break them apart, succeeding only after Ferret had been flung into a bank of monitors and Sergeant Shiva replaced him with his greater bulk and authority.

"What the hell is the matter with the two of you?" the Captain demanded.

Atlas looked befuddled, like he was emerging from sleepwalking. His face was flushed and bleeding from minor scratches. Gorilla shook his bald head to clear it.

"I-I don't know, Captain," he murmured.

"Gorilla, he . . . he . . ." Atlas stammered. "Gorilla, he . . . *looked* at me."

C·H·A·P·T·E·R
TWELVE

DAY TWO

H-Hour for insertion.

"Suck it in, DRT-bags, it's show time," Sergeant Shiva announced.

The crew donned pressurized space suits and helmets over our chameleon cammies and crawled on hands and knees, one at a time, through the airtight lock into the tiny shuttle pod and strapped ourselves into individual G-seats. Some of the seats were situated in front of the miniaturized control panel, where the Captain, as pilot, began switching toggles to start the undocking sequence. I heard a hydraulic whine. Panel lights began blinking.

Sergeant Shiva entered last and secured the hatch before taking his place. The chamber went dark until the interior lights came on. The area was so cramped that the taller men slumped in their seats to prevent banging their helmets against the overhead, and if we moved otherwise we barked our elbows and knees against the surrounding bulkheads. We went into OPSEC silent running. Secure commo sets plugged into our helmets provided intercom.

The craft was point-computerized for the fastest and most effective landing approach. It was designed to negotiate a low detection entry, morph into a glider configuration, dive in slow flight to the water, level out, and "control crash" into the sea where it became a submarine. All of which was computer initiated and controlled. After undocking, and until we landed in the water, passengers were mostly along for the ride, dependent upon a "pilot" constructed of microchips and electric micro energy.

Because of our unfortunate historical roots in Indowy technology, Zentadon were less comfortable with machines and artificial intelligence than Humans. I was particularly uncomfortable with it and felt my muscles tensing and taa dripping into my system as Captain Amalfi activated the cycle that would fire the pod away from the Stealth and plunge us downward toward the Dark Planet. Keepers at the orphanage, bless their Zentadon souls, always said I had the heart of a poet. Poets were cautious of things you constructed to think for you.

"This is going to get a bit hairy," Captain Amalfi warned through the intercom. "Barf bags are built into your helmets. Listen to the bell. It tolls for thee."

He fired the pod after a final systems and safety check.

It shuddered, the lights dimmed. It shot away from the Stealth like a bullet from the muzzle of a Grav rifle. There was minimal gravity at this altitude above Aldenia and no atmosphere, resulting in little discomfort for those of us strapped into the projectile. About an hour of weightlessness followed, filled with some idle chatter but mostly with quiet as we riveted our attention upon the viewscreen.

"Piece of cake," Atlas quipped. That was one of the grunt's favorite lines.

The ride really began when the pod touched the edges of Aldenia's thick atmosphere. The "pilot" flew like it was insane. That was in case the Blobs were watching. It was programmed to execute random barrel rolls and flips and to make flaky course changes in order to simulate a meteor entering the atmosphere. It tumbled, yawed and skittered first one way, then the other, slamming us against our restraints. Heat shields armored the vessel, but the temperature inside rose anyhow to the steamed-seafood level.

"Vomit . . . comet!" Ferret moaned. He sounded sick.

Plastic wings sprouted from the landing pod once we hit good atmosphere. The viewscreen showed us flying through high storms, which gave us another good jostling. Lightning cracked and popped. A wind tunnel caught us and sent us plummeting and spinning wildly toward Aldenia. We were out of control.

"Aeeeiiii . . . !" Ferret gasped.

We struck the ocean with the impact of a can of

processed vegetables dropped from the top of the Triple Trade Towers on Galaxia. Splat! I shook off a moment of unconsciousness. The craft was being tossed about like a small boat in a gale, which was precisely what it had become. A monster that resembled some kind of eel with sharpened teeth the size of pickaxes loomed so suddenly on the viewscreen that Sergeant Shiva recoiled from it with a grunt of surprise and Maid emitted a startled scream. It sank again into the sea, leaving the screen filled with savage mares' tails whipped by ranks of demonic clouds among which lightning engaged in firefights.

"What the hell was that?" Atlas exclaimed.

"I think we've been properly welcomed," Team Sergeant Shiva said and began a head count.

"Captain Amalfi?"

Captain Bell Toll gave him a look.

"Kadar San . . .?"

"Yes."

"Gorilla . . .?"

"Uh . . . Whew!"

"Atlas . . .?"

"I was wrong. That was no piece of cake."

"Gun Maid . . .?"

"I'm with you."

"Ferret . . .?"

". . . sick."

"Blade . . .?"

"Fu-uck."

"Very well," Captain Amalfi acknowledged, taking over the ship from the auto pilot. "All accounted for. Crew, prepare to dive."

Gorilla checked his panel. "We have watertight integrity, Cap."

"We're still picking up no signals, sir," Maid reported.

"Nothing?"

"That's what I said, sir." She sounded testy. "Not even static."

"Very well. Dive . . ."

That was as far as he got. A throaty voice whispered into the intercom, indistinct and hollow like it was belching out of the black depths of the planet itself. A shudder wracked my body. I not only heard and felt the presence, whatever it was, but an image of something otherworldly and indescribably hellish, of death and torture, perversion and brutality, flashed for an instant in my brain. I almost cried out.

"Who said that?" Captain Amalfi asked.

We all looked around, half-expecting something to have entered the pod with us. Something beyond the worlds any of us knew.

A barely audible chuckle slithered through the intercom. A chuckle without humor, dry and raspy. It would have possessed scales if it were visible.

"What's so fuckin' funny?" Blade challenged.

A single explosive burst of sourceless, maniacal laughter. Then, only silence and the lingering odors of ozone and rot.

Maid was the first to find a voice. She sounded shook. "The . . . the Blobs know we're here."

I shivered, although the temperature in the pod must have been over one hundred degrees Fahrenheit. Sergeant Shiva and Ferret drew their Punch Guns.

"That was no Blob," Gorilla said in a low voice. "I don't know what it was, but it wasn't sentient. It left no signature on the LF indicators. Captain, we all heard it, but there wasn't anything here."

C·H·A·P·T·E·R
THIRTEEN

Maid attempted to explain it once she recovered her composure. "We're under OPSEC. All commo is locked down. The only way I can explain it is that we must have picked up a dead transmission that has been floating around space for heaven knows how long. Otherwise, I'm picking up nothing."

"We aren't in space now," Gorilla said.

He exchanged his reentry helmet for the special combat one that fed environmental data directly into his large brain for analysis. After a moment, he reported a negative.

"Same on the LF," he said. "No other life form within the vicinity."

There simply was no room in the pod for a stowaway, and certainly no place for it to hide in such a compact environment.

"Sergeant Kadar, your assessment?" Captain Amalfi requested through the intercom. He sounded distrustful, his misgivings unquestionably fueled by the talk he had had with Lieutenant Snork aboard the *Tsutsumi*. The sown seed growing.

I had already scoured the pod and the immediate vicinity outside the ship, using my particular Talent. Whatever presence I previously sensed was no longer among us. In fact, the environment seemed scrubbed, so non-threatening that it made me even more uneasy.

"I . . . Negative," I responded.

"Nothing?" Captain Bell Toll pressed. "Can you explain it?"

My senses were telling me . . . something. Like in a language I could not quite comprehend.

"I am as baffled as anyone," I admitted.

"Fu-uck," Blade's rough voice barged in. "Why the fuck did we even bring him along?"

If someone removed that particular vulgarism from his speech, it would reduce his vocabulary by half.

Captain Amalfi professionally relegated the odd event to the back of his mind since it couldn't be explained at the moment. With cool efficiency, he punched our target coordinates into the pod-turned-submarine, checked the systems and said, "Dive! Dive! Dive!"

Submerging, the submarine "flew" through the water within a vacuum created by its own remarkable speed, making a sound approaching that of a constant, but low-volume sonic boom. We encountered no more of the eel-shaped creatures or, at our speed, any other aqua life that showed up on the viewscreen as anything other than small, disappearing blurs.

In spite of our meteor-like arrival and the surface storms, we had landed within a relatively short distance of our land debarkation point. Thanks to the computers. Sonar revealed a deep glacier-formed harbor and a river emptying into it. The water became darker, murky, turbulent at the river's mouth, reducing the effectiveness of the viewscreen and forcing us to rely on the ship's nerve center to avoid obstacles and underwater stone banks. The skipper reduced speed to a crawl. We proceeded up the river like a blind fish. My senses tingled like raw nerves.

Captain Amalfi pulled power. "Okay, DRT-bags. We're here. Now we go overland."

The craft sank to the bottom. Atlas shot core anchors into the riverbed to hold the pod securely in place and out of sight. The crew prepared in a businesslike manner to go ashore in a hostile environment. The edginess, the pre-mission jitters -- whatever it was -- appeared to have dissipated. The team returned to its old bantering character. Even I felt more at ease.

Chameleon cammies were activated. They were of a remarkable lightweight material that assumed the nature of the surrounding environment. Clad in helmet, hood, and mask, you could stand in a forest and blend in perfectly with it, so that you couldn't be seen until you moved and then it was like part of the forest moved. There were two drawbacks: their properties of camouflage lasted only a relatively short time, even with an energy source, and they precisely mirrored immediate surroundings so that when you walked next to a particular bush, you became another bush in the exact image of the first. Double vision. Atlas crouching next to Maid in the confined space of the pod powered up his cammies first, and suddenly there were two of Maid side by side. Except Atlas hadn't donned his battle helmet and mask shield and the image he reflected was of his own blond head attached to Maid's body. Ferret guffawed.

"If you had a body like that all the time, big man, I'd give up Naleen for you."

"That prolie slut's already given you up for the home guard, Ferret."

Ferret laughed. "Just so they don't wear it out before I get back."

"You can't wear those things out," Gorilla put in, joining the banter. "I've tried."

"Is that right, Gun Maid?" Ferret leered. "What do you get, about a million miles or so out of one?"

"Pervert."

I laughed, the low Zentadon purr that passed as a chuckle among my kind. Maid shot me an astonished look.

"That's a wonderful sound!" she exclaimed.

"He sounds like a tomcat in heat," Blade rumbled. "Watch out for him, Gun Maid. Next thing you know he'll be humping your leg and trying to jump your bones. I'll bet he's got a tail curled up inside his crotch instead of a set of . . ."

" . . . which I'll neuter if I catch him sniffing around." Atlas glowered.

Gorilla ejected a sensor robot from a hatch in the pod's side to swim ashore and take a look around before Captain Amalfi committed the team. The bot was an off-the-shelf design that resembled a large pill bug. It was about a foot long with a series of rapid legs that could be remotely adjusted for walking, swimming, or even climbing trees. As soon as it was free of the craft, it popped to the surface and stuck up a thin detector rod for a look-see. Huddled around the monitor inside, DRT-213 took its first close-up look at Aldenia.

The Dark Planet was appropriately named. The river water was a black coffee color, obviously stained from tannin leeched from the forest. Above its surface, the atmosphere was dark gray and clutching, hovering like a noxious and dangerous cloud, boiling with stabs and flickers of lightning. We had landed in the middle of one of the numerous storms and it was raining. Not so much that it was raining, but that everything *was* rain. The river appeared at flood stage; it was probably always at flood stage.

The gen-bot swam toward shore on the rain-churned

surface, dodging flotsam hammering swiftly on the current toward the nearby sea. The monitor revealed logs and huge floating boulders bearing down upon the bot, so imminent and present on the screen that Ferret actually ducked. He grinned sheepishly.

The bot reached shore and clambered onto solid, if not exactly dry, land.

"Pan out for a big view," Captain Amalfi instructed Gorilla.

The panorama showed a small grassy clearing — the grass was black — surrounded by a forest thick with spindly, cycad-looking undergrowth and thin, twisted forest giants whose moss-crusted tops disappeared into the cloud cover. Rain and cloud scud swirled. No more forbidding place could be imagined. No wonder the planet spawned an aura of evil, even without the additional ignominy of the taa camps and experimental labs run by the old power-mad Indowy.

"It's like Earth before time began," Maid breathed, staring at the monitor screen.

"It's not Earth in any of its stages," Blade objected. "I was here before. It's more like Hell."

The bot nosed around as it was programmed to do, scouting in a series of expanding concentric circles starting from its initial position. A half-hour passed without incident. Blade grew bored at the repetitive scenery of forest, rain, and creeper mosses writhing in the storm, and broke out his Gauss to give it a last-minute cleaning and checking.

A bolt of lightning struck a tree with a terrific crack. The tree splintered but remained standing in several reduced renditions of itself as wind howled through them. I realized lightning was the reason why the taller trees were so thin-trunked and twisted.

"We're really going to get a charge out of this mission," Ferret quipped.

The bot moved upriver near the bank, then swung into the forest in another sweep that brought it out on the bank downriver. The monitor revealed a large flying creature soaring low above the river, apparently hunting while it ignored bolts of lightning snapping around it. Spotting the bot moving, it dropped low and circled it a number of times. They were apparently curious creatures.

"A pterodactyl," Maid breathed, awed.

"More like a giant dragonfly," Gorilla corrected. "The area study describes four basic forms of local fauna, the most prevalent of which are families of insect-looking creatures in varying size, color, pattern, configurations, and methods of locomotion and sustenance. Some crawl like millipedes, some fly like dragonflies, some build enormous webs and are like spiders, others walk or scurry or run. They are the largest and most dominant of the planet's life forms."

Atlas grinned wryly. "Thank you, Mr. Universal Geographic."

"I'm not through yet. You're going to like this. Most

thrive on foliage or are scavengers, but there are also predator insects that resemble monstrous, mutated hellgrammites the size of lions and water buffalo, with lobster-like pincers and mandibles that are perfectly capable of making hors d'oeuvres of any one of us with one snap."

"Sounds appetizing," Ferret commented.

"There isn't enough of you, Gun Maid, or the elf, to make a hors d' oeuvre," Blade chided.

The second basic life form described by Gorilla was giant predator reptiles. Lizards the size of ground vehicles, toads like boulders, snakes forty feet long -- all with their special adaptations to Aldenia's environment.

There were also fish and unknown creatures in the rivers, lakes, and oceans, one form of which we had caught a glimpse of upon splashdown.

Finally, there were the innocuous mammals. Small, hairy, rodent-like creatures upon which the predator class apparently fed.

We watched the view screen as the giant flying insect receded into the distance, darting and diving as dragonflies will. It was replaced, as though in illustration of Gorilla's impromptu lecture, by a swarm of insect creatures ambling down to the river and preparing to swim across. Comparing their size to the surrounding foliage, I estimated the larger individuals to be about six meters in length and two meters in height. Their carapaces came in three parts. The rear two plates were a reddish-maroon in color, while the front section humped forward over a small shovel-like head and was darker and cream-striped.

"They look like Goliath Beetles," Sergeant Shiva said.

"There is an old, old Earth expression," Maid said, winking at me, "which postulates that if an ant were the size of a man, it could take a few buddies and carry off every building in New York, piece by piece. Here, the ants are bigger than cows."

"With corresponding strength," Gorilla assured us. "Which makes even the plant eaters formidable. Is anyone still wondering why the first two DRTs never came back? They didn't necessarily have to encounter the Blobs."

Blade patted his rifle affectionately. "A depleted-uranium round from this baby will squash any of those like a cockroach under my boot sole."

Sergeant Shiva shrugged. "Maybe."

Gorilla neglected to mention the fifth and sixth life forms now existing upon the planet, perhaps because they were so obvious; the Blobs and us. To these categories I might even add a seventh, more threatening than all the others, if our experiences with the strange laughter, the Presence, proved valid.

"Sergeant Shiva," Captain Amalfi said, "get these DRT-bags ready to move . . ."

He suddenly froze, his attention glued to the monitor. The screen was going crazy, like something had snatched up the bot and was shaking it like a dog shaking an old rag.

The bot's three-sixty wraparound vision had failed to detect its assailant.

The screen went blank.

FOURTEEN

The bot's destruction like that, without forewarning, shook the team speechless. Everyone stared disbelievingly at the blank screen. Finally, Maid breathed what we were all thinking, "It didn't stand a chance. How could whatever it was have struck without our seeing it first? That bot had orbital sensors."

"Maybe we weren't looking," Atlas offered. "Maybe we had glanced away."

Gorilla shook his head. "I was looking the entire time."

"It was fast, damned fast," Ferret said.

Master Sergeant Shiva's scar looked drawn and inflamed.

"The Blobs," Blade growled. "It was the fuckin' Blobs."

Captain Amalfi shot me a look. "Kadar San? Was it the Blobs?"

I had experienced a slight jolt of taa in the split instant

before the attack. I couldn't be sure if my intuition had picked up something, or if the incident had occurred so suddenly that my system was merely reacting. I reached out now with my mind and searched the entire area. I only read emotions, sensed them, if the target were sentient and expressed emotion. I found nothing out there.

Oh, God. Kadar, we have to depend on you. We're doomed.

The thought, fully focused, nearly knocked me off my feet before I realized it came from Maid. I looked at her in amazement. It was the first time I had actually received telepathic communications from a Human in a fashion I recognized. She must also possess the Talent, whether she was aware of it or not.

"Doom is a little harsh," I said to her. It was her turn to look shaken.

"What are you talking about?" Sergeant Shiva demanded impatiently.

I hesitated. "I do not think it was the Blobs. I can sense them now, but they are faint and in the distance."

"Then, what was it?" the Captain insisted.

I had no answer for that.

"What the fu-uck does the elf know?" Blade snarled. "He can't sense his own bad breath."

No one defended me, but Maid kept looking at me.

I'm sorry, Kadar San.

"Apology accepted," I said.

She blushed. "You're reading my thoughts."

I smiled and left it at that. It was safer for me if they all concluded that I could read what they were thinking.

"All right, all right," Captain Amalfi said in frustration. "It had to be one of the insects. Prepare for debarkation. The bell tolls. Send out the other bots."

Sergeant Shiva extended the landing tube to the river's surface, then nudged its sealed exit to the bank and secured it. Viewcams fed back to the monitor the image of the grassy clearing surrounded by forest. The grass was actually purple, but it was so dark it looked black. Nothing moved on the screen. It was still raining as hard as ever. It drummed on the tube.

Four more "insect" bots, larger than the first, these equipped with self-defense mechanisms, were ejected out through the tube and deposited into the clearing. They immediately scurried different directions into the forest to set up a security perimeter and feed their observations back to the submerged pod. After several more minutes of nothing happening, Ferret the point man picked up his weapons and ruck.

"Luck," Atlas said.

"Luck," Ferret said back, crawling on his belly into the tube where its force field quickly committed him to the drenched clearing.

He was virtually invisible to the normal eye in his chameleons. Infrared detectors in our combat helmets picked up his life presence and fed it directly into our central nervous systems. We watched him on the screen as a red energy source.

He first checked the perimeter to make sure the bots hadn't missed anything. Then he did his own squat in the trees to employ his sensor implants against the environment. After awhile, he passed back the word and the rest of us prepared to cycle through the process of debarking.

"Is there an old, old Earth expression for this?" I asked Maid.

She smiled ruefully through her tension. "Yeah. It's called 'Now the shit will hit the fan.'"

The team transported alert and edged into the clearing in the driving hard rain. Lightning cracked and sizzled. The debarkation tube contracted out of sight into the submerged landing pod. It was a bit unsettling, this closing off our escape route. From hither on, the pod's computers were programmed to respond only to the ranking team member still alive. If no orders were received after nine days, it automatically reactivated itself, no matter that we were alive or dead, and returned to the orbiting Stealth. The *Tsutsumi* would recover the ship and pod for analysis of the daily data log the team fed back into the pod's memory banks.

It was going to be a long nine days.

I looked warily about, "seeing" through the infrared only the heat sources of my companions. I felt with my mind, probed, but there seemed to be nothing out there.

At least not nearby. Still, I had the feeling that we were not alone, notwithstanding that the bots had checked out the area and that Ferret had re-checked. I kept thinking of the crazy sourceless laughter. The presence, the *Presence*, which was how I began thinking of it.

The others also had a case of the nerves. I sensed the transformation as the team reverted to its previous edginess. Atlas spun around and around in defense. Taking stock. He lumbered into Blade and Blade roughly pushed him away.

"Asshole."

"Who's the asshole, asshole?"

Instead of intervening to maintain military discipline, as he should have done, Captain Amalfi stood back and observed with . . . amusement? He left it to Sergeant Shiva to restore order and get the march lined out.

"Moving Overwatch," the Team Sergeant ordered.

The team moved out in two elements, one leading and one tailing to "overwatch" the first. Captain Amalfi ordered me to stay with the command element, which consisted of the CO and the radio operator, Sergeant Gunduli. Ferret automatically assumed point with one of the scout robots, with a second bot in advance of them. Atlas dropped back on Tailend Charlie. The remaining two security bots ranged one on either flank. It was an efficient way to march and, under the circumstances, as safe from surprise attack as could be expected.

It no longer mattered what had occurred back on Galaxia. Politics, prolie problems, Homelanders, traitors . . . That was all behind us now. Here on Aldenia we either functioned as a team and trusted each other, or we perished separately and became the third lost DRT.

Our destination was about three days' hard travel away, through some of the most inhospitable country in the galaxy, as we had already seen. The previous two DRTs had landed within a day's march of the range of mountains in which the Blobs' signature had been localized — and neither returned. It was assumed the Blobs had discovered them upon insertion and eliminated them, thus the explanation for our longer distance.

We trekked through a thick wet wood where rain drumming on the foliage muffled sounds of our progress. In places, the vegetation grew in such abandon that Ferret had to hack our way through with a laser. It would rain and rain hard for long periods, then stop suddenly in the middle of raindrops. The fog disappeared almost immediately, as though sucked away by a giant vacuum. Sunshine never actually appeared, just a kind of translucent gray light that made the planet seem slightly less forbidding. Apparently, the short rain-free intervals provided sufficient light, combined with the hot house warmth, to allow wantonness of foliage.

Then the rain started again.

Gravity here was slightly stronger than on Galaxia, but

much weaker than on my home planet of Ganesh where I weighed in excess of three hundred kilograms. For all her small size, Maid wouldn't even be able to get out of bed on my planet. The atmosphere was breathable, although we remained temporarily on manufactured air to reduce our susceptibility to toxicity. We would gradually accustom our bodies to the thicker, coarser atmosphere of Aldenia until by the second day we were weaned from the bottle.

There were many streams, naturally, most of them shallow, and almost as many lakes, around which we lost time detouring. After several encounters with unusually aggressive purple water snakes as big around as city water mains, we learned to steer back from the large bodies of water. Giant dragonflies also hunted the lakes, landing on water surfaces like helicopters and skittering across in the manner of air cushion boats. Herds of Goliath Beetles browsed the lakeside grassy swamps. Symbiotically, they attracted scavengers, who lured out small furry mammals, who were in turn pursued by predator insects and on up the food chain to meat-eating scorpion-things and dinosaur-like lizards. I dreaded what might happen were we confined on Aldenia longer than expected and our chameleons expired so that the local fauna might actually see us.

All this raw unsettled real estate, like vacant lots everywhere, was available for a reason.

Gorilla's pack required a big man to carry it, and Gorilla was the big man. His ruck was stuffed with all kinds of techno gear: sensors, receivers, materials for more bots ranging from the size of a normal mosquito to a children's pet guinea pig. The human males with all their macho muscular enhancements and implants were all enormous specimens. I felt . . . elfin in comparison, never mind that the density of my natural bone and muscle furnished me strength far beyond my size. Especially in less gravities than on Ganesh.

We halted frequently to give Gorilla a chance to work his techno magic for the Blobs. His gadgets proved of little value at this range, what with the thick atmosphere charged with the ozone electricity of almost-constant lightning. I stood to one side, outside the circle of Humans, and attempted to work my own magic. I felt around in the low range of mountains occasionally visible through a break in the forest and cloud cover, probing with my mind for some contact with another sentient being.

Whenever I managed some fleeting bond with the Blobs, they felt slimy and sinister, although not exactly evil, and left a bitter and unpleasant aftertaste. The connection was always weak and there seemed to be no distinction between individuals. It was like they were a single entity with multiple forms. Even so, they seemed to be in many fewer numbers than should have been the case were they building an advance base for the invasion.

"They are not so near," I assured Captain Amalfi. "They have not moved from their original location."

"You are sure, Kadar San?"

"Of that I am sure."

I was much less certain of the Presence that seemed to come and go within our midst. The others were not so much aware of it, I observed, as they were reactive to it. Tension suddenly spiked whenever it appeared, almost as though it were mocking us. The air thickened, the light darkened, and the wind stilled, even though hanging mosses and lianas continued to grasp and grope. Team members clawed and snarled and snapped at each other; the aftertaste in my senses went beyond slimy and sinister.

"Fu-uck!" Blade bitched in exasperation when Ferret on point held up a halting hand and suspiciously sniffed the air with his built-in hypersensitivity. "What the fuck is it now? Put me on point if the bastard is scared of his shadow."

"Fuck yourself," Gorilla retaliated through the helmet intercoms. "The only reason you weren't eaten before when you were here is because you're enough to turn a maggot's stomach."

I didn't think the Presence, whoever or whatever it was, had the power at the moment to cause us physical harm, although its strength appeared to be growing. At first, as on the pod, it appeared for only a few seconds. Those periods were growing longer until by the end of the day and the approach of the shorter of Aldenia's two nights, it was with us a few minutes at a time, leaping and flitting about us like a hate-filled poltergeist begetting mischief.

I feared that whatever its intent, it was with us until we departed this cursed graveyard of my people.

C·H·A·P·T·E·R
FIFTEEN

DAY THREE

We came to a river, black and swollen and crashing through the jungle. Although Aldenia had two moons — orbiting each other, but still two moons — as well as two suns, their ambient and passive light could not penetrate the cloud cover. Night, when it fell, would be total. Captain Amalfi called a halt while there was still enough light to make camp.

"We'll cross when it's daylight again," he decided. "Don't get too comfortable. It's going to be a short night."

About two hours, actually. It was the first of the two nights.

Gorilla set up the bots on perimeter security and activated a hand monitor through which he maintained perimeter surveillance through the robots. Ferret took off his helmet and sniffed the air like a hunting animal. Both soon declared it safe enough that the team could deactivate chameleons while in camp to save them for the more dangerous marches. We emerged into each other's view as actual figures rather than simple energy heat sources.

The team quickly erected individual pop-up bivvies against the ubiquitous rain and warmed rations with energy tabs. It was a convivial meal time, the Presence choosing not to honor us with its company at the moment. Maid went on her encrypted com channel to relay the day's report back to the pod's computers. Atlas and Ferret went back to battering each other with good-natured verbal swords, to the amusement of the rest of the team. I almost felt a part of the group. I was also a bit envious of Maid's sitting next to Atlas.

Gorilla suddenly stiffened at a silent perimeter alarm. My own special senses were dormant; they didn't seem to work on bugs, most reptiles, and furry creatures.

"Penetration! Three o'clock!" he warned.

The team switched to defensive mode, swiftly and automatically from long practice working together. Ferret, Gorilla, Maid, and Sergeant Shiva locked into a circle around camp, weapons facing outward. I joined Captain Amalfi, Blade, and Atlas on the ready reaction force. We moved out hurriedly, but cautiously, toward the machine that had emitted the danger signal.

We drew near to a furious thrashing about in the underbrush and saw our bug-like sentinel engaged in combat with one of a pair of giant hunting hellgrammites. Robots were programmed to defend their controllers. The first carnivore had instinctively counterattacked. It and the bot were locked in a manner similar to mating insects. Although the hellgrammite was many times larger than the little bot, the bot was putting up a pretty good fight.

While the second predator warily circled the combatants looking for an opening, the little bot latched itself onto the juncture between its enemy's head and its enormous yellow-green carapace. It shot out monomolecular spikes, its primary weapon, and literally shredded the hellgrammite's head. The creature's deadly mandible flew free. Green-pink fluid sprayed the surrounding foliage and us. The dying insect continued to thump and quiver, shaking the bot free and hurling it into the grasp of the other creature.

The second terrible beast, larger than the first, made short shrift of the robot. Micro-energy innards and metal exoskeleton exploded in different directions. The creature worried the larger pieces with its mandibles for a few seconds, mindlessly attempting to consume it, before it gave up. It reared up and its multi-faceted eyes on stems looked around for more appealing prey. They fixed on us. We had left camp in such a hurry that none of us had donned helmets and activated our chameleons.

Curious about what sort of meals we might make, the enormous insect advanced, swiveling its eye stems down toward us like microscopes examining microorganisms on a slide. Captain Amalfi took aim with his Punch Gun, a blobby-looking submachine pistol that fired an energy rod that obliterated anything it struck. It was deadly effective within fifty meters or so, but useless at ranges beyond that.

Eager for a kill, Blade beat him to the trigger. The Gauss sniper rifle came issued with auto-tracker Hornet ammo, which sought out its target with incredibly accurate sensor tracking. However, Blade's vanity in his marksmanship refused to allow him to use anything other than old-fashioned "dumb" ammunition. The seven millimeter projectile with its high velocity and extreme range capability, which could reach out to ten thousand meters to touch somebody, virtually exploded the hellgrammite at such close range, spraying us with a disgusting blood slime. What was left of the creature lay in two main twitching parts, while other pieces of it dangled like ornaments in the surrounding trees.

Blade swaggered over, hacked up a goober from his throat and spat it at the remains. He patted his rifle. "Told you this baby would squash 'em like cockroaches."

Captain Amalfi seemed in deep thought as he holstered his Punch Gun. I managed to read him in a general way. He was concerned about security for the team, about accomplishing the mission. After less than ten hours on the planet, we had already lost two of our five robots to hostile attacks, and we still had days to go. When the robots were gone, we came next.

"You are wondering now what could have dispatched the first robot at the river so quickly," I said.

"Look at those things," he replied. "They're enormous, yet the bot managed to kill one of them. What sort of . . . of thing must it have been to destroy a bot so easily?"

C·H·A·P·T·E·R
SIXTEEN

DAY FOUR

I was growing more sensitive to the Presence — or it was getting even stronger. It wasn't with us all the time, or even most of the time, but I always knew when it arrived and when it left again. The others spoke occasionally in hushed tones about the ominous laughter on the pod. In some subliminal way, they seemed aware of something, but at the same time quite unaware of its being the motivating factor behind the sporadic bouts of dissension and quarrelsomeness within the team. Maid attributed the volatile mood swings to the planet's malevolent atmosphere, the ubiquity of threat from the local giant fauna population, and the anticipation of possible action at the Blob site.

Kadar thinks it's something else. What?

I could now read Maid's thoughts more often than not when they were fully formed and not just wool gatherers or random cogitation. Sometimes I even caught fleeting reverie from the others, especially from Ferret and Gorilla who seemed more open and straightforward than the others. I tried sending mind messages to Maid, but they only seemed to make her uncomfortable without getting through.

"You're reading my thoughts again," she accused, mildly rebuking me.

"What naughty thoughts they are," I teased.

She blushed. "I don't believe anybody can really do it. Can we conduct a test?"

It was meal break. Atlas had been sent to check the perimeter. I set my food aside.

"I think you also have the Talent," I said. "You must learn to develop and use it."

"Okay," she challenged. "I'm thinking of something you shouldn't know. Tell me what it is."

After a moment, I purred, my ears twitching with the pleasure of her company. "It's on the right cheek of your behind. A tiny tattooed flower."

She blushed again. "Kadar!"

"Am I right?"

"It's called a rose. You must have peeked when I was down to my panties for the time couch."

"You still had your panties covering it."

"You're naughty, Kadar."

She was a wonderful and lovely creature with her wide

blue eyes and that thick crop of thatched black hair. She was built beautifully too. I liked to watch her when she shed the baggy cammie uniform in camp and wore only a skin-tight body suit while she administered to her hygiene. It wasn't even the Zentadon breeding season, but I nonetheless felt a powerful urge to breed. After all, I was half Human. I was beginning to think I knew which half, too.

"Humans don't call it 'breeding,'" Maid corrected when I tried to explain Zentadon customs in mating. "We call it 'romance.'"

I tasted the word. "Romance. I do like it, Pia. And you Humans cohabit as well? I have seen pictures in which your pet dogs come to resemble their masters after a period of cohabitation."

She laughed in that delightful open manner that simply tore at my heartstrings, as the Humans put it.

"It's true that married people come to resemble each other after a period of . . . cohabitation," she said.

"Married? I know. It is an old, old Earth expression."

"Actually," she replied with a touch of sadness, "it's an old, old Earth custom in which a man and woman take an oath to 'love, cherish and honor beyond all others . . . till death us do part.'"

"I see. An exclusive breeding contract. Do you have one, Pia?"

Her eyes softened. "No one has called me Pia in so long."

"Then I shall call you Pia always."

She glanced up. Atlas was returning from his perimeter duties and walking across camp toward us. Rain began to fall again.

"It's better if you call me Maid, like everyone else," she said brusquely as Atlas approached.

"The Captain needs you for commo, Gun Maid," he said. "He's trying to run an encrypt through the Stealth to the *Tsutsumi*."

"I've told him it's useless to try in this atmosphere."

A bolt of lightning struck nearby, crashing and splintering a tree, as though to stress the point.

Atlas shuddered. "Damn this lightning."

He waited until Maid was out of earshot. He glared at me. "Stay away from her," he warned in a steely tone. "I see the way you look at her."

"Do you have an arrangement?" I asked.

"You're stepping on thin ice, elf."

"An old, old Earth expression?"

"You're about to fall through it."

He stalked off.

It rained some more. It rained almost constantly as we slogged relentlessly toward the mountain of the Blobs. Lightning kept the atmosphere electrified and our nerves frayed. Everyone seemed to cocoon in on himself during those tense periods when the Presence walked among us. Once or twice, a lesser predator slipped past the outrider bots, which were spread thin by the decimation of their numbers, and had to be destroyed. The planet's monsters could see us when we deactivated our chameleons.

One of the hellgrammites was almost upon Atlas, its mandibles slashing and its giant armored legs threatening to pin him for the kill. Taa surged through my veins. I snatched the Viking from the very jaws of death, as Ferret later dramatized it, and deposited him safely to one side before he realized what was happening. Sergeant Shiva dispatched the beast at close range with his Punch.

The team stared at me, disbelievingly.

"I . . . I couldn't even see you move," Ferret stammered, awed. "What kind of enhancement is that? I have got to have it!"

"It's no enhancement," Maid corrected him. "It's taa, isn't it, Kadar?"

She shivered. Then she smiled, came toward me, and kissed me on the cheek. "Thank you," she whispered.

Atlas scowled at her. "This changes nothing," he said to me before he stomped away. "You know what I mean."

"I don't understand what's happened," Maid said, watching him go. "He's usually so happy-go-lucky and good-natured . . ."

I had to sit down on a log. The use of taa left me temporarily weakened.

"Are you all right, Kadar San?"

"I will be fine in a few minutes."

She sat next to me. Atlas and Sergeant Shiva were

examining the dead insect-beast, what remained of it, and the others were returning to their places in the march. Maid looked worried.

"What's happening to all of us, Kadar?" she asked in a strained voice. "We seem to be ... well, different. Growling and snapping at each other, even fighting. All of us except you. You know what it is, don't you, Kadar San?"

I decided it was better that I not share my suspicions, even with her, until I could be more certain. How did one explain feelings about a presence that could not be seen or, with that one exception aboard the pod, heard or detected in any way by Gorilla's sophisticated gadgets?

"Sometimes . . ." Maid hesitated, her brows knitting. "Sometimes it's like I feel somebody else ... Something ..."

It's like the planet is coming alive . . . she thought.

"I overheard Atlas and Blade talking," she confided presently. "They think the trouble is you. They think you're communicating with the Blobs to lead us into a trap. They think you are a Homelander and that the Homelanders are conspiring with the Blobs."

"What do you think?"

"Captain Amalfi says there's no proof of that. Ferret and Gorilla go along with whatever he says. Sergeant Shiva is ... well, he's Sergeant Shiva and handles problems when they develop."

"And you, Pia?"

She looked directly at me. "You wouldn't have saved

Atlas' life if you wanted us to die."

She turned away, then turned back again.

"Kadar San, does what's happening to us have something to do with the insane laughter in the pod?"

"I cannot be sure."

She looked at me for a long, searching moment. I felt her uncertainty, her confusion, her determination. I felt *her*. It was like I went inside her and she inside me. I sent her a thought message: *I will let nothing harm you, Pia.*

C·H·A·P·T·E·R
SEVENTEEN

DRT-213 reached the lower foothills of the Blob mountains and began to climb. The hills were smooth and rounded and the vegetation thinned out some the higher we climbed. Storms actually seemed to die down during the short periods of darkness, but always returned with the watery dawn. From the top of a rocky promontory, we looked out over a wide purple-black valley to another ridgeline on the other side. Lightning popped and crashed and snapped like a pen full of caged Ganesh two-headed tigers. A spectacular and awesome display that kept nerves jagged. It wasn't only the weather, however, that kept the DRT-bags of the team popping and crashing and snapping.

We selected a bony ridge to follow down-valley toward the area where previous sensors had localized Blob activity. Eventually, we came to a series of caves which afforded cover, concealment, and shelter against the weather. Captain Amalfi designated it an ORP — organizational rally point — from which scouting parties could be sent out to find the Blobs and recon them.

The valley should have been full of soldiers and activity if the Blobs were really building an assault base from which to launch an invasion of the galaxy. You couldn't hide an entire invasion army in a valley no bigger than this; you couldn't even hide an advance element from all the sophisticated aids, detectors and sniffers the team had brought along.

Gorilla's molecular detector picked up no indications of Blob genetic material, nor could it uncover plastic or oil molecules that signified an alien robot presence. Maid sifted the air electronically for communications signals, without success. Gorilla dispatched one of the bug bots along the ridgeline to scout. It found . . . nothing.

Patrols returned to the cave to report the same failure. Ferret sniffed the water-clotted winds. He listened through the rumble and bang of lightning. Even though his body was equipped with various enhancements to the five natural senses, he finally shook his head in defeat.

Blade was an excellent tracker with something of the predator's mien about him. He gave a go at picking up a Blob spoor. He and one of the bots examined the ridgeline in both directions. He returned disgruntled.

"Fu-uck," he said in response to the Captain's unspoken query.

The scar on Team Sergeant Shiva's jaw looked taut and inflamed when he removed his helmet and faceplate to scan the valley basin inch by inch through powerful electronic binoculars.

"You're a Sen," Captain Amalfi said to me. It was almost an accusation.

My ears involuntary twitched in frustration. It puzzled me that my senses were unable to detect much activity in this mountainous valley basin in which the alien Blobs were supposedly concentrating their advance base.

"There is a Blob down there," I said finally.

The Captain frowned. "A Blob? There should be hundreds."

"I detect a single Blob."

"What is he doing?" Sergeant Shiva asked.

"I cannot be sure. He is hardly doing anything. It is . . . almost like he is on autopilot or suspended animation . . . He is quite unconcerned. There is no martial feel to him. It is like he is simply going through the motions."

Captain Amalfi paced back and forth at the mouth of the cave, agitated and puzzled. "It doesn't make sense," he fussed, talking mainly to himself. "A single enemy Blob does not build an advance assault camp. Nor does a single enemy account for the disappearances of the previous DRTs. DRT-418 was a strak team."

That acknowledgment produced a minute of restive silence contemplating the fate of those who came before us.

It began raining harder than ever, so that the rain across the cave entrance resembled a live curtain. Lightning flashed so brilliantly it lit up the entire cave and deposited among us the acrid odor and taste of ozone. Sergeant Shiva, who had gone outside to glass the valley yet again, returned through the rain curtain, dusting water off his cammies and shaking his crewcut free of rain.

"Maybe they're building it underground," he suggested.

"Sen," Captain Amalfi said. "Would underground interfere with your . . . your reception?"

"The Blobs communicate telepathically," I said. "I should be picking up something even if they have burrowed to the planet's core."

Atlas moved near, glaring at me suspiciously. "How do you know what the Blobs feel like? Where do you feel them at? In your brain, in your nuts?"

I thought I heard the Presence's baleful snigger, but it was faint and none of the others heard.

"It is a gift, a Talent."

"Fu-uck," Blade rumbled.

A spider's electric web crackled across the dark dome of the low sky outside the cave's entrance. I felt hostility all around me, but none of it came from the valley. Even Maid looked at me in an odd way, like she didn't quite trust me either.

What are you hiding, Kadar San?

Blade stepped up. "The elf is lying," he said. "Can't you

see that, any of you? He knows something he's not telling the rest of us."

A discussion with Blade was like talking to a rock. Another old, old Earth expression I learned from Maid. As I had to avoid overt behavior at all costs — the Humans already distrusted me sufficiently — I reverted to passive aggressive defense and turned my back on Blade. It was a sign of disrespect among both Zentadon and Humans.

"We're being sucked into a trap!" Blade roared. "Ask this tailless elf."

He grabbed my shoulder to spin me around to face him. I planted myself. He was unable to move me. I chuckled with satisfaction. Blade stepped back in astonishment that his muscular enhancements seemed to have failed him. I turned slowly on my own to look at him.

Captain Amalfi interceded before Blade could collect his thoughts. I suspected collecting his thoughts would be a major challenge for him.

"At ease, Sergeant Kilmer," the Team Leader commanded. "That will be all of that."

"A trap," Blade reiterated. He glowered at me, then walked off, deliberately fondling his Gauss.

"The Blobs are up to something," the Captain pondered, staring out past the rain curtain. "It'll be dark again soon. Place the bots on near perimeter with a constant monitor watch. We'll scout the Blobs when it's light again."

I offered to take first monitor watch as a gesture of peace.

"Ferret will take it," Sergeant Shiva interjected. "Followed by Gorilla, Blade, Atlas, and Maid. In that order."

That said how much he trusted me.

"I'll be doing a monitor watch on him," Blade said, jabbing a finger at me. He patted his Gauss for emphasis.

This time I knew I heard the snigger.

C·H·A·P·T·E·R
EIGHTEEN

DAY FIVE

Captain Amalfi and Sergeant Shiva called for a move the next morning; we had thoroughly scouted out this particular AO — area of operations. We continued down-valley with the intention of crossing over to the far ridgeline and taking a look there. A wildlife trail led through the forest on the side of the ridge. Three inches of rainwater turned it into a miniature river, but it was still easier going than cutting fresh trail. The downpour reduced visibility to a matter of yards. Out front on point, Ferret was forced to depend upon the robots for early warning. The crack of lightning, the snapping and writhing of struck trees, the bellow and boom and din of the continuing storm all but negated the effectiveness of his hypersensitive implants.

"When this is over," Atlas complained, "I'm moving to a desert where it never rains. Want to go with me, Maid?"

She didn't answer.

From the middle of the march with the C&C element, I looked back and ahead when the trail opened up and saw most of the team. I noticed that our chameleons were beginning to fail. One or the other of the team would suddenly flicker into full view as a Human form rather than the IR heat source our helmets provided, then just as suddenly merge back into the surroundings. I assumed the dreadful weather was causing the dangerous little glitches.

It was no problem as yet, as long as none of us flashed into view at a critical moment, such as when we ran into a Blob patrol or encountered a predator. I gently probed Captain Amalfi's thoughts and discovered he was also concerned about it. The intervals of uniform failures and our coming into full view of all and sundry were bound to lengthen until they became more than an inconvenience.

"Ferret, I see you," Gorilla hissed.

"Close yours eyes. The damned cammies are going."

We had almost reached the point where the trail cut up the ridge and down into a narrows to cross over to the other ridgeline when Ferret gave the danger signal. He barked crisply through the intercom: "Off the trail!"

The team split to either side, SOP. I was on one side of the trail, Maid on the other. Her chameleons flicked off, making her visible not only to me but also to anything else that happened by. What was happening by was a beast that we had not come across before. I watched it as it approached along the path, passing Ferret and Gorilla without noting their presence. Their chameleons were functioning properly. The imposing creature was about the size of a tracked land rover and resembled some hellish cross between a desert fanged scorpion and a horned dung beetle. Its long, ridged tail of a blistered orange in color curled up over its back and rode at alert above its triangular head. A barbed harpoon protruded from the end of its tail.

It paused when it detected Maid. Its four antennae swept back and forth, swishing aside foliage. Venom dripped from its harpoon. Maid frantically worked with her cammie controls as the beast crouched, preparing to spring.

Maid disappeared from sight. The scorpion-thing relaxed, confused.

She reappeared. The huge predator emitted a type of squeal and again crouched to attack.

Captain Amalfi prevented Blade from shooting it, snapping, "The Blobs'll hear."

Mission always came first.

Terrified, Maid edged away from the trail, attempting to melt into the jungle. I again experienced an explosive rush of taa. Thousands of generations of selective breeding had engrained into Zentadon males the need to protect and preserve females. Zentadon breeding season was fast approaching, a time when young Zentadons' attention spans for most matters shortened and their . . . well, lengthened. Besides, this female in danger was virtually the only member of 213 who had shown me any kindness or friendship, and I had promised to protect her.

No bug, no matter its size, was equal in speed to a young and vigorous Zentadon under the influence of taa. I moved too rapidly for the Human eye to follow. I appeared next to Maid and deftly whisked her to concealment behind a growth of large ferns. To the disoriented insect, it must have seemed its quarry simply vanished.

Another victim appeared running in the trail, however. Lovelorn Atlas had deactivated his cammies and thought to distract the scorpion away from Maid by running directly at it. The poor brave Human was willing to sacrifice himself for the woman. For an instant, I thought to leave him to the attentions of the vermin. That would free Maid from him. I had my weaknesses of character. After all, I was half-Human.

That I even considered letting Atlas cede his life showed I might be no more immune to the unseen influence of whatever entity had linked itself to this mission than any of the others. After only the one thought, however, I left Maid among the ferns and in an instant deposited Atlas beside her. The three of us hid while the scorpion-thing quivered in lost anticipation. Its antennae searched the rain-driven air. Then, as though shrugging, it dumbly scooted on down the trail and out of sight.

"Kadar San, we owe you our lives yet again," Maid cried, hugging me.

"Spare me the sentimentality," Atlas flared. "I had it under control. I didn't need him. It was a piece of cake."

He reactivated his chameleons and moved off like a shifting image. Maid rubbed my arm.

Kadar San, you're the better man.

With that one thought left behind as consolation, she jumped up and went after Atlas. I wasn't sure which weakened me most, the burnout of taa in my system or the choice Maid apparently made.

Gorilla patched a micro-electrode replacement into Maid's cammie suit, but even he admitted it was only a stopgap measure. There would be other failures. He had insufficient replacements to repair them all. It was only a matter of time before all the suits went.

"Captain, we need to get this recon done quickly and return to the pod," Gorilla proposed, worried. "If the chameleons malfunction entirely, which they're starting to do . . .?"

"Bugs gotta eat too," Blade said.

Atlas laughed a little too shrilly. He gave Maid a spiteful look and slapped Ferret on the back. "Don't worry, little man," he gibed, still looking at Maid. "If the fauna get you, I'll take care of your little prolie slut for you. I won't let Naleen get lonely."

It required quite some time for a Zentadon's body to replenish itself following the use of taa. One other time, long before the attempted sabotage of the *Tsutsumi*, I had witnessed a Zentadon go into instant lintatai from the prolonged use of taa and explode. The incident occurred during a crisis when little Zentadon children were trapped inside the flames of an interplanetary shuttle that crashed. The Zentadon teen rescued four of the children, but it was too much for his system when he started back into the fire for more. There wasn't enough of him left to wrap in soul-cloth to be shot into burial space.

I felt shaky and substandard for the rest of the day's march and took every opportunity to rest. It was a welcome relief when we came to the ruins of an old Indowy encampment and Captain Amalfi called an early camp.

Centuries ago, the town must have been a spectacular achievement of architecture and construction. Time, however, along with the relentless rain erosion and the wrecking bar lightning, had reduced it to piles of rubble with here and there a wall still standing encrusted with lichen and snarled with lianas and vines. Giant spider creatures, black with red legs, had spun webs out of strands of silk as thick as hawsers. Abandoned webs stretched across many of the trees. They looked like fishing nets and were coated with a substance so sticky that we had to literally laser Ferret free when he stumbled into one.

After the Humans' Great Revolution succeeded, the conquerors started the initial destruction of the Indowy by nuking the towns and settlements and systematically laying waste to the Indowy war technology so that it could never be used again. Today, remnants of the Indowy technology, unsurpassed in either of two neighboring galaxies, were literally invaluable and brought huge prices on the black market. Space bandits, pirates, scavengers, pot hunters, and other restless ones sought to enrich themselves by finding and exploring old ruins for their secrets. Few of them, however, ever came to Aldenia. Aldenia kept its remaining Indowy and Zentadon skeletons.

A giant dragonfly lifted into the clouds from the dome of what appeared to be the only structure that offered some relief from the storm. It circled lazily above us, as though curious and sensing us even if it could not see us in our chameleons.

"It's like a vulture," Maid commented through her helmet intercom, watching it.

I selected her channel to talk to her in private. "A vulture?" I inquired.

"It's an Earth bird, a carrion eater. It circles over the doomed and waits for them to die for its meal."

"A pleasant Earth thought."

"This place gives me the creeps, Kadar San."

"Duly noted, Sergeant Pia."

Water circulated out of hidden rooms and ate runnels through rubble. Rain slashed at walls with empty window panes.

"How did the Indowy manage to build camps here and live in such a horrid and dangerous place?" Maid asked me.

"You would think it would take a miracle to survive."

"Technology is a sort of miracle," I replied. "The Indowy erected force fields around the camps through which nothing could enter . . . and nothing could leave. During the time that the Indowy bred Zentadon to fill the ranks of their soldiers, there is record of only one escape. A brave and rebellious Zentadon named Ghia San."

"What happened to him?"

"It is supposed that he was eaten by the predators."

"A pleasant Zentadon thought," Maid murmured.

The team crowded into the domed structure. It was small, moldy, and empty of all furnishings. Soon, my energy restored, the relief I initially felt at bivouacking early turned to apprehension. I suspected the camp must once have been an Indowy experimental compound holding Zentadon slaves. That impression was strong in my genetic memory. The character of the evil place slowly seeped through our skins. I felt the Presence stronger than ever. Stronger than in the pod when it emitted its chilling death's laughter.

I recognized its reflection in the faces of the others as we ate, helmets on the floor at our sides. Rain splashed in sheets outside the open door and lightning flashed hard shadows and light, transforming Human features into ghoulish masks. Atlas glared at me for no discernible purpose, considering that I might have saved his life, twice. While I didn't expect him or my other teammates to throw themselves at my feet in supplication for what I had done, considering their mistrust of me, I had thought someone might at least acknowledge it. Instead, exhausted from the long, continuing trek and the constant strain of environment, we huddled together in individual isolation.

Sergeant Shiva, his scar ragged and gorged like a war leech, snarled at Gorilla. "You eat like a pig." He issued a dry and raspy chuckle, an echo of that we had suffered aboard the pod. I half-expected him to burst into maniacal laughter.

Even Maid's tanned and pretty face was not so appealing in the presence of the Presence. I couldn't stand to look at her.

"Fu-uck," Blade said. He stood up, looked contemptuously at his teammates, replaced his helmet and went out into the rain to rummage around in the running dark water that had cut gullies, ditches, and channels among the ruins.

"Are you trying to get rich by finding Indowy war treasures?" Gorilla chided him through his helmet intercom.

"Fu-uck."

It was a cold and silent camp. I lifted my head once, thinking I heard the eerie chuckle of the Presence. It seemed I could never focus on it, study it, because the moment I became aware of it, it was gone. There was nothing there except Ferret at the door taking his monitor watch.

Perhaps it was only my imagination and rain washing relentlessly off the dome and skeining the open door.

C·H·A·P·T·E·R
NINTEEN

It was against military regulations for a soldier to scrounge planetary artifacts with the intent to black market them for personal gain, but sometimes the temptation proved too strong to resist. Especially here on Aldenia where the Indowy war technology had once flourished. Greed was a difficult drive to resist. For some.

Curious about Blade's rummaging around in the old camp alone, I slipped out of the domed shelter. It was not yet dark, but rain fell in such layers, drumming hard, that vision was reduced to a matter of yards and the only sound was of the downpour. Lightning crashed on the Blobs' mountain. I picked up Blade's spoor telepathically. He seemed to have left his thoughts and emotions momentarily unguarded. Within him I also sensed the Presence, whose repugnant signature I was beginning to recognize. It was almost like they were one. Conjoined, as Mina Li might have put it.

Something about the place, undoubtedly its sordid history, at least in part, gave me the jitters. Among these now-rotted remnants of walls and spires, domes and towers and degraded electronic barriers, the Indowy had kept Zentadon herded and confined under deplorable conditions while they experimented on them like laboratory animals. The entire galaxy suffered the result: tailed devils of superhuman strength under the complete control of a madman race intent on sacrificing the Zentadon population in order to eradicate populations and dominate the planets. The Zentadon had been a large and prosperous people prior to the Indowy death camps.

I almost walked up on Blade before I actually saw him. He wore his helmet as protection against the rain, but his chameleons were deactivated. A monster dragonfly materialized out of the wet gray, but Blade jumped up and waved his arms and the insect skidded across the sky, swirling water, and made a few curious circles before making its retreat. At least the dragonflies had proved, so far, not to be a direct threat to us.

I crouched out of sight behind a crumbled wall. Blade returned to digging and pilfering among the rubbish. He seemed to be frantically looking for something. I picked up his thread of impatience and ill temper. Then, to my surprise, I actually received his thoughts, they were so powerfully projected. I couldn't read them completely, but enough fragments came through for me to understand. It was almost like my Talent received a boost once we landed on Aldenia. I had first noticed it in exchanges with Gun Maid.

Blade appeared to be having a thought quarrel with himself. With a shock of understanding, I realized he was communicating with the Presence, but in such a way that he likely wasn't even aware of it. He probably thought the conversation originated within his own fertile mind.

. . . Was here . . . know it was here . . .

Fu-uck . . . idiot . . . know where it was when I get . . .

I saw him . . . buried it here . . . Right here. Fu-uck!

. . . fucking lizard got him . . .

Not the lizard . . . fed him to the lizard . . . Killed him and . . .

Fu-uck. Stanto . . . Stanto dug it up again . . . Stanto wanted . . .for himself . . . Cheatin' sonofabitch . . . He took it. What did he do with it?

. . . Buried I t. . .buried . . . on high ground near base camp . . . before killed Stanto . . .

Horror wracked my body. Blade and the Presence had encountered each other before and found themselves compatible. This Stanto must have been a member of the explorer mapping team Blade accompanied here years before. Apparently, the team had found something important, something valuable here in this camp. The impression that came in strong was of quarreling and bloody fighting that decimated the team. Violence and death spurred by greed and emcee'd by the Presence.

Just as the Presence now choreographed dissension within DRT-213.

I assumed this Stanto Human ended up with the treasure, whatever it was, and reburied it elsewhere. Blade didn't know where it was because Stanto was dead. But the Presence knew where it was.

. . . On the high country east of here . . . Remember . . .? Near the explorer camp . . . If I hadn't killed . . .

The Presence was trying to tell him, but Blade listened only to himself. I felt the Presence's slimy tentacles burrowing deeply into Blade's soul.

It's there! That's where it is . . . near where I dumped Stanto off the cliff . . .

It's not here . . . It's there, damn you . . .

It was difficult to distinguish which voice was whose. What I now knew clearly was that the fauna of the Dark Planet had not entirely destroyed Kilmer's mapping team. The members had got to fighting among themselves and killed each other. Blade Kilmer was the last man standing.

Now he was back and still seeking the "treasure." The Presence apparently intended to assist him as much as it could.

I glimpsed movement from the corner of my eye. Blade also sensed something, for he immediately clamped down on his thoughts. He snapped erect. The globe of his helmeted head ran with water and his face was barely visible through the glass as he peered intently through the rain.

Off to my right, a figure in deactivated chameleons flitted behind an outcropping of weathered stone and darted into a maze of standing walls. It was a small figure that could belong only to someone like Ferret or Gun Maid. It occurred to me that I was being followed even as curiosity had sent me looking for Blade.

I eased away from Blade without being spotted, then ran an intercepting course to cut off the spying DRT-bag member. Few Humans were as fleet as a healthy Zentadon, even without our use of taa. I leaned casually against a wall, arms and legs crossed, looking as nonchalant as possible. Maid sneaked out of the dilapidated buildings, concentrating on her back trail. She jumped and gave a little startled cry when I spoke up.

"Looking for me?"

She recovered quickly. She straightened herself. After another glance back in Blade's direction, she responded with her own question. "Why should I be looking for you? Can't a lady go to the john?"

I must have looked puzzled.

"The john," she clarified. "The bathroom."

"Did you find it?"

"Close enough. I'm going back to shelter now. I'd advise you to do the same. I saw Blade out using the john also."

"Blade *is* the john."

She chuckled.

"Why were you following me?" I asked bluntly.

"Why were you following Blade?" she countered.

For a fleeting moment, it occurred to me that Blade was the second Human form I saw with Mishal at the hangar, along with the female Human that might have been Gun Maid. Blade and Maid, conspirators with the Homeland Movement? Conspirators now in attempting to recover some unknown treasure?

Preposterous!

Yet . . .

I probed her mind, finding it remarkably clean and centered now only on getting out of the rain and finding a place as dry and comfortable as possible. Was she so good at mind control that she could project to me the thoughts she wanted me to hear while covering up all others?

He's a Zentadon . . . she thought. *He's a Zentadon* . . .

As though she had to keep reminding herself that a Zentadon could not be trusted. I was thinking the same thing in a slightly different context. Whom among the Humans could I trust?

"Walk back with me," she invited. "I thought you didn't read other people's thoughts without being invited."

"Lying is sometimes a fault of mine."

"Do you often lie?" she asked.

"Only during the breeding season," I quipped to divert her.

I was wrong about some things. Politics, prolie problems, Homelanders, traitors . . . DRT-213 brought it all with us to Aldenia. It still mattered, more than ever. The team was falling apart. And in this harsh and inhospitable land an individual alone had about as much chance of surviving as a live organism shot into an airless vacuum.

Rain almost stopped during the short night, but the paradiddle of sprinkles gave way in a bang of lightning to a serious drumming once daylight arrived. Everyone had been pushed hard mentally and physically. I was as anxious as the others to complete the mission and return to the pod waiting in the black river. Even the cramped confines of the Stealth seemed luxurious compared to living in a waterfall.

We located the Blob base at midday.

We were traveling the military crest to avoid silhouetting ourselves. Gorilla deployed one of the bots to the top of the ridge to check out the valley and the side of the ridge facing the valley. The robot relayed feed to a miniature monitor. The screen displayed the narrow glacial valley heavily forested, revealed where it curved abruptly back to the north. At its bend were caves — and definite movement among the caves.

"Captain?" Gorilla said in a low voice.

The way he said it was an alert. The rest of the team immediately deployed into a security perimeter. I huddled with the command element — now Captain Amalfi and Sergeant Shiva — around the monitor with Gorilla.

"The base?" Sergeant Shiva asked.

"It has to be," Gorilla acknowledged.

Gorilla manipulated the robot to climb a tree and zoom in on the caves with its close-up lenses. The rest of the team breathlessly viewed the scene through their helmet monitors. Curiosity consumed us as the camera uncovered intense activity. None of us had ever seen the enemy before other than in rare photos, and now Blobs seemed to be everywhere in the valley. Higher-higher was apparently correct in their assumption of an advance Tslek base on Aldenia.

Verti-form maintenance robots coasted about checking and repairing an obvious force field around the base. Roving security balls flew back and forth above combat bots unlike anything I had ever seen. These were huge tracked machines bristling with weapons protruding from various orifices. Gorilla's tech gear also exposed transmissions from placed sensors and smart mines, along with low-level energy transmissions from aerial space defensive weapons.

"It's heavily fortified," Captain Amalfi murmured appreciatively, "and so sophisticated it's virtually undetectable except at very close range."

A phalanx of Blobs on patrol appeared on the screen, moving in wedge formation around the outer boundary of the fortification. They were huge individuals, fully Gorilla's height but even bulkier. They appeared solid and heavy. They were gray to black in color, wore no clothing, and appeared to be forming and reforming themselves to the terrain as they oozed rapidly, covering territory. Each individual carried several strange looking weapons in retractable appendages.

"Good God, they're ugly!" Ferret breathed through the intercom.

"You haven't seen a mirror in awhile," Atlas responded with a trace of his old humor.

Gorilla was engrossed in the screen. "Record it, sir?" he asked.

"In detail," Captain Amalfi concurred.

The monitor transmitted the recordings directly to the waiting pod's memory system, so that a record would be made in the event something happened to the team on the way back and the pod took off without us.

"Sir, we've got it all confirmed on tape," Gorilla reported directly. "We got what we came for. I suggest we return to the pod via the most direct route."

"Hallelujah!" came Ferret's voice. "I'm going back to my baby!"

The news revived the team's morale. In a moment, everyone except Blade was laughing and bantering and the helmet intercoms were buzzing. Blade looked preoccupied, nervous.

"At ease!" Captain Amalfi said sharply. "Your assessment now, Sen?"

My ears prickled. Why couldn't I sense that these beings were even Blobs? Had I somehow lost my extrasensory abilities?

"I sense one Tslek, sir. One."

Captain Amalfi looked at the Blobs on the screen. He looked at me. "One?"

"Sir. One."

His brow creased. The scar-faced Team Sergeant squatted in front of Gorilla's monitor. He jabbed a thick finger.

"Are you crazy, Kadar? Look. You can see at least a hundred or more," he growled.

I said nothing. My ears twitched.

"Fu-uck," snarled Blade's voice in my helmet. "If the only DRTs to return from a Blob patrol had a Sen along, it's a cinch it wasn't one like this fucked-up elf."

"The Blobs divide and reproduce themselves," Captain Amalfi speculated. "Could it be that the reproductions don't communicate, don't think or feel so that you can pick up their thought patterns?"

That wasn't the intel we received at the mission briefing. Each cloned Blob was supposed to be a perfect being with all the qualities of the parent. I pointed that out, adding that I didn't have to read thought per se in order to feel

DARK PLANET # 153

the presence of another sentient. Thought didn't matter anyhow, since I didn't understand their language whether it was thought or spoken.

The Captain remained silent while he digested my input.

"There could be a very large invasion force hidden inside the ridge," Gorilla said. "They may have the technology to hollow out that entire mountain and fill it with warships and troops. The sooner we get back and report it, the sooner our fleet can act and nuke the bastards.'"

"They're there," Atlas argued. "We can see them. Let's get out of here before they spot us and we blow the whole mission."

"I need a closer look," the Captain decided to a general round of protests from the team. "At ease, DRT-bags. Gorilla, bring some of your tricks. You and the Sen come with me. Sergeant Shiva, prepare the rest of the team to move out in case something happens."

He gave me a hard look. "Sergeant Kadar, if you're not right . . .?"

"One," I replied. "One Blob." My senses couldn't be mistaken, could they?

"Cap'n, the elf is setting a trap. He'll get our asses waxed . . ."

"Shut up, Blade."

Captain Amalfi led the way scrambling to the ridgeline, followed by Gorilla and me. Cautiously, we found a place among a pile of boulders where we could see into the valley.

Curtains of rain swept up and down it. Through helmet binoc-vision, we studied the activity around the Blob camp. Patrols coming and going. Unconcerned pickets.

"They're thick down there," Gorilla breathed.

"What do you have in your bag, Gorilla?"

He had a viewster, a small biotic bot that resembled a gerbil or a large rat, complete with fur, tail and whiskers. It would likely go unnoticed among the other rodent-like mammals. Gorilla launched it piggyback on one of the sensor bots, which carried it rapidly down into the valley and released it near the Blob garrison. The bigger bot returned. The viewster was programmed to scurry through and among the other pickets, find Blobs and make near contact with them. We saw everything it encountered through its bionic eyes on Gorilla's monitor. The scenes in turn were relayed to the pod's memory.

The tiny viewster easily penetrated the Blobs' outer security by engaging in all the natural things little animals did on their own: feeding, excreting, sniffing and scampering about. Apparently, the Blobs' sensors were not designed to respond to non-autochthonous life forms. It was simply one among many small mammaloids in the area. Further in, there might be "clean" zones which even a mouse could not access, but so far, so good.

A herd of the monstrous Goliath Beetles rumbled through, pushing over trees and creating a pathway through the rain forest, their armor carapaces shimmering maroon and black in the downpour. The insect beasts went out of their way to avoid the Blob force field. The viewster scrambled out of the way.

"Damn!" Gorilla muttered, unable to get his LF sensors operating. There was increasing concern that our equipment might not survive Aldenia's charged atmosphere long enough to get us back to the pod.

The viewster discovered a small animal trail and followed it to within a few hundred yards of the caves. There was enough Blob activity that it shouldn't have to wait long for contact. It began feeding, upturning small stones and scratching around rotted logs, munching on insects that resembled pillbugs. I hadn't realized until now that there were insects on the planet smaller than tigers and one-family dwellings.

Soon, a Blob patrol came by, moving as silently as wind ships passing in dark space. Gorilla manipulated the viewster into the line of march. The Blobs continued moving, paying it no attention. The viewster halted directly in front of the patrol. Through its eyes, we watched on the screen as the Blobs descended upon it, amorphous and imposing, but clearly oblivious to their surroundings.

"They'll discover it!" Captain Amalfi hissed.

Suddenly, Gorilla's monitor went blank. We lost all contact with the viewster and, through it, with the Blobs.

"It's out of the bag now," Gorilla hissed.

Captain Amalfi studied the distant camp through

binoc-vision. "I don't know," he said. "They haven't set off an alarm. The viewster might have malfunctioned or hit a force field that crippled it. We have to send a patrol down."

"Sir, do you think that wise?" Gorilla asked.

"No. But it's necessary."

C·H·A·P·T·E·R
TWENTY ONE

Ferret and one of the remaining security bots took point across the marshy lowland basin from our ridge to the Blob mountain. Vision inside the forest was minimal, as was hearing because of the constant howl of rainfall and the flashing boom of lightning. Sergeant Shiva led the patrol. I went along as a sensitive to pick up Blob telepathic signs. Blade brought up drag with his Gauss 7mm. Sergeant Shiva thought we might have need for his long-range marksmanship in case we ran into an unavoidable confrontation.

I felt uneasy with Blade at my back, considering what I had learned snooping through the rubbish of his mind. It seemed clear to me that he murdered at least some members of his long-ago explorer mapping expedition over a mysterious treasure. I thought I was comparatively safe, at least for the time being, as long as he remained unaware of what I knew. It was something I dared not share with anyone else until we were back aboard the *Tsutsumi*, or until and unless the Presence led him to the artifact over which the Humans of a previous mission had met their doom.

Maid and I had beat Blade back to the domed shelter last night. When he returned, he spoke briefly to Ferret on monitor watch at the door. Ferret glanced back into the dark room where Maid and I merged in the shadows with the others, I sitting alone, as usual, while Maid took her place next to Atlas and pretended to be sleeping. Blade swaggered over to me.

"It's dangerous out there by yourself, elf," he snarled. "One of those big ol' bugs or snakes could eat you up and nobody'd ever known what happened to you."

It was a not-so-subtle threat. Ferret must have told him I had followed him outside. He assumed that it was I instead of Maid he sensed while he was busy digging.

Don't taunt him, I warned myself. But his insolent and badgering nature was something hard to resist.

"Verily, though I walk through the Valley of The Shadow of Death," I quoted from an inscription I once saw on a prolie's t-shirt, "I will fear no evil — for you are the meanest sonofabitch in the valley."

Blade looked at me. I smiled innocently.

"Fu-uck. One of these days, elf, you're going to let your pellet-sized asshole overload your cannonball mouth."

He was probably right about that. Now, I felt his eyes

boring into my back as the patrol made its way cautiously across the floor of the basin toward the Blob stronghold. I knew he was wondering if I might have read his thoughts and if now might not be a good time to get rid of me.

Ferret up front slowed the pace as we came near the Blobs. We waded knee-deep up a stream with high, wooded banks. Rain churned the surface of the water. Creepy-looking leeches hung from the overhanging tree branches like parasitic intestines. Ferret sliced one in two with his laser-machete. It squirted black blood in a thick spritz for thirty meters. Out of the blood erupted tiny intestine leeches, hundreds of them, which wriggled frantically into the stream and tried to attach themselves to our legs with teeth as sharp as needles.

We fought them off and got out onto land. A short distance later, Ferret gave the danger signal.

Two combat robots, each about the size of a small land rover, were running purposefully across a clearing directly toward us. Our chameleons obviously didn't work against non-life forms that used sensors as their primary mode of identifying targets. Both bots bristled with weapons suddenly hammering and winking death. Heavy lead and missiles cut swaths through the trees, splintering branches and exploding clouds of leaves, bark, and twigs. Little bombs and grenades detonated in a deadly circle of exploding steel to our rear.

I had not been in combat before. Instinctively, I

dropped on my belly into a shallow depression. For some insane, incongruent reason, I recalled one of the holographic cartoons back on Galaxia in DRT-213's team room. Two soldiers were lying behind a single small tree branch while enemy fire burst all around them. *I can't get any lower, Ivan,* one was saying to the other. *Me buttons is in the way.*

Me buttons were definitely in the way.

I controlled my taa output with an effort, telling myself that our attackers were merely machines and that the Zentadon moral prohibition against killing sentients did not apply to bolts, nuts, hard drives, and microchips. I drew my Punch Gun as the two combat bots split up and charged into the trees to make short work of us.

Behind me, Blade took cover behind a tree trunk and was trying to get a piece of target as the bots flitted in the jungle. I heard automatic Grav fire forward from Ferret. Sergeant Shiva was shouting, "Envelope! Envelope right and left!"

Envelope right and left? What the Human Hades did that mean?

All I knew was that I had to fight off lintatai while fighting off the robots. Okay. Deep breath. Now move.

I jumped up and ran to my left. Was that an envelope? I dodged and darted on minimum taa, running between the hard fire and laser energy. Bolts of light streaking. Brilliant explosions. Trees erupting. Ground torn up. And the din of it all! A grunt once told me that a single combat bot carried firepower equal to an entire old line infantry company. I believed him now. These Blob bots sounded like they were equivalent to a battalion. A battalion was bigger than a company, wasn't it? How could anything possibly survive such a barrage. I was glad now that I didn't have a tail. It would only have made of me a larger target.

I ran through the forest tangle to engage the robot on my side of the woods. It was chattering away. The world was exploding all around. Yet, miraculously, I remained unscathed and completely in control of my taa output. What was all this about war being Hell?

I glimpsed a sheen of green-black mottled metal. I dropped to my belly and crawled forward, pulling myself with my elbows and pushing with my feet. A Punch had a limited range. I had to make sure my first round did the job, or the bot would do the job on me.

I saw it. Eight feet tall and, curiously enough, built like a metal Human man. It looked like the Tin Man in the ancient Wizard of Oz film. The Tin Man on steroids with enhancements and fitted with enough artillery to knock down a dreadnought. Old Earth movies were something else the Human side of me liked, along with cocktails. Much of what I knew about my Human half came from their movies.

The Tin Man hammered away with a cannon in each hand and two machine guns sticking out of his belly. I crawled close while it was occupied shooting at my team-mates. Just as I took bead with my Punch Gun, I noticed that the bot was shooting high. Shooting over our heads!

Its sensors picked up on me. It whipped around in my direction, guns blazing. Taa would have given me the ability to easily escape, but I didn't bother.

Sure enough, the Tin Man shot into the forest canopy over my head instead of at me. It didn't even attempt to lower its fire. I stood up and coolly shot the bot with a single round from my Punch. Pieces of it spurted from a center core of blinding light. I ducked to avoid flying metal.

The woods went silent with the Tin Man's demise. Blade or one of the others must have likewise assisted the other robot into its component parts. I stood with the Punch Gun hanging from my hand, marveling at my own courage in the face of danger. After all, I hadn't known until the end that, for some incredible reason, almost like the mechanical monster was partly blind, it had been pro-grammed not to kill us.

A snicker of mechanical laughter grabbed me by the throat. I wheeled to confront the Presence and found Blade instead. He stood not thirty meters away in real life form after having turned off his cammies. Rifle raised, muzzle pointed at me, finger on the trigger. His eyes burned through the faceplate of his combat helmet.

"I can drop you now," he said. "I want you to know it's coming and to see it clearly when it happens. I'm using a

Hornet round. You don't have enough taa left to get away from it."

"Good work!" Sergeant Shiva called out in intercom, scuttling through the woods in his chameleons with a burst of infrared energy. "Wha . . .?" he said when he realized Blade was holding me at rifle point.

Blade slowly lowered his Gauss, but his eyes continued to burn through the helmet facemask. He had missed his moment.

"There are Blobs in the other treeline," he explained, pretending that he had been aiming at them.

I left it at that. My ears flicked wildly, but now was not the time for a confrontation when no winners other than the Blobs could possible emerge.

Sergeant Shiva quickly reconsolidated the patrol; no one was injured, except for a minor shrapnel scratch on Ferret's arm.

"I'm a wounded hero," he crowed. "Naleen will love me."

"If she still remembers you," Blade poked at him, still ill-tempered.

The clearing ahead of us, across which the battle bots had charged, rose in an incline toward a distant treeline. Beyond the trees loomed the ridge into and at the foot of which the Tslek were constructing their advance assault base. We burrowed into cover and gave the open park a good optic-glassing before deciding on further action. Sergeant Shiva had also noticed how the Blob bots appeared to lift their fire to avoid hurting us.

"They had us dead to rights," he pondered, troubled. "Why didn't they finish us?"

"Did you see the big bastard Kadar shot?" Ferret exclaimed, still on an adrenalin high. "He was built like a real man. The other was Blob-like, but this guy had legs and arms."

"And a machine gun for a dick," Blade added sourly.

"It must have been a bot the Blobs stole from us on one of their raids and converted," Sergeant Shiva guessed. "Why aren't they sending more forces out against us?"

A particularly heavy deluge of rain obscured the distant ridge. Lightning splintered a nearby tree. Then, suddenly, the storm lifted and light weakly touched the tops of trees and the crest of the mountains.

"I vote we've seen enough," Blade said. "Let's get our holy asses out of here while we still have them. We know there are Blobs here. That's what we came to find out. What more do we need?"

Sergeant Shiva slowly shook his head. "There's something wrong," he said. "It's almost like we're intentionally being let go. Why?"

"I don't care why," Blade shot back. "We need to return to the pod with what we've got."

"Galaxia is at stake," Sergeant Shiva said. He stood up and squinted against the sprinkling rain. "We can't afford to go back without a full and complete report. Sergeant Kadar, what is your take on it?"

"I still sense only one enemy," I said. "One Blob."

Blade jumped to his feet and pointed angrily toward the ridgeline, now clearly visible below the lowest cloud. "What the hell do you call those?" he demanded. "One, two, three . . . six of the obese motherfuckers all in a fucking row. What are they, huh? Mirages? Hallucinations?"

I couldn't explain it either. Blobs were indeed moving openly about among the rocks and pastures high on the slopes. Blade cranked the Hornet round out of the chamber of his Gauss and, with a sneering look at me, replaced it with a magazine of dumb rounds. He dropped into a sitting shooter's stance, looped his left arm into the rifle's carrying strap for support, and took careful aim over the iron sights. It was another of his eccentricities that he disdained use of scopes and holographic sights. With a true sniper, he boasted, it was more sporting with only you, your weapon, and your target. The range approached eight thousand meters.

"Hold your fire," Sergeant Shiva ordered.

"What for?" Blade responded. "After all the shit that just happened, the cocksuckers know we're here."

Sergeant Shiva couldn't argue with that. He looked at the busy Blobs. He looked back at Blade. He made a "go ahead" gesture. Blade rewarded him with a tight-lipped smile before ripping off his helmet to get a cheek-to-rifle stock sight picture. He drew in a long breath, let half of it out, and held the remainder. The rest of us watched through helmet optics. A party of three Tslek was moving across a mountain opening.

"Three fat Blobs in a free-fire zone," Blade quoted with grim amusement. "Hand in hand, going home. Last in line goes home alone."

He caressed the trigger. The sound of the shot reverberated in diminishing echoes across the basin.

"You missed!" Ferret exclaimed, disbelievingly.

The three Blobs continued their stroll as though nothing had happened.

"Fu-uck."

Blade took even more careful aim and fired.

"They're still up," Sergeant Shiva announced.

Blade stared. He shook his head. It couldn't be. He settled deeper into his stance and took so long aiming that the unperturbed Blobs were almost out of sight among concealing rocks. He popped a cap. The bullet rode the shock wave across the basin. It ricocheted off stone and screamed painfully into the drenched heavens.

Three fat Blobs in a free-fire zone hand in hand kept going home.

"I don't miss," Blade protested, stunned. "I'm telling you. Them motherfuckers are all three dead but still moving."

"Ain't no flesh can take a direct hit from a Gauss round," Sergeant Shiva pointed out.

"I did not miss."

Sergeant Shiva nodded without further comment. He took off his helmet to scratch the scar on his cheek. It looked inflamed and gorged with blood.

"We ain't got much choice now," he said presently. "We have to know what's happening up there. Saddle up. We're going up the ridge."

C·H·A·P·T·E·R
TWENTY THREE

The security bot on point with Ferret located the same small animal trail used earlier by the missing viewster. As the viewster had, we followed the path to within a few hundred yards of the Blob caves. All four of us were back in full chameleon camouflage, using secure helmet intercoms for communications. We were not challenged, although several of the glowing security balls bounced and flew past as though ignoring us. Ferret suggested we might be invisible to them after all due to our camouflage. Somehow, I doubted it. There had to be a better explanation for why the battle bots refused to eradicate us from the planet, and for why the Blobs hadn't gone on full DefCon security alert following the fight at the clearing.

Presently, we came upon the viewster. It was blind and scurrying aimlessly about, bumping into trees and things.

Sergeant Shiva radioed Gorilla at the rally point on the other ridge. Gorilla programmed the little warm-blooded mechanical creature to find a hole, crawl inside and die. Specially-bred bacteria would dissolve it in less than three hours. At some level, everything was disposable.

"Enemy!" Ferret hissed. He was strung so tight from tension his voice sounded ready to snap.

A Blob patrol appeared literally out of nowhere and headed directly toward us. We blocked the trail, invisible that we might be in cammies. My surprised comrades prepared for a fight. I heard firearms rattling.

"Hold up," I said quietly. These things were not sentients; they project no brain waves at all.

"Hold up, my ass!" Blade growled.

"Don't fire!" Sergeant Shiva interjected. "What is it, Sen?"

I stood erect and deactivated my chameleons so there could be no doubt about my being readily seen. The Blob patrol seemed not to notice. It kept coming, neither changing direction nor pace. I began to explain.

"Did you observe that they are five and in the same configuration as those we saw on the screen before energy blinded the viewster?" I asked. "They appeared at the same location as before. Now, watch."

The swift-moving beings oozed on, approaching, paying no attention to me. It seemed they would march directly over me in their path. For a moment I became enveloped in a transparent and insubstantial thickness. The Blobs kept going, leaving me entirely undisturbed. I turned and watched them go.

"Holograms!" Sergeant Shiva exclaimed. "Excellent holograms, but still nothing but light."

Everything became clear. This was why my Talent appeared to fail in detecting only a single entity on the mountain. The entire Blob advance base was a fake, a trap, a decoy populated by a lone Blob to operate the camp's accessories and leave a life form signature to make us think the Tslek were building an invasion site on Aldenia. It was all very cunning. We were not meant to be harmed, only driven back before we discovered the nature of the camp. The two previous insertion teams were not killed by the Blobs; they were destroyed by the hostile Aldenia environment before they reached the compound and reported back on it.

That might have been fortunate for the Galaxia Republic. Otherwise, a Deep Recon Team sans Sen would have taken first readings and images and described a large enemy facility concealed in the valley and inside the mountain. Higher-higher would then have put that intel together with other reports, some of which were undoubtedly also deceptive disinformation, and sent the bulk of the Galaxia space fleet to intercept the invasion route at Aldenia, when in fact the Tslek were invading by another route, straight toward Galaxia and the unprotected Galaxia Capital and

Republic headquarters.

Clearly the Tslek had not counted on a Zentadon Sen exposing their little ploy. The killer bots had not killed us, because the Blobs *wanted* us to escape and report on the decoy invasion site.

Sergeant Shiva brought up Captain Amalfi on the commo link and advised him of what we had.

"Withdraw," the Captain ordered. "Let the Blobs keep thinking they have us fooled."

I felt vindicated for having stuck with my intuition and my senses that this was not a large Blob buildup after all. I also felt a certain told-you-so pride.

"The galaxy owes you, Sergeant Kadar," Captain Amalfi said simply, with feeling, when we returned to the rally point. "Now, let's get these DRT-bags back to the pod. Galaxia needs this intel as quickly as we can get it there. The invasion is not coming from here; it's coming from somewhere else."

Blade glared at me as though still pointing the rifle at my head.

"Fu-uck," he said.

C·H·A·P·T·E·R
TWENTY FOUR

DRT-213 had two compelling reasons for being in a hurry on the way back. First, the fates of Zentadon, Indowy, Humans, and other Republic Federation peoples depended upon the timely transfer to higher-higher of the intel we had recovered from the counterfeit Blob invasion site; second, we were eager to reach the pod for our own personal comfort and safety. For all we knew, having been cut off from outside communications for the past four Galaxia days, Republic battle fleets might already be on their way to Aldenia, leaving other invasion routes open and unguarded.

I added a third compelling reason: Blade. If he got the chance, he was going to wax me for a trophy. I could tell during his unguarded moments that he suspected me of having read from his mind the guilt of his previous crimes. Blade faced execution for the murders if I knew and I made it back alive. It was safer for him if I died by accident or in a firefight.

There was also the matter of the artifact, the "treasure" for which he had been searching in the Indowy camp.

"Did you come this far the time you were here before?" the Captain asked him.

"No," Blade lied, casting a glance at me. "We saw other camps, but not this one."

"What did you find?" Gun Maid asked deliberately.

"Nothing important," he lied again.

I attempted to interrogate Maid when I caught her alone.

"You were not following me that evening we camped in the Indowy ruins," I accused mildly. "You were watching Blade. Why?"

She looked at me with startled blue eyes. "Why would I do that?"

"That is what I am asking. Blade was looking for something. You know what it is."

"No." Her thoughts told me she was telling the truth, which puzzled me, because I also read that she at least was trying to hide something from me.

Kadar San is a Zentadon. Kadar San is a Zentadon.

That was her way of blocking my exploration of her thoughts. I wondered how she learned to do that.

"Whatever he was looking for," I said levelly, "I think he knows where it is now. If he finds it, we are all in danger."

A Zentadon cannot be trusted . . .

"I can be trusted," I said.

She blinked. I read sudden fear.

"Why are you afraid, Pia?"

"Kadar San, we will be off this planet in two days. Then perhaps we can have a sit-down talk."

"And a cocktail when we reach Galaxia."

She smiled, calm again. "Perhaps. When we reach Galaxia."

The route cut back through the low hills we had intervened on the way out. We followed game trails paralleling the ancient remnants of mountains. Foothills of taller mountains beyond appeared as shimmering mirages through the raveling skeins of rain. We often forsook caution for speed and, as a result, experienced several close calls with the local fauna, both insect-like and reptile-like. Fortunately, reptiles, most of which were savage predators, were far less numerous than insects. We encountered only an occasional giant snake, a big spider and, once, a pack of thickly-built lizards with rows of saw-like teeth. Gorilla continued to urge more haste, as our chameleons were rapidly deteriorating. We were constantly fading in and out of view.

So far, the Presence had caused us no direct threat. It simply was with us at various times, spreading its corruption like an undiagnosed malignancy. Now and then I thought I glimpsed it, dark and vaporous, less substantial than a wisp of fog, standing or moving among us. At other times, an entity seemed to be within the rain itself, within stone or forest. The moment I became aware of it, it was gone, leaving only tension and anger and disagreeableness within the team.

Increasingly, I began to sense a second presence, this one weaker and less defined than the original, more difficult for my mind to grasp onto and catalogue. Although it seemed somehow less rancorous, it unnerved me to think that the Presence might be growing and attracting other entities who fed upon something dark within the Human psyche until, like malevolent parasites, they took over completely.

We came to a deep, strong stream and followed it downhill to a point located by the scout bot where we could cross without having to construct a rope bridge. The water was shallow at this point and the river narrow. We ran across it on line to get to the other side as quickly as possible without attracting any of the teeth and stingers we knew to inhabit bodies of water.

When the longer of the two Aldenia nights overtook us, Captain Amalfi called for a camp with our backs snug against a towering cliff and our faces toward the stream. It was not a good camp, tactically, as the sounds of the stream could mask the approach of intruders while it lulled tired sentries to sleep. Although darkness fell so completely that even the local fauna rarely moved from their beds unless disturbed, providing a modicum of safety during the

Aldenia nights, Captain Amalfi took no chances.

Since the incident with the holographic Blobs, I seemed to have partly won the trust of at least the majority of DRT-213, those being the Captain, Sergeant Shiva, Gun Maid and Gorilla. Captain Amalfi started assigning me turns on night monitor watch along with the Humans, displaying his newly-discovered trust in my loyalty. Ferret, as usual, was noncommittal; Blade remained openly contentious, hostile and suspicious; and Atlas was jealous and resentful of any contact I might have with Maid.

I drew first watch, along with Gun Maid. For additional security on the way back, because of approaching exhaustion, we doubled up on night guard. Atlas glared at me, not liking my pairing with Maid. He sullenly took his pack and, not speaking to anyone, tented near the cliff face.

I sensed in Maid's emotions a certain excitement and anticipation that, to my discomfiture, I associated with mating. Ardor in Human females, I decided, was not so much different from that of Zentadon females during the annual season of breeding, for all that the Zentadon females' long, sensuous tails made them more expressive. Humans might well have done better socially with tails of their own. Sometimes I felt cheated, even partially muted, by having lost that particular part of my physical legacy when my parents succumbed to passion and produced a hybrid line of half-breeds. But, as Maid once said in an old, old Earth expression, we all had our crosses to bear.

Her excitement transferred itself to my Human side. I looked at her and caught my breath.

What will he think if I'm too forward? Will it frighten him off?

Try me! I sent back. The returned thought seemed to jolt her, as though she had actually received it. That puzzled me. Why was my ability to read thoughts growing stronger on Aldenia? Was it, as Commander Mott suggested before he dispatched me to DRT-213, because close association with Humans opened up my receptiveness to them?

Fu-ucking elf! Maybe a bug'll get him tonight.

That from Blade. It shook me upright and I looked across the camp in his direction. I couldn't see him in the darkness, but I felt his illogical hatred of beings different from his own and for me in particular. For reasons I couldn't even guess, and perhaps which he couldn't himself explain, he despised me from the beginning. Now he had a real reason to fear me, and to hate.

Suddenly, I was no longer sure I wanted to read others' minds, with or without their permission.

We had deactivated our chameleons before nightfall in order to save them for when we were on the march. Maid donned a wide rain hat over her black hair. She smiled at me before she assumed her post downstream. In the quick-covering night, I erected a pocket bivvie to offer refuge from the rain, but left all sides open. I caught rain in a tin folding cup and added some ground harrow herbs. Grasping the cup in both palms, I concentrated on the contents until they were of a temperature to my taste. I sipped the hot tea and nibbled on a prepared LR/DRP meal of vegetables. There was nothing moral in my vegetarianism. It was simply a preference cultivated among all Zentadon in order to temper the predation of our ancestors. A consolation, perhaps a conciliation, to civilization.

I sensed Maid's approach after the others slept, although I failed to detect her light step in the rain. Lightning shimmered on the surface of the river, a spectacular display, and in the flickering she joined me beneath my overhead shelter. I moved over and in the aftermath of the electrical fanfare, felt the warmth of her small muscular body settling on the boulder next to me.

I had never bred before for all my wiseass macho bragging, so was unfamiliar with its rituals of "romance", especially as they applied to Humans who pursued them much more ardently than the Zentadon. I felt her heart racing and her breath catching in her throat and the rise of her body temperature, all certain indicators of passion. I became aroused by feeling her aroused. It was not yet the season for Zentadon coupling, so it surprised me that my Human side responded so readily.

"If the mountain won't come to Mohammed . . ." she quipped in a thick voice.

"I know. Another old, old Earth expression."

". . . then Mohammed must go to the mountain," she finished with a nervous laugh.

I'm shameless, shameless . . .

I offered her tea, my trembling hand almost spilling it. That was me all right; worldly and coordinated. She sipped from my cup. We sat side by side in the total darkness between lightning flashes.

"It's raining cats and dogs," she said presently. We both chuckled. "I like the purring way you laugh," she said.

I felt comfortable with her while at the same time uncomfortable with her being here. Atlas and his jealousy could make trouble for us. Cross-mating, or even the appearance of cross-mating, was against both Human and Zentadon law.

She tried another sip of my tea.

"What is this?" she asked, thrusting my cup back and pulling a face.

"You like it then?"

"Does it come from Ganesh?"

"Yes, but the Zentadon on Galaxia also pay the prolies to grow it for us."

"Do you miss it?" she asked softly. "Ganesh, I mean?"

"There are times," I admitted. "Have you been there?"

"No."

"If it were not for the cloud cover, if we could see the stars, I would point it out to you."

"Could we also see Earth from here?"

"If we knew where to look. Do you miss Earth?"

"I have never been there either, but I have seen movies and visited through VR."

"It is a magnificent planet, seen from space."

She gave a start. "You have visited? How is it? Is it as ruined as they say? Is there still the aftermath of the war contamination?"

"No one lands there anymore, Pia. Parts of it are still uninhabitable, populated by dreadful and savage mutants. Still, there are isolated points where Humans have struggled to make a comeback. After all, they sent colonists into space. Galaxia is proof of that."

"If the Blobs reach Galaxia," she said in a quiet voice, "they will destroy it too. Maybe it is Human destiny to keep moving from planet to planet like interstellar gypsies."

"They will not reach Galaxia," I reassured her. "In two more days we will be off Aldenia and able to warn the Republic."

She shivered against me.

"You are cold?" I said.

"The chameleons are losing all their properties, beginning to leak and let in the weather. It's almost like they're rotting while we're wearing them. Gorilla fears that we might not reach the pod before we become visible to everything."

She shuddered. She recalled her close call with the scorpion-thing when her cammies malfunctioned and it saw her. I knew what she was thinking.

"Here," I offered. "Let me touch you."

She said nothing. I took that as permission. I placed my hands carefully on either side of her neck. She was cold. I felt her heart racing again. I made myself concentrate. She gasped.

"How do you do that? It's like sitting before a campfire."

I gave the Zentadon purr. "Yes. I am Sergeant Kadar San, campfire."

"You're not having sex with me or something?"

I snatched my hands away, causing her to giggle.

"Please, Kadar. I was only teasing. Put them back on my neck. They're warm."

I did. She sighed with pleasure.

"When you awakened from cocooning in the dreadnought . . .?" I began.

I felt her smile. "You were there dressed in green," she said. "You looked like a wonderful Irish elf with gold hair and big green eyes."

"I was wondering, "I said, teasing. "The VR you were experiencing must have been X-rated. That is how you describe it — X-rated?"

"You read my mind."

"No. Your lovely nipples were hard."

"Kadar San!"

She grew very quiet. I took away my hands. We sat, comfortable with each other. Lightning played on the storm's surface and thunder coughed and growled.

"You have a mating contract with Atlas?" I finally asked. "You didn't answer when I asked you before."

"He would like it to be. But, no, we do not have a relationship."

"Is a relationship the same as a romance?"

"Perhaps not. A relationship is about sex. Romance is when a man and a woman fall in love and . . . surely you have romance on Ganesh?"

"We mate," I said, defensively.

"How do you mate?"

"It . . . it is arranged during the breeding season."

"How is it arranged, Kadar San?"

"Our respective representatives meet and they decide the terms . . ."

"I see. Your seconds? Like a duel? How long does the mating season last?"

"Nine days, sometimes shorter. It depends upon the female's ovulation and . . ."

"That's a true relationship," she said, appalled. "How do you do it?"

"It is our custom . . ."

"No. I mean *it*."

"It?"

"You know." She seemed embarrassed. I received a mental picture of a male and female naked together.

"Oh." It was my turn to be embarrassed. "Well . . . do

you really want to know?"

"I'm interested," she said bravely.

"Well . . . The female assumes the position on her hands and knees. Then the male places her tail over either his left or right shoulder. Over the left if he would like the 'relationship' to continue. Over the right if not. Then he . . ."

"Doggie style. Wham bam, thank you, ma'am. If he places her tail over his left shoulder, does that mean they are married?"

"It means they are exclusive. But exclusive does not happen often."

"What does she do with her tail if she rejects his offer of exclusivity?"

"That is her choice. She will move it to his right shoulder."

"What does the male do with *his* tail?" She giggled. "Providing he has one."

I felt my face burning. "Nothing."

"Are you exclusive?"

"I have never mated."

"Why not?"

"I have been away from Ganesh for awhile. I . . . I . . ."

"And this . . . arrangement occurs only once a year?"

"That is so."

"What do you do for the rest of the year?"

"We work. We study. We . . . things."

"But you don't make love again."

"When the season comes again."

"How awful! Do you think I am too forward, Kadar San?"

"Yes."

She giggled. "So do I. You don't have the urge except during the breeding season? You, personally, I mean?"

"I am half-Human," I pointed out, defensively.

"You have the urge?"

My ears went into spasms. I was glad she couldn't see them. She moved close.

"Kadar San, I haven't properly thanked you for saving my life."

She placed her lips over mine. My eyes widened in surprise just as a magnificent bolt of lightning spidered from horizon to horizon. In the sky's afterglow, Pia said, "You're supposed to close your eyes. Haven't you ever been kissed?"

"Well . . ." I stammered.

"You haven't, have you? Did you like it?"

"I do not know," I lied. "Shall we try it again?"

C·H·A·P·T·E·R
TWENTY FIVE

DAY SIX

At daybreak, during a hurried breakfast away from the rain in our individual bivvies, I looked out and saw Blade walk over to Captain Amalfi's tent and bend down to go inside after announcing himself. All the other bivvies were sealed against the rain.

A moment later, Gun Maid stuck her helmeted head out from the opening of her shelter and looked quickly around, as though to make sure no one was watching. I closed my opening to a mere peep hole. Maid emerged, hunched against the rain, and made her way covertly to the commander's bivvie. She crouched behind it out of sight, obviously eavesdropping on the conversation inside.

Although my powers as a sensitive had grown during my time on Aldenia with the Humans, there were certain occasions on which I drew a blank. Such as when Humans were talking to each other. Perhaps it was because they didn't think when they were talking.

I was as curious about the content of the conversation between Blade and the Captain as Pia. I donned my helmet as protection against the storm and slipped outside. Gorilla and Ferret had drawn last watch, but withdrew at first light to eat and prepare for departure. No one was out and about to see me as I crept from camp and returned against the cliff wall behind Captain Amalfi's overnight domicile. Gun Maid was so engrossed that her first awareness of me came when I threw one arm around her waist and snatched her off the ground. My free hand clamped over her mouth to prevent an outcry.

I carried her into the hidden protection of an outcropping of rock.

"It is me," I whispered into her ear.

She stopped struggling.

"I will let you go," I said. "Keep your voice down, little spy."

She whirled angrily to face me as soon as I released her. "I am not a spy!"

My eyebrows lifted and my ears gave double flickers. She blushed, then took a breath.

"Okay. I'm a spy. You caught me. Are you going to report me?"

"Would I do that after last night?"

"Would you?"

"Pia, we have to trust somebody. Let us start by trusting each other."

She studied me.

"Are you a Homelander?" she asked bluntly.

"Why would you think that?"

"I saw you at the hangar with the Homelanders trying to sabotage the *Admiral Tsutsumi*," she accused.

"Wait a minute," I recoiled. "I saw *you* with the Homelanders."

"You couldn't have seen me with them, Kadar San."

"Same here, Pia Gunduli."

We looked at each other.

"We have apparently had misconceptions," I said finally. "Okay. Who goes first?"

Can I really trust him?

"You first," she said.

Nothing ventured, nothing gained. An old, old Earth expression. Rainwater pouring off the cliff and beating past the sheltering overhang covered the sound of our voices. I hurried through my explanation. We didn't have much time before the camp was up and ready to move out.

I told her about Mina Li, how I had gone to the safe house to reason with Mishal, only to have been taken prisoner. I escaped and intercepted the terrorists on post while they were attempting to bypass the security robots.

"You were the one throwing rocks!" Pia exclaimed, giggling. "I saw you back in the shadows. I assumed you were the lookout. But it was you who triggered the alarm by throwing rocks!"

She sounded relieved.

"A skill I learned from a misspent childhood. I saw a female with the terrorists at the hangar. That was not you?"

"I'm not saying I don't have a certain sympathy for the Homelanders' aims for a planet of their own on Ganesh," she began seriously. "I'm acquainted with some of the Homelanders. I got to know them through volunteer social projects working with both Human and Zentadon prolies. I'm afraid I'm a bleeding heart."

"Bleeding heart?"

"It's an ..."

". . . old, old Earth expression."

"It means I want to see misery alleviated wherever I see it. To abbreviate a long story, a Zentadon prolie friend contacted me the night before we set sail from Galaxia. A Human man and woman were inquiring as to whether or not the Homeland Movement was interested in buying a secret Aldenia device that would give the Homelanders the power to overthrow the Republic government of Ganesh and return the planet to the Zentadon. My friend didn't know what the device was, but she described Blade and this woman he associates with. Blade hinted to the Homelanders that he had the device hidden on Aldenia and was returning there to pick it up. He said the device should be worth millions of credits."

"All the more reason why Blade would not want the *Tsutsumi* blown up," I reasoned.

"Exactly. Sometimes there isn't much coordination between the Homeland bands. I learned that Blade and his lady friend, who's a medic specialist in another DRT, were supposed to make contact with Homelanders to receive a down payment on the device. So I followed them. Instead, it seems Blade had been warned that another Homelander group was going to sabotage the dreadnought that would take us to Aldenia."

"How bizarre! So . . . Blade and the female were at the hangar to try to stop the sabotage? The female was who I saw with them?"

"Yes. She and Blade argued with them, but Mishal was going ahead with it. Some of the terrorists, maybe even most of them, are very naïve when it comes to the Blob threat. They think it's a ploy manufactured by our government. Blade was about to play the big hero and cut loose on the saboteurs when . . . Well, you know the rest. Stones began flying."

"I do not know *all* the rest," I said. "Why did you not go to CD with this?"

"Why didn't you? I could be implicated because of my contacts. I simply ran away. No harm was done to the *Tsutsumi*. Besides, it would be my word against Blade's. I've been trying to find out what Blade has hidden here and where it is. It's the only way I can get the proof of what he's doing and stop him. While I might be a bleeding heart, I'm a patriot who wants to see justice done without destroying the Republic."

"You are a Zentadon lover," I said.

She looked at me. "Maybe. So where do we go from here?"

"First, tell me what you learned from your little pre-breakfast sortie." I indicated Captain Amalfi's tent.

She frowned. "Blade seems in a hurry to get back to the pod. He persuaded Captain Amalfi that an easier, faster route exists if we move over toward the steppes. His mapping team used it before."

"What did Captain Amalfi say?"

"We're going to change routes."

I watched it rain. I heard movement down in the camp.

"Do you suppose Blade has already found the item?" Maid wondered.

"I doubt he has it yet," I decided after a moment of consideration. "But it does sound to me like he knows where it is. That is why he went to Captain Amalfi with the new route. Whether he has it now or whether he picks it up on the way out, I think we are relatively safe as long as the team doesn't know about his little secret."

I gave her a briefing on Stanto and my suspicions that Blade had murdered the members of his previous expedition in order to obtain the mysterious artifact. Maid listened while the blood drained from her cheeks.

"This has to remain between you and me," I cautioned. I started to say "between you and me and the Presence," but I didn't have time right now to explain it. "That means we don't do anything to make him suspicious of us. Let him get the item and keep it until we're back aboard the *Tsutsumi* where we can go to CD and have him arrested. Good enough? No more snooping around and spying?"

"Good enough," she agreed with a tremulous smile.

"Now, let us return to camp before Atlas misses you."

"Kadar San?"

I paused.

"Kadar San, I'm happy that you're not a traitor."

"I am happy that you are not a traitor, Pia Gunduli."

C·H·A·P·T·E·R
TWENTY SIX

No one questioned Captain Amalfi's change of route to take us into the more open steppes to the east. Blade glowered me a menacing look as though daring me to protest. I ignored him and treated the change with enthusiasm to throw him off, even going so far as to comment that I was all for anything that would bring us to the pod faster. Maid did likewise.

We climbed until nearly midday. The forest thinned out into large savannahs and meadows where herds of herbivores, mostly Goliath Beetles, browsed and dug for grass roots. Once or twice we spotted predators: a lizard, a couple of the scorpions with their blistered orange tails, a spider, and a hive of giant wasps. The hive was at least four stories tall and constructed of a waterproof paper-like material secured between two trees. The wasps were bright red and resembled fighter aircraft swarming around an air-and-space port, their wings beating the rain into a smoky mist. The predators kept their distance, eyeing us with curiosity as we passed. We circled wide of the wasp hive and the spider.

The Captain called for a break. Shortly after we resumed travel, the robot on point picked up a power energy source from the east. Blade rushed forward with the commander to check it out.

"After last night," I privately joked to Maid through the intercom, "the energy source it is picking up might be us."

I loved the way that brown female human giggled. She didn't have to have a tail.

"Sen?" Captain Amalfi sent back the request.

I moved up to the Captain and Blade. The three of us continued forward to where Ferret had conducted an alert squat. His malfunctioning cammies flashed in and out of sight. One moment he was a duplicate of the rain, virtually disappearing except for the IR signal he made through our helmets. The next, he knelt hunched against the weather with rain streaming off his helmet, through the faceplate of which I discovered his axe blade face sharper than ever.

"It might be more Blobs, Cap," Ferret said. "The bots don't pick up energy sources from the critters. It simply shows them on the monitors."

I sensed it now. The Presence. Stronger than ever, strong enough for the bot to pick up, as though beckoning

us. Blade's IR signature blazed with tension. He knew
what it was.

"What is it, Kadar San?" Captain Amalfi asked.

"It is not Tslek, sir."

"What is it then?"

I hesitated. I also knew. I felt it through the Presence
and through Blade's excitement.

"I sense only that it is there," I said. "I suggest we
avoid it."

"No!" Blade thundered.

"That's my decision to make, Sergeant," Captain
Amalfi said.

He gazed reflectively in the direction of the pod waiting
for us in the river. We had five days remaining before it
automatically activated, surfaced, and blasted off without
us. The commander frowned and his eyes shifted toward
the source of the unknown vibrations. I gently probed
and found his thought patterns not entirely rational. It
occurred to me that the signals were being transmitted by
the Presence. Apparently unable to communicate directly,
limited to using only its "influence," the Presence was utilizing this method to attract not only Blade, but indeed the
entire team to the treasure. At least that was my initial
assessment, my fear.

But why this way? I had only a minute to mull it over
while the commander made up his mind. I tried to reason
it out. Did the Presence understand somehow that Pia and

I were on to Blade and that we intended to stop him once he carried the item aboard a Republic starship? If everyone on the team knew of the treasure, then Blade would have to act overtly now in order to preserve it to himself. Apparently, greed, jealousy, and strife — created by the Presence? — had infected Blade's old expedition, as it was infecting this one, and led to wholesale carnage.

The Presence wanted the artifact to surface among the peoples of the galaxy. Blade's rapacity was merely a tool for that transmittal. Something had happened last time that resulted in the treasure's being left behind. This time, *this time*, it would not be lost, even if everyone had to die in order to ultimately release it from Aldenia isolation. Everyone, that is, except the messenger, Sergeant Darman "Blade" Kilmer. Used once, used again.

Against the Presence I possessed a major advantage which the Humans did not have with their less developed sensitivities. I was aware of it. I could fight it, resist its takeover even while the rest of DRT-213 seemed to be moving inexorably, even against their wills, to come under its domination.

"We have to investigate," Blade insisted.

"It could be following us," Ferret suggested in a chilling voice. "It's better to confront it now in the open where we can see it."

"No!" I countered. "We will be at the pod tomorrow. It is more important that we return to the ship with the intel about the Blobs."

Mine was a lone voice against. Even I had to admit that I was curious about this thing that had already led to death, and would likely do so again.

In the end, as I suspected, Captain Amalfi decided our duty lay in investigating. I heard a dry, raspy chuckle, but when I looked there was nothing there.

"Pia?" I said to her privately.

"Go away!" she snapped. The Presence had got to her as well.

The Presence became so powerful in my mind as the team drew near the power source that even I had to struggle to resist it. Its taut, greasy tentacles probed every area of my brain. A spring screwing itself into my core. My entire body felt horned and crusted with filth and transferred sin.

The bot on point cautiously entered another Indowy ruin from the bad times. There was little left of the settlement, but it must have been one of considerable size judging from the mounds covered by stunted forest out of which rose fragmented plascrete walls. The evil that is done, I thought, lingers long after the doer is gone.

I still sensed nothing alive, just something there. *Here.* Like the harpies of old human lore luring ships to wreck on the shoals.

It's alive.

I whirled toward Pia.

"Let's leave this place! Now!" she warned suddenly,

resisting the power.

"Shut the fuck up, cunt!" Blade rumbled.

Like the trained hunting machine that it was, the bot made its way to one of the smaller mounds and stopped on top of it, indicating that it had localized the energy source. Then, unexpectedly, for no apparent reason, it exploded with a terrific bang. Pieces of it whizzed in all directions.

Everyone hit the dirt. Weapons appeared ready for use.

"What the fuck . . .?" Blade exclaimed.

My heart thudded. "Will you listen?" I pleaded. "Whatever it is, leave it be."

"It was an old mine that exploded," Sergeant Shiva reasoned.

"It was not a mine," I argued. "Remember the first robot? It also went off like that for no reason."

Both of them had detonated, I thought, because they came too near the Presence and its voltage. What kept it from doing the same to the team? Had it other plans for us? A somber thought.

"Chickenshit elf," Blade said.

He got up and climbed to the top of the little mound and began digging. None tried to stop him. They were as curious as he, mesmerized by the Presence and its unrecognized objective. We had been deliberately led to this evil place. I backed off as taa squeezed into my system. My ears tapped anxiously against the sides of my helmet.

Gorilla called up one of the two remaining bots to help

with the excavation. It went to work without suffering the fate of the previous robot. Within a short time, the powerful little machine burrowed into the mound. It pulled out of the hole and into the light a rather thin plasteel case. It was black, about a half-meter long, slightly rectangular, and was equipped with two queerly fashioned handles for carrying. Gorilla's sensors remained silent, no longer picking up an energy source.

Blade threw off his helmet. He pounced greedily upon the little case. A quick cleaning revealed a control panel on one side. Sergeant Shiva took the case from Blade and thrust it at me.

"You understand Indowy," he said. "Read the inscription."

I balked at even touching the thing. I looked at Blade; he already knew what it was. It was what he had been looking for.

"Read it, Sergeant," Captain Amalfi ordered, his patience tried.

They all stared at me. Glared. Even Gun Maid. Although they should have trusted me by now, they seemed more wary and suspicious than ever. I looked at the case, reluctantly. A wave of dizziness overcame me when I saw what it was. A *lindal*. I jerked back from it in horror.

"I cannot," I said.

A lindal was one of the damnable creations the Indowy had invented long ago to induce taa in the Zentadon and to master us. I suspected it could also be used, in the wrong hands, to affect similar hormonal imbalances in other peoples in order to control them. It was one of the most hellish finds imaginable, one that empowered its possessor to literally rule the galaxy, as the Indowy had done. No more powerful military device could be imagined than one which obligated the unquestioning obedience of entire populations, while at the same time investing their soldiers with super strength and abilities. The Homelanders would indeed pay untold millions of credits for it. So would a dozen other renegade and dissident groups and governments, including Human ones. Including, I also suspected, the Blobs.

"It's something important, isn't it?" Atlas surmised, walking around the case and looking first at it and then at me. "Indowy technology is always worth a fortune. That box can make us all rich; a cool billion credits at least."

"Back off from it," Blade warned. "It's mine. I found it."

His eyes fixed greedily upon the case. Big scar-faced Sergeant Shiva reached out and touched the object with his fingertips, as though to verify the treasure as actually real. Atlas and Ferret knelt by it, their eyes wide with avarice.

I looked around for allies. Considering the present temperament, Gun Maid was the only one I could hope for. After all, she and I had experienced something special together, hadn't we?

"Pia?" I petitioned. "You Humans have a folklore about finding a magic lamp with a genie inside."

Three wishes?

Yes. Three wishes.

This is not a magic lamp.

She read me! I sent my thoughts and she picked them up! She indeed had some of the Talent herself.

Listen to me . . .

It's hard . . .

I reverted back to speaking. "Pia, you remember how you said this planet had a feeling of evil to it? That you felt it?"

I pointed at the box. My hand trembled.

"That is at the core of the evil," I said, grabbing her by the shoulders and trying to shake the Presence out of her. "Rubbing the magic lamp never brings anything but tragedy. That lamp contains an evil genie who may ultimately destroy Humans the way it almost destroyed the Indowy and the Zentadon. That case is more dangerous to civilization than all the Blobs in the universe."

She refused to listen. None of them listened, so transfixed were they by the prospects of the unholy find.

"Smash it now," I urged. "Then bury it again, so that it will never be found."

"Fu-uck," Blade growled. "Fuck off, elf. This thing will make us rich. Make *me* rich. I was the one who found it, wasn't I? Wasn't I?"

He took a step back and brought the sniper's rifle to port arms, prepared to defend the treasure if he had to.

The mad laughter of the genie who led us here shrieked through the rain. DRT-213, to a Human, ignored it.

C·H·A·P·T·E·R
TWENTY SEVEN

A type of insanity seemed to catch the team in its grip following the discovery of the Indowy artifact. I couldn't help believing that the genie in the lindal was already struggling to freedom and that it and the Presence might be the same thing, that the moment we entered Aldenia airspace we became part of some grand evil design that was now starting to play itself to some climax. The treasure was as red meat thrown to starving animals. Each became suspicious of the others and their designs upon it.

Indeed, the black case represented a life of wealth and comfort and power to whoever possessed it. Not merely a life . . . *lives*. A Human that wealthy could transport to Kali and have himself rejuvenated as many times as he wished. When rejuv finally failed, he could have his brain, his soul, transferred to a different body and start a new life. He could be a woman, if he desired, or a bisexual with the accouterments of both sexes — screw herself himself, as Gorilla joked obscenely — or a multi-sexual like the Posleen. All this, especially if the billions of credits did not have to be shared.

The excitement called for an early camp so everyone could have a chance to look over the find. Sergeant Shiva designated the bivouac area on high ground within a field of boulders, some of which were as large as small Zentadon dwellings. No one ate. Blade's gaze seldom left the plasteel box that Captain Amalfi appropriated in the name of the Galaxia Republic.

"It's mine," Blade protested. "You're not giving it up to them. Captain, we can split it among us. Nobody has to know. We're all rich, *rich*."

Splitting the proceeds was the last thing Blade intended doing. He glared at me. He knew I knew.

I felt isolated and shunned as the Presence worked its shitstorm within a team that was no longer as close as belly button to asshole. It wasn't even a team anymore. Jealousy, greed, resentment, suspicion. I felt these dark emotions insinuating themselves among the DRT-bags like a malignant slime.

"Watch out for Cap'n Bell Toll," Gorilla whispered to Ferret. "He'll keep it for himself."

"You're the biggest and the strongest and the smartest," Ferret shrewdly observed. "Are you sure you don't have designs on it yourself?"

No one sought shelter from the rain because that meant the lindal would be out of sight. I had to physically pull Gun Maid from its orbit. She attempted to jerk away from me, so completely had she been dominated. I heard the Presence howling through the camp like a chill tempest.

"Pia," I hissed. "You must listen to me. This is the same thing that happened on Blade's explorer mapping mission."

"We are all rich, Kadar San," she said, almost in a daze.

"We are not rich, Pia. Do you not remember? We were safe as long as Blade alone knew about the lindal . . ."

"Is that what it's called, a lindal?"

"Concentrate, Pia. Resist. We must watch out for Blade. He's going to make sure that none of us reach the pod. It happened when he was here before. Only this time he will succeed in taking the genie off the planet with him."

"Wonderful little genie," Pia said, smiling. "You're just sour grapes, Kadar San. We're a team. We'll share like a team."

Out in the camp, Gorilla took offense over something Ferret said and went off on him like a charge of nitro with a short fuse. He grabbed the smaller Human and threw him completely across the bivouac area. Ferret landed in mud and water, cushioning his fall. With a shout of rage, the black Human leapt across the opening and landed on Ferret's chest with both feet.

"There's your team," I snapped, jumping up to intervene

and prevent what was obviously about to be a slaying.

Atlas darted in front of me, pointing his Punch Gun at my face.

"No!" he said.

"Captain Amalfi?" I petitioned, backing off at gunpoint.

The Captain seemed content to stand by and let the two teammates go at each other. He wore an enigmatic smile that twisted his lean face into a perverse mask. I looked to the others for support and received much the same reaction. All of us were now in deactivated chameleons, our helmets removed for camp and all expressions visible, zombie-like and without apparent concern.

Pia sat down on a rock and nibbled an energy bar while rain water ran off her cheeks. Blade occupied his own rock outside the circle, the ever-present Gauss resting across his knees as he checked it for weather corrosion and lubricated it. I sensed in him the joy of a sadist at a mass execution.

That was precisely the image that popped fully formed into my mind — mass execution.

Blade's eyes shifted to meet mine, as though aware of my intrusion into his thoughts. Even under the circumstances of two men fighting and a gun in my face, it startled me how completely he shut down, as though slamming a psychic steel door in my face.

Ferret managed to wriggle free of Gorilla and was grabbing rocks and slinging them at his opponent, keeping the larger man temporarily at bay. Atlas' attention was on me, not them. He jabbed me in the chest with the muzzle of the Punch Gun, forcing me backwards into the clearing among the boulders, as onto center stage. His voice began in a quiet tone of fury, erupting quickly into a continuous shriek of jealousy and rage that shocked Gorilla and Ferret into a standoff.

"Him!" Atlas bellowed. "Him . . . and her! They're criminals! They think they're so smart. I saw them together last night. They committed a crime. They were together."

Veins popped out on his handsome face like cicatrix scars.

Maid sprang to her feet. "Captain Amalfi, listen to me. Nothing happened. I . . . I kissed him to thank him for saving my life. That's all. It was a simple spontaneous emotion. I regret it now."

I looked at her. She regretted it?

"She is telling the truth," I confirmed, feeling unexpected sadness weeping into my soul.

"Execute the pair of them," Blade suggested coldly.

Captain Amalfi seemed annoyed at having to deal with this issue on top of everything else. He contemplated for a long minute, his eyes on me. I couldn't tell what he was thinking -- whether he believed us that nothing happened, or if he were actually considering Blade's recommendation. Finally, he took the easy way out.

"Both of you," he growled. "Consider yourselves under house arrest. We'll conduct a hearing on this once we're back aboard the *Admiral Tsutsumi*."

"Do it now!" Atlas shrilled. "They broke the law. She was screwing a Zentadon. You can't get lower than that."

He wanted us lynched on the spot. I looked into the muzzle of his Punch Gun. I thought he was about the pull the trigger.

"Put the weapon away," Sergeant Shiva commanded sternly, stepping forward. He was an imposing man with the scar and the steel-like quality of both his hair and his eyes, a man accustomed to being obeyed. "They'll be seen to in due process, if they're guilty."

"Oh, they're guilty as Hell, all right," Atlas said.

He wrenched himself away with an effort, holstering the Punch. Maid turned her back on me to underline her complete rejection of the charge that she might have had anything to do with an oversexed elf.

I'm sorry, Kadar. Oh, God, I'm sorry . . .

That settled, the camp temporarily at peace, the splintered team dourly turned itself to preparing for the onslaught of nightfall, only minutes away. Blade glanced around balefully and stepped out of camp to relieve himself. I watched him, all my senses screaming warnings. The others were busy in the rain erecting pop-up bivvies and rolling out waterproof bedrolls. Captain Amalfi still had the lindal.

Blade disappeared from sight. I stiffened as I received a visual reception so strong that it immediately injected a load of taa into my veins. It wasn't as though I sensed by any telepathic means the presence of danger. It was like I was being warned of it in a manner that instantly prepared my defenses.

I saw the image of a fanger, a giant predator of the planet Shartan. It was springing at me for the kill. It was already in mid-leap. Fangers killed for food — and they killed for pleasure.

Already pumped with taa, I turned in time to see a neural grenade hissing deadly through the sheets of rain, flung hard into the camp specifically to reduce my chances of acting against it.

TWENTY EIGHT

I would have perished if it hadn't been for the fanger warning, from whatever its source. Because of the releasing jolt of taa speeding up my entire metabolism to Humanly unbelievable levels while in the same process converting the environment around me to apparent slow motion, I was able to consider alternatives while the neural grenade was still in the air.

The Punch Gun I carried holstered at my side was incredibly lethal at short range. Capable of firing invisible energy "bullets," it would literally eliminate all matter in its path. It would destroy the target and surrounding matter, everything collapsing into the vacuum with the sound of a thunderclap. It was a noisy weapon.

I eliminated the Punch as a choice. Crucial was the moral and legal prohibition that Zentadon no longer, under any circumstances, kill another sentient being. This derived from the Indowy use of us as killing machines. Even providing that I overcame my inbred compunction against taking life, it was highly unlikely I could draw the weapon and locate a target before the grenade exploded, wasting us all.

A second choice was to catch the grenade and hurl it away. Impossible. I had tried baseball with Humans once. I was never good at catching fly balls. Even if I caught it, we were all still dead. The neural grenade detonated immediately upon contact with anything in its path.

I thought to save Pia's life. I had promised myself to keep her safe. She was on the far side of the camp. I could never reach her in time to whisk her to safety, even with taa speed.

That left one final pick: Save myself.

The entire scene unfolded before me in heartbreaking slow time frames, almost as though it were a still-life museum tableau. Although Blade had slammed the grenade like a baseball in that stupidly boring Human game in which a pitcher sometimes intends to bean the batter and put him out of commission, it was barely inching through the air in my perception. I saw my team members in the last instant of their lives, each unaware of impending calamity.

Pia, sitting with her back to a rock, bent over to shield from the rain the energy bar suspended halfway to her mouth; Atlas agitated, not mollified by Captain Amalfi's decision concerning Pia and me; Gorilla and Ferret squared off at each other across the camp, silent but still engaged in eye warfare; Sergeant Shiva chiseled huge and with the scar on his face inflamed in the gray, wet remnants of the day, busy erecting his bivvie; and Captain Amalfi only partially registering how traitorous fate manipulated by a traitorous subordinate had selected him for death. His eyes riveted on the grenade, following it as it slugged directly at him.

They were all dead. They just didn't know it yet.

The Captain still gripped the lindal by its handle. He had been studying the inscriptions on it as he prepared to put it in a safe place for the night. That was what Blade was after. If he eliminated everyone else, he had the treasure to himself. It wasn't enough to strip us of our weapons and gear and turn us loose for the savage local wildlife to take care of. Everyone who outranked him had to be eliminated in order for the pod to accept him and let him board for blastoff back to the orbiting Stealth. That meant witnesses had to be taken care of as well.

Blade had it all figured out. He returned to Galaxia a hero, ultimately a very rich hero, while claiming the rest of the team perished violently during the mission. His greed would unleash upon the galaxy once again the depraved curse of the evil genie.

I experienced a flicker of intense sadness over the team's fate, especially Pia's. That little brown Human female had touched me and awakened my Human side to a depth that her recent rebuke of me under the influence of the Presence in no way dissipated.

Then I acted upon the only choice left to me if the evil in the Indowy case were to be contained. I had to take the case myself and destroy it. I summoned the full depths of taa, acknowledging even as I did that I might go into lintatai and be destroyed by the overdose.

Captain Amalfi could not have seen me as I acted. I used a knife hand strike to release his hold on the case, breaking his wrist bone. I snatched the prize with the other hand. I dived for the nearest boulder with it, propelling myself over with my free hand. My fingers dug into the solid stone, leaving it scarred.

The neural lash of the exploding grenade turned the rain to red fire. Erupting air ahead of the lethal core threw me the rest of the way across the boulder and slammed me hard to the ground out of the blast radius. I landed hard on my shoulder and felt a sudden wrenching burst of pain in bones and muscles. The red snarl of the detonation blossomed above me and merged in a hellish crack with a bolt of lightning.

Panting to prevent lintatai, I rolled desperately on the soaked and water-puddled soil, clawing for my Punch Gun. I popped up and fired toward what I assumed to be Blade's hide in the rocks, the place where I had seen him disappear. I justified the defensive action under the guise that I wasn't shooting at a sentient. I was shooting at a stone. If a vile

Human just happened to be hiding behind the stone . . .

The boulder disintegrated with a mighty bang, along with anything behind it.

It wasn't a kill. Not really a kill . . .

I stood in the rain looking miserably upon the wreckage. They were all dead now, although a couple of the bodies were still twitching. Maid wasn't moving. She lay on her back, as though only napping. A neural grenade did not rip and shred flesh, as other explosions might. It simply demolished the central nervous system of any exposed living thing within its detonation radius. It was incredibly effective.

The burning of taa always left me weakened, reducing what powers remained to a level equal to or only slightly above that of the average Human. Blade with his implants, intensity of purpose, and expertise with weapons, driven by greed and simple cussedness, could never be considered average. He was a worthy combat adversary.

Underestimating him was almost the end of me.

He had used an old infantryman's ploy — disappearing behind one boulder as a diversion, then reappearing behind another at a safe distance, from which he hurled the grenade. He was now lying quietly in hiding to make sure the enemy was dead or, if one were alive, to finish him off. I had foolishly fallen for the trick, inexperienced in combat as I was.

My diminished senses failed to pick him up; perhaps he was blocking me as he had demonstrated himself capable of doing. I received only a warning from somewhere -- the fanger again! To my surprise and later consternation, self-preservation proved stronger than my prohibition against killing. I ripped off an antimatter Punch shot in the general direction I assumed the sniper to be hiding. A boulder exploded into its individual molecules. Trees beyond all but vanished in a white core of released energy.

Blade's shot came from somewhere else entirely. I had expended my current production of taa. I felt like I was now moving in slow motion. I half-turned toward the crack of the rifle. He couldn't miss. He used a Hornet round that tracked on a heat source once it was fired, like an anti-spaceship missile. It left the barrel at a relatively low velocity, then went into supersonic speed upon acquisitioning its target. It contained a tiny core droplet of antimatter in a depleted uranium coating. It could tear the guts and bone out of a Galaxia mammoth sloth at ten thousand meters.

Fortunately, I still wore my battle harness. Its defense sensors spotted the round and emitted high-intensity protons in an EMP field to shut down much of the bullet's impact energy. It still slammed into my torso at more than one hundred meters per second. It knocked me to the mud in a paroxysm of agony. It felt like every bone in my body was broken. I couldn't breathe and for several seconds it was all I could do to retain consciousness.

Pain wracked my entire body as, verging on lintatai, I pulled myself into the rocks, expecting another "smart" round to follow the first and finish me off. When it did not come, I lay panting and spent behind a slide of moss-covered, rain-slick rock and shale. It occurred to me then that Blade had no more Hornets. I remembered the arrogance he always expressed in his marksmanship. All he had left were "dumb" rounds. He was waiting for me to show a piece of myself as a target.

"Elf?" he called out from beyond the range of my Punch Gun.

I waited, remained still, hoping he would show himself and move in closer if he thought me finished.

"Can you hear me, elf?"

I felt nauseous at the thought of killing him. My stomach muscles contracted with dread and revulsion. I lay silently. From where I hid, I saw only a corner of the camp. The background hum of Human life had vanished, snuffed out like flames from a row of decorated scented candles. Gun Maid's body lay with the rain beating down into her face in the last gray of daylight. How small she looked, dead. I recalled the wonderful sound of her giggle, how she was always coming up with her old, old Earth expressions.

I was now in command, being the ranking living member of the team. Due to the way the landing pod was programmed, Blade could not leave Aldenia without first killing me, and he had five more Galaxia days to do it in before the pod took off without either of us. Besides, I had the treasure for which he had just murdered six of his teammates.

I rolled over on my back to study the terrain above. I still felt weak and nauseous, and not only from the afterburn of taa. Blade's Hornet round had undoubtedly cracked my chest plate. Add to that the wrenched shoulder from where I landed on it and I was reduced to the level of an ordinary Human. Say an ordinary one hundred-year-old Human who had never received rejuv.

The rain had slackened into a steady drizzle and bolt lightning had turned to sheet lightning. I batted my eyelashes against the rain. The high ground stuck up above me like a giant leg bone supported by beds of boulders that resembled skulls in the dwindling light. An observation point anywhere up there provided a clear view of the camp and its litter of dead Humans.

I sensed the sniper out there. Somewhere. Near. I was unable to pinpoint his precise location in my sapped condition, but his energy source appeared to be moving uphill from his previous location. That meant he did not intend to come directly into camp to check on me and finish me off, wily predator that he was. He was circling above, out of range of my Punch Gun, to look down and take care of me at long range. Long range was his deadly specialty.

Darkness on Aldenia always came quickly, but it would not come quickly enough tonight. Long before the cover of night fell, Blade would have reached a point from which he could pick me off. I almost felt his sights burning into a point between my shoulder blades.

I slithered in the mud to the other side of the rock slide, but the feeling of being targeted persisted. I looked around for an option. Further downhill, the twisted thick forest resumed. A flock of giant dragonflies settled into a copse of taller trees near a stream, their gossamer wings beating the rain into a mist that surrounded them like sheer lace. They were roosting ahead of the approaching night.

"Elf?"

It came from upslope.

"Elf, throw the case out into camp and I'll let you live. Do you hear me? I know you're not dead. Yet."

What kind of fool did he take me for? He couldn't leave Aldenia without killing me first. But — I glanced north toward the river and the pod — I *could* leave without him. If I could reach the pod first.

Before long, before night came, unless I did something, the sniper would have found a good hide and the next sensation I felt would be that of a slug blowing out my heart.

The choices were downhill or uphill. If I broke contact and reached the forest downhill, chances were that I might evade and prevent his getting a shot at me until I recovered my strength. Then I could make a break for the pod.

Terrain on the high ground was more open. Zentadon were descended from fleet, heavy-grav predators. Ordinarily, there would have been little contest in my outrunning a heavy-muscled Human. These, however, were not ordinary times.

Better I take to the low ground that offered more cover and concealment.

I required survival items from the camp: food, helmet, shelter, medical supplies, sensors. I had bolted when the grenade came in with only my battle harness, the Punch Gun, and the plasteel Indowy case wrenched from poor Captain Amalfi's fist. My chameleons wouldn't even camouflage without the power source contained in the helmet. I needed Gorilla's tech gear to reconfigure the bots' sensors so that I could utilize them. I glimpsed one of the robots perfectly inert on the other side of camp where it had been posted as sentry. Useless as an old fuel can in a trash dump.

Without basic subsistence and defensive items, I might just as easily fall prey to the planet's feral fauna as to Blade's rifle. I shuddered at the prospect.

"Elf?"

I didn't answer.

"Fu-uck."

The way I saw it, Blade had all the advantages. He was much more experienced in the field than I. As the old, old Earth expression went, he had more time in combat than I had in the chow line. In fact, other than the Blob battle bot encounter where we hadn't really been targeted, this was my first time being shot at. Shot at and hit. His rifle had one hundred times the max effective range of my Punch. He had been to Aldenia previously. Somehow, he survived when his expedition was annihilated; he probably killed them himself as he had just killed his fellow DRT-bags. On top of all this, he had access to the camp supplies and I did not. My dashing into camp for the items I needed was out of the question. Blade surely had the camp covered. What he didn't take he would likely destroy when I cleared out.

To kill him, if I could summon the resolve to override the veneer of recent Zentadon civilization, I would first have to survive, then get in close, past the long-range deadly accuracy of his Gauss and battlefield sensor implants. If he killed me, he took possession of the case and the potential power of evil it contained.

Either way, one of us had to die -- or we both died.

I looked across at Pia's body, stifling the emotion that welled in my throat. I had an old, old Earth expression for the sniper: Make my day.

C·H·A·P·T·E·R
TWENTY NINE

Runoff water turned the hill into a waterslide, fortunately for me since it required little of my waning strength to belly downhill like a salamander and escape the trap that the campsite had become. It took me out of Blade's range, at least for the moment, and into the dripping forest. Night came with a suddenness that always surprised me. I thought to continue moving through the short night, using the lightning flashes to guide my way. Few deadfalls clogged the wildlife trails since lightning strikes splintered the forest giants into smaller versions instead of dropping them. The remarkable adaptability of nature, no matter the planet.

However, when I struggled to my feet, everything whirled around me and I thought I was going to black out. In my debilitated condition, it would be an easy matter to fall into one of the deep ravines and break more bone and cartilage, providing I could make any progress at all. Or blunder into a sleeping predator and really piss it off. I decided to opt on the side of caution. I doubted Blade would attempt to travel either in the dark. He was probably digging in for the night and devising plans after discovering that the elf had disappeared with the precious Indowy gadget.

I dragged myself cautiously along a game trail, feeling the way with my hands, until I came to a small waterfall made by drainage across a rock ledge. Strobe lightning revealed a sort of cave up underneath the ledge behind the waterfall. I crawled inside and found a small dry area. I desired nothing more than to rest, close my eyes, and escape into sleep. I forced myself not to succumb until I had taken complete stock of my predicament and devised some kind of plan myself. The military had drilled into me that you accomplished nothing without a plan. Undoubtedly, Blade was an expert at OpPlans.

I was wet and miserable without my helmet, which controlled not only my uniform camouflage but also the life support system within the uniform that kept the wearer dry and comfortable. The helmet also contained various sensors, such as the one that allowed me to see in infrared the heat emitted by someone else wearing full-activated chameleons. What this meant was that my enemy remained dry and comfortable and blended into his environment, at least as long as his chameleons continued to work. He could see me; I couldn't see him. Predators could see me; they couldn't see him.

The first thing I did was check for wounds. I stifled a cry of pain when I touched my ribs. I heard and felt crepitas, crushed bones grating against bone, but the battle harness EMP field had blocked Blade's bullet from penetrating. My shoulder felt sore and inflamed. Obviously, ligaments were torn. It would take a number of days, even weeks for me to fully recuperate. By that time, this deadly little game between the sniper and me would have ended, one way or another. I simply had to play the game, like it or not, while enduring handicaps.

I mentally compared our respective weapons.

Blade was armed with the Gauss 7mm sniper rifle, the high point of Republic infantry technology, with a maximum effective range of 10,000 meters, over three miles. While my battle vest possessed the capability to defuse "smart" rounds and reduce their power, it was useless against straight "dumb" rounds.

I had the Punch Pistol, incredibly lethal, but only up to fifty meters, seventy-five at most.

Blade was probably at this moment sacking the camp, loading up for the duel with rations, extra weapons, and anything else useful. He would most certainly have access to Gorilla's LF tracker capable of picking up complex nervous systems out to several hundred meters. This, on top of his own tracking skills. I was sure he would destroy everything else in the camp he didn't need and then booby-trap the vicinity should I attempt to circle back to it.

I had never lived off the land before; I understood only the rudimentary survival principles taught during military basic training. In any event, this was an alien planet with exotic fauna and flora whose edible properties were totally unknown. One bite of the wrong thing might cause agony and death.

Comforting. It was said in basic training that when you got hungry enough you would eat your own combat boots.

So, give my enemy the advantage of food, concealment, experience, health, superior equipment, and firepower. What did that leave in my column?

I was of a higher intelligence level than the Human. So what? Deceit, cunning and a 7mm round from Blade's Gauss were more than equal to brain mass.

Taa was a two-headed beast, at best. It was good only for a burst every several days, after which it left me weak and vulnerable for some time. Besides that, taa could be a destroyer. Zentadon sometimes went into lintatai and self-destructed during an emotional crisis or while under great stress, no matter that for generations we had been taught control of it. Many younger Zentadon even used it as a "recreational drug," ignoring its dangers.

Finally, I was a Sen. Although my telepathic powers seemed to be expanding for some strange reason while on Aldenia, *were* in fact growing, I had discovered Blade capable of blocking my mind probes. If I couldn't read his thoughts and emotions, decipher his intent, then I was hard put to counter his moves.

That was the situation. I was lucky if I lasted tomorrow on the run. I again considered getting up now and trying to put some distance between him and me, but when I attempted it I was so stiff and spent that I could hardly drag myself to where the waterfall formed the door to my cave. I sank back. I probably wouldn't make a hundred yards if I fled for the rest of the night. I needed rest first.

One final option remained. I examined the lindal, more by touch than sight in the cave's darkness. Hiding it somewhere was out of the question, as the mysterious Presence had already located it once for Blade. Destroying it seemed even more improbable. First of all, the thing felt, and probably *was*, near indestructible, at least considering what I had to work with. Even if I somehow smashed it, say pushed a mountain on top of it, the Presence could still find the pieces so the damnable thing could be reconstructed.

That left it and I conjoined at the hip, so to speak. The only way to prevent the genie from unleashing its corruption was to take the case with me. That set Blade and me on a collision course from which only one would walk away. If Blade won, his greed over the lindal would turn the galaxy into a virtual Hell.

But at least, I thought wryly, I didn't have to worry about the Blobs. Apparently, there was only one of them on

Aldenia; he would likely remain neutral on Blob mountain, continuing his job as decoy, no matter what, not interfering either for or against me as long as neither of us invaded his territory.

I listened to the constant mutter of the downpour. I listened for Blade's coming. He shouldn't be underestimated. Lightning flashed and made a living silver curtain of the waterfall and, beyond it, brought into stark relief the reaching arms of the ghoulish landscape that surrounded me. Thunder crashed and reverberated over the forest.

How was I going to handle this?

The predator runs for his dinner, I thought wryly, while the prey runs for its life. Perhaps that was my advantage.

I decided to head for the pod in the river at first light. I could take off and leave Blade stranded if I reached it first. If not, I would leave him dead — if I *could* kill him.

The thought caused taa seepage, which I controlled with a mental effort.

On the other hand, Blade must certainly expect me to try for the pod and strive for his own checkmate. But as long as I was alive, Blade was stuck on this planet, whether he obtained the case from me or not.

I had one other alternative. I could start running in a direction away from the pod and keep running until time ran out and the pod took off on its own at the end of the ten days. Both of us would be left on the Dark Planet to perish. Better that both of us die than that the lindal leave Aldenia and eventually release its evil.

That I must consider only as a last resort. After all, it was only a stopgap measure. Sooner or later other explorers would land on this planet; as long as the lindal remained on Aldenia, the Presence would be ready to guide the next Blade to it.

I found a length of cord in a pocket of my battle harness. I tied it to my belt and put a single knot in it. Day one. In four more days, the pod would automatically fire up and take off. The DRT-bags of DRT-213 would be considered lost and dead, the same as the two previous DRTs. No one would bother to look for us.

I breathed deeply, even though it hurt. I used mind control to relax every muscle in my body. I needed rest. Daylight required all my faculties if I were to stand any chance in this deadly contest.

Before I drifted off, I wondered briefly about the fanger warning and how it had been delivered like that in time for me to act. It also occurred to me that I no longer sensed the Presence.

C·H·A·P·T·E·R
THIRTY

The Presence came to me in the night and made my short sleep fitful with dreaming. The way I understood it, Zentadon dreams were so much more forceful than those of Humans and so real that Zentadon often ascribed to them the properties of an alternate dimension. The older Zentadon, the spiritual among us, believed that when we died we simply began another life in our dreams. In fact, the present life was only the dream of a previous existence and that in turn the dream of an even more previous life. Humans called it reincarnation, except that in reincarnation Human spirits, souls, survived to occupy new bodies. Both were interesting theories. I had no desire to test either at the present. What if, when you died, there was nothing, not even blackness?

At first, in my dream, I was running in that painful,

impossible nightmare way when you are being chased. DRT-213, led by Blade, was chasing me. The members were all dead, except Blade, who appeared to have transformed himself into some kind of Dark Planet humanoid monster.

"Give it to me! Fu-uck! Fu-uck! It's mine. Give it to me!"

Shooting me again and again. Pain as sharp as slivers of ice doubled my wretched body into that of a permanent cripple.

"Fu-uck! Fu-uck! Fu-uck!"

Next came Pia with her pretty brown face dead and turned ghastly. One blue eye hung out on its stem. Flesh sagged in putrid lumps, revealing greenish bone and sockets underneath.

"I regret it! I regret it!" she screeched in pursuit.

Ferret and Atlas were even more repulsive, having risen from their graves half-rotted.

"Prolie slut! Prolie slut!" Ferret yammered.

"Execute him! Execute him!" Atlas shrilled.

Sergeant Shiva was one big ugly skeleton with the scar hanging from his skull like one of the intestine-leech things we encountered in the stream at the bottom of the Blob basin.

"Fresh meat! Fresh meat! Fresh meat!"

Gorilla became something indescribably hideous with his black hide blistered and cracked and peeling off his big yellow bones.

"It's out of the bag! It's out of the bag!"

Captain Amalfi's bones rattled as he brought up the rear, his head having turned into a giant bell with skin and a face stretched tightly over it. The bell rang madly.

"It tolls for thee! It tolls for thee!"

Kadar San? said an apocalyptic thought-voice. I jerked in my sleep at the odor and the muculent feel of the Presence. *You are experiencing a preview of your future. When you die today, as you surely must, I will transport you permanently into this new dimension dream life. You will live it fleeing from the risen dead.*

What do you want? I asked, already knowing, but wanting it to answer.

Give up the lindal.

It is evil.

So? What do you have against evil?

Why do you not take it from me, if you are so powerful?

You are trying to trick me.

Take it. I dare you. You cannot take it.

Before the day is over, you will beg to give it up.

We shall see.

It was like the Presence smiled inside me, although I could not see it and its smile tasted simultaneously oily and bitter. It took a different tack.

I can do things for you, it said.

Suddenly, the dream changed. I was back on dry Ganesh, out of the infernal Aldenia rain. I lived in a luxurious mansion overlooking a lake reflecting the incredible beauty of the Ganesh star-heavens. I knew I was both rich and powerful, that I could have anything I wanted simply for the asking. Rich food, rich surroundings, a rich life of luxury, forever rejuvenated.

I was in a bedroom then with a wide window overlooking the lake and the stars. Silk from Earth, sheen from Ganesh, and other rare and expensive fabrics canopied the enormous bed raised upon a pedestal of what appeared to be gold. The carpet felt as soft as a cloud under my bare feet and was the color of a blue morning sky. I looked down and I was naked and I was throbbing, embarrassingly erect.

Maid entered the room. My breath caught dry in my throat and I stared. She posed inside the door frame, one hand on her curving upthrust hip, the other arm gracefully raised to permit me an undisturbed view. All she wore were a warm smile and the blue bikini panties she had worn into the time couch. Her nipples were pink against rounded brown breasts, her merry eyes so blue they were almost deliciously painful to look into. Strands of fine black hair escaping from the V of her panties were the same color and texture as the short-cropped thatch of hair on her head.

My groin ached.

"I am not a virgin," she said. "I can teach you many pleasures that the Human side of you should experience."

I couldn't speak. I only stared.

"Ohhh . . . look at it!" she whispered, looking. "It's so hard and so ready. Is it breeding season?"

"I-I do not know," I croaked.

"Let's try it," she suggested.

She walked nearer. She seemed to flow. I caught the delicate scent of the little rose tattooed on her butt cheek, which she now revealed by slipping thumbs underneath the band of her panties and easing them down past the patch of hair to her knees. She lifted one leg, long and brown and clean, out of the tiny underwear and flipped the bikini across the room with her toes. She stood before me wearing only the smile.

"Shall we conjoin?" she teased, reaching out and grabbing me as if by a handle.

"Humans call it romance," I corrected.

She led me that way to the bed. She lay down on it naked and spread her legs for me. I stared, dry-mouthed and breathing heavily. I knelt over her on the bed, both knees between her legs, and looked at the precious split jewel of hair and pink-brown flesh and drew in the exciting aroma.

She reached and guided me toward it, caressing it slightly and still smiling up at me, her eyes half closed in anticipation. I lowered myself toward her silken brown body. I was almost crying from pleasure.

Suddenly, she vanished. So did the mansion and the view from the window. The Presence shrieked with awful, mocking delight.

You can fuck her all the time, it said. *Fuck like a Human.*

I realized I was being tempted in the wilderness. First

threatened, then tempted. Why did the Presence even bother, if it possessed powers as it claimed?

Then I knew. Its powers, whatever they may be, were nonetheless limited.

You fear me, I said.

I was being chased again by the ghoulish Captain Amalfi and his dead DRT-bags.

You will join them in another day, the Presence cried.

Whatever you are, I responded, *you are afraid of me because I can win.*

He is the more evil man.

That is why I will win.

Take the lindal yourself and become rich. I can help you. You can have everything.

Everything except my soul.

You will die.

You fear me! I laughed. The Presence shrieked in rage. Then it was gone.

C·H·A·P·T·E·R
THIRTY ONE

The Presence was still with me when I awoke. Unseen, but not unfelt. The chill of this invisible entity piercing to the marrow — the stubborn, psychotic, thorny spirit of piercing its beleaguered prey even unto death. Like an invisible, scabby prolie from the Human slums of crime and degeneration.

I also felt something else, yet another presence. It didn't feel dark and venomous like the first; it did not gag me when my thoughts tasted it. A counterbalance to the Presence, the antithesis of the evil I felt in it? Pia had said it before, and it was also something ubiquitous in Zentadon culture, this philosophy of opposites. For dark, there was light; for right, there was wrong; for good, evil.

Then they were both gone. For every presence, an un-presence.

I was hungry and stiff. The mournful trees through the little waterfall huddled massed in the liquid gray light. I went through the pouches of my battle harness looking for food. I found a protein processor that converted virtually any organism to food. I also found a squad radio, but assumed it useless with the team gone. The processor was just as useless; Blade's bullet had damaged it beyond repair. I tossed it aside. Soon, I would have to take the time to forage and eat organisms unprocessed, for which I presently lacked inclination.

Watchful and guarded, I left the shelter of the waterfall and crouched in forest undergrowth for a long five minutes, examining my surroundings for a bush that showed double, a reflection of rain against itself, a mirage movement of a part of the forest. Satisfied at last, I took the Indowy case, much as I already despised it, and continued downhill toward a stream I heard rushing through the canyon.

The stream was broad and black. I assumed one stream led to a larger, and the larger to yet a larger until one of them emptied into the sea. This particular one flowed toward the black river where the landing pod was moored. I contemplated building a float of some sort and riding the current, but immediately dismissed the idea. Building a craft, like foraging, took time. Besides, the water, as we had already seen, was as infested as the land with strange and dangerous monsters. Though Zentadon were smaller than Humans, we were significantly more dense of muscle and bone. Few of us ever mastered swimming, even the half-breeds like myself. I would drown should something happen to any boat I hoped to build.

I continued on foot. I started out at a fair pace, following the stream as the day's storms built up and rolled across the menacing skies. I quickly tired. What I hadn't counted on was the debilitating extent of my physical injuries. A Zentadon's chest plate was not merely ersatz ribs, as a Human's. It was both protection for the vital organs and a node center that served the same function as the nerve center in a Human's spinal column. The amount of pain I suffered warned me of nerve damage.

Also, the plate's qualities as a diaphragm for taking in adequate air during periods of high exertion were severely limited. I realized I was lucky for the time being if I could move as fast as the sniper, much less outrun him. The most I could hope for was to maintain my small lead.

I tested my senses, let them sniff around through the high country in hopes of picking up Blade's spoor. Blade erected in his mind an icy barricade against my probing. I almost felt him sneer at my puny efforts. I sensed him, always nearby, but when I sensed him it was almost like he and the Presence were one. The trouble was, I couldn't tell where he was. Just that he was there. Near. Coming. Relentless. Like the skilled hunter he was.

The best I could hope for was that my Talent act as a barometer for his emotions, that I might judge the rise of his excitement to determine exactly how near he was. He had thrown a rage after having botched the assassination and allowing one of his targets to escape with the prize, but it was not a mindless rage. Quite the opposite. Although his fury reached such extremes that, in spite of his blocking efforts, I actually palpated it with the fingers of my senses, his thoughts remained cool and calculating and focused. I could tell now that he knew from my slow progress that I was hurt and my abilities to resist limited.

I felt him as a predator excited by the distress of his injured victim.

My feet left deep, lasting impressions in the crusty forest floor. Water quickly filled the prints to leave a track readable from a hundred meters away by a blind man. Blade didn't need the sensors and the LF tracker scavenged from the dead. It wasn't even necessary that he be an exceptional tracker to follow my trail as I made an obvious beeline for the pod.

I attempted to place ridges between us in order to foil the LF. I waded streams and backtracked to cover my trail; but still I felt him and the Presence always with me, driving me toward the pod. I even took a rocky canyon that led off at a tangent from the due north azimuth that pointed toward the black river, but Blade refused to be fooled. He seemed elated that I was in more open country where his chances at a sure shot increased.

Alarmed, I returned to the forest where my chances

of fighting back with the short-range Punch were better. Blade seemed to anticipate my every action.

I recalled from the old histories of the Human Rebellion how the ill-armed and outnumbered Humans had won their freedom from the Indowy and we Zentadon warrior slaves through the general utilization of guerrilla tactics. Roving bands of Earthling fighters tormented the enemy with ambushes, sudden raids, sabotage, assassinations, and terrorism. They appeared as unexpectedly as birds of prey, then disappeared like smoke.

One of their most effective tactics was the use of what they referred to as "booby traps." Entire areas of the battle zone on Galaxia were made off-limits to Indowy troops because of man pits, sharpened stakes, mammoth whips . . . The Humans used everything available to impale, maim, injure, and kill the enemy by enticing him to trip the traps himself.

My battle harness contained a small clasp knife. The blade was too short to be considered a weapon. As I walked, fleeing, I cut lengths of a tough bamboo-like plant, each about two feet long, and sharpened them on the ends. I collected about a dozen before I lay my trap.

First, I left a trail of footprints across a small open marsh. That was the bait. In the forest on the other side I selected a tough, springy branch that reached across the trail about chest-high to a Human man. Using the knife, I inserted the sharpened stakes at intervals of two inches for the entire length of the branch. Finally, I cut a tough vine with which to pull the branch into tension, and a much thinner vine to arrange a trip wire across the trail. The dripping rain from the trees, tendrils of fog, and the dimness provided by cloud cover and the forest canopy made the trip wire almost invisible, merely one of many such plants intertwined. If my luck held, the next thing Blade Kilmer felt was the teeth of the whip lashing out to skewer him through and through.

It troubled me that I had it in me to coldly calculate the slaying of another sentient, but I assuaged my conscience by telling it that what I was doing was for the good of all in the galaxy, not for mere self-survival. The power of the Indowy lindal must not be released. Besides, it wasn't actually like I was killing him with my own hands. Concentrating on that thought kept my taa contained.

I felt Blade coming. I felt him near. He was cautious, wary, suspicious. That was his nature. That was the nature of anything that would survive on the Dark Planet.

I ran hobbling deeper into the forest. Drenched foliage lashed at my face. I had to get as far away from the actual killing field as possible to avoid lintatai. I made my mind go blank.

The whip triggered with a force that shook the trees involved. I suppressed the sudden taa that threatened to burst into my system. I experienced a moment of satisfaction, if not exactly elation. Blade had fallen for the trap. I stopped and looked back.

A peal of maniacal laughter swept through the jungle. It was difficult to determine where Blade left off and the Presence took up. Chills engulfed my body. He — they — were still coming. The trap had not got him.

If the Presence feared me, it wasn't something that showed.

C·H·A·P·T·E·R
THIRTY TWO

My heart pounded. Drawing my Punch, I hid underneath the low concealing branches of a tree to examine my back trail. I waited, my throat dry and my chest wracked with spasms of pain. I saw him. A mirror image among the trees, the telltale presence of someone wearing chameleons.

I aimed the gun. My hand shook at the prospect of killing. Again I verged on lintatai. Which was the mirror and which the mirrored? Now would be the time for his chameleons to malfunction, for my benefit if certainly not for his.

Lightning cracked, reverberating and rumbling across the sky, strobing into the forest. A breeze rustled one side of the mirror but not the other. That meant it wasn't him after all. I collapsed with relief, the moment of truth postponed, and felt the hard rough bark of the tree grinding against my forehead. It suddenly occurred to me that my gold hair must shine in the dark forest like, well, gold. I cut off part of a leg of my cammie trousers with the clasp knife and tied it around my head like a scarf, leaving my ears free to twitch. They had reason enough to be active.

What with the sensors in Blade's possession and his training and experience on the battlefield, I had about as much chance of waylaying him in an ambush as I did of reaching Galaxia without the pod. His canniness had aided him in surviving my booby trap whip. I felt him out there, patient, waiting now until all the advantages were on his side, playing with me.

I turned once again into the forest, desperation driving me. Looking back over my shoulder, expecting him.

Absorbed as I was, I literally ran into one of the snake-like creatures stretched across the path. It was of a thickness equal to my height and so black it gleamed dully in the rainwater washing off its sides. It was hard and muscular. When I bounced back, its entire amazing length converted into a lashing whip. Its tail hurled me thirty meters through the air and into the trees. When I landed, the breath knocked out of me, its triangular head lifted high among the trees, darting and probing, searching for the interloper. Tongues, for it had four of them, flickered like mercury, testing the air.

I didn't know if the thing could climb trees or not, or if

I could climb fast enough or high enough to escape it, but the treetops seemed my only hope. I scrambled painfully to my feet and made it to one of the forest giants. Because of lightning strikes, the trees were exceptionally tall but also exceptionally slender. Dropping the black lindal at the foot of the tree, I hugged the trunk and began shimmying up it like a simian.

The ebony head slithered through the trees. I swung out onto a branch just as it struck. Rows of teeth ripped off bark just above my hands, leaving a bright gash in the trunk. The head cocked for a second strike. Lidless black eyes the size of plates sized me up. Contemplating the little animal that was about to become lunch.

What difference did it make if I gave away my position to Blade if I were to be killed and eaten by this creature anyhow? Hanging onto the branch with one hand, I drew my Punch Gun and fired. The creature's head and half its body blew up, showering the surrounding forest with purple-gray blood and shredded flesh.

A moment after, a bullet ripped past my head so near and with such velocity that it seemed to suck out my breath. Twigs and leaves exploded. I had no taa left, so I merely reacted. I let go the branch.

Underbrush cushioned my fall. Luckily for me, I managed to hold onto my gun. I scrambled around in the snake's gore until I found the Indowy case.

"Elf!"

Blade's grating voice, diffused and multiplied, seemed to come from all around me, as though it were the voice of the dark forest. Bruised and scratched and breathing heavily, I listened on hands and knees.

"Give it up, elf. This is one you can't win. You can make it easier on yourself by turning the case over to me now. Or we can do it the hard way. Either way, you have to die."

I tried to think of a brave, snappy comeback, something like *I have just begun to figh,t* or *Damn the starships, full warp ahead*. All I came up with was one word. I shouted it from the bottom of my lungs, hurling it back at him. "Fu-uck!"

I plunged deeper into the forest with the black box, laughing almost hysterically. I was going mad.

Soon, however, I was again nursing a core of loneliness and fear. I had grown up in a civilized, rather protected environment. Taa was something I only experimented with occasionally, cautiously, aware of its danger. Now, here I was, taa-depleted, wounded and battling for my life. One damned thing after another, to coin one of Pia's endless old, old Earth expressions.

It occurred to me that Blade didn't have to kill me in order to get the case. Aldenia's savage denizens could do it for him. Either way, he had the prize and a clear claim on the landing pod.

I paused and looked at the case. I had to make sure he didn't get it, no matter what happened to me.

I found an outcropping of rock and smashed at the

case with the largest stone I could wield. As I expected, the thing proved virtually indestructible. I beat on it without even marring its glossy surface. No wonder it had survived the centuries and still functioned.

I thought about throwing it in the stream and letting it sweep out to sea. It floated. I even contemplated hiding it. In the end, however, I kept it. Sooner or later, the energy it emitted with the Presence's help would lure Blade to it. If not him, then, someday, another Blade. The genie contained in the lamp possessed such evil that only the vastness of space was large enough to bury it.

Survive, said a solemn voice fully formed inside my head, *if for no other reason than to get rid of the case for all time.*

That, I promised this new Presence, *I would do.*

The shorter of the two Aldenia nights was almost upon me. I halted, thinking. My tracks were leading Blade in the direction of the pod. No matter what tricks I used in attempting to shake him from my back trail, I felt him doggedly back there. It was almost like an electronic string led from me to him; it was much more than the LF tracker, which was precise as to locations only at short distances. The Human was good at tracking, I had to hand him that. Sooner or later, the way things were going, he was bound to win.

I should reach the river early in the morning after the coming short night. If I reached it, Blade was toast. I was out of here like a bad dream, leaving the sniper behind to see if he could survive Aldenia a second time.

He couldn't let me do that. So what was his next move?

All he had to do was forge ahead — he had no problem getting ahead of me in my weakened condition — and set up an ambush between me and the pod. I might survive one ambush, perhaps even a second. But he would eventually score.

But what if the prey did the unexpected, the unpredictable . . .? As long as I was heading for the pod, the only game in town was "Blade wins." Changing rules in the middle of the game might extend the chances against me from perhaps one in four or five, to perhaps one in eight or nine. Play the odds. Another old, old Earth expression. Make my day. They would have amused lovely Pia.

"You ain't seen nothing yet," I murmured, pleased at the phrase and still thinking of Pia.

Mind made up, I turned away from the north and toward the east. The stream I had been following faded behind me into the trees and I looked for rugged, rocky high ground that would both challenge Blade's tracking skills and prevent his getting another shot at me.

C·H·A·P·T·E·R
THIRTY THREE

The strength and endurance of a Zentadon did not come without costs. Although the chemical analog our bodies used instead of ATP was more efficient, the lack of long-term energy storage meant that after a day or so of high energy activity without food our bodies began drawing entirely upon muscle mass. Plant matter might be high in complex sugars, but there was minimal usable protein in it. The grueling events since the neural grenade went off in the rocks, along with my injuries, had taken a lot out of me. If this pace continued, I needed food, real food. Meat.

The thought caused my stomach to roil.

The matter should all be academic tomorrow anyhow — if my ruse worked. There was plenty of food on the pod.

Before night fell in the higher country, I committed to memory exact details of the fastest route to the black river.

Crouching under cover of rain-dripped stone, I traced in my mind a wide ravine down from the ridge that I had been traveling. It ran half full with water, naturally, but the swiftness of its passage and frequent flooding cleared its banks of most foliage. Negotiating it at night would be possible.

The ravine opened onto an open plain lush with purple-black grass swept with rain and dotted with various giant herbivoric insects. Animal life on the planet slept at night, so the big bugs should be no problem. The real problem lay in the band of thick forest that lay between the marshy meadow and the river. It would make tough going in the dark, but as long as I continued north I couldn't miss the river. A left turn should then bring me to the pod in short order.

An extremely hazardous undertaking in the total locked-in-the-closet darkness of Aldenia, but it appeared at the moment to be my best hope of escape, and perhaps my last hope.

I studied the route one final time before the shorter of the two nights descended. Far to the west, I made out the dark hint of the sea where we had landed barely five Galaxia days ago. The black river snaked through the jungle to empty into it. In a briefing while DRT-213 was still orbiting in the Stealth, Captain Amalfi explained how the pod extraction worked. You didn't have to be a small craft pilot. Once the senior living member of the team approached, the pod read his DNA signature and automatically extended the debarkation/embarkation tube for boarding. Adjusting a few computer settings released the pod from anchorage. It guided itself back to the sea, became a surface craft, then blasted off for re-docking with the Stealth in orbit.

I was thinking of that and of food when night fell like a curtain and the storms, as usual, slackened somewhat. I went through the pockets of my cammie vest and combat harness, hoping to find something to eat I had overlooked, but discovered only the tiny watch-sized squad radio intended for emergency communications within the team. It was useless now. Wet, miserable and enduring almost as much hunger as pain, I had to settle for the relative shelter of a rock ledge and no food. I shivered from the wet and the cold.

Before going into meditation and self-hypnosis to relax my muscles and thus help their regeneration, I sent out my mind to probe for Blade. My shivering increased. I found the Presence; it and Blade seemed immutable, melded together. In my mind's eye, I saw a pair of giant baleful eyes staring at me in the night, as though reveling in my misery and anticipating my end.

The Presence, I thought, must have specifically selected Sergeant Blade Kilmer to do its bloody bidding because Blade was the most susceptible to evil. He was a good choice. Toward what ultimate end the Presence aspired I could only speculate, other than the releasing of the lindal's dark powers once again into the universe.

I tried to find the Good Presence. It must be sleeping — or it had abandoned me. I touched upon another sentient, however. Fleetingly, but it was there, only with insufficient strength to be identified. Then it was gone too and I slept in the rainy night for exactly one hour.

C·H·A·P·T·E·R
THIRTY FOUR

Day was still another hour away when I awoke, feeling somewhat rejuvenated. I twisted a second knot into my string, the beginning of my second day on the run. Four days to go before the pod took off on its own. Which shouldn't matter in another three or four hours anyhow, once I boarded the pod with the case.

I set off in the dark along the route I had earlier plotted and memorized. Blade wouldn't expect me to start moving until daylight. An hour's head start, with luck, should be all I needed.

Traveling Aldenia rainforests was exhausting going under the best conditions, almost impossible in the dark. Sheet lightning illuminated the way ahead, briefly, then plunged me back into even greater darkness by the contrast. I slipped and slid down the ravine, once or twice falling into

252 * CHARLES W. SASSER

the rushing water and almost being swept away to a horrible drowning death. I attempted to use my psychic powers as a type of sonar to guide me, but it failed miserably and I was soon battered and bleeding from stumbling into rocks and trees.

Daylight brought new hope. Goliath beetles and other herbivore types were already in the meadow when I reached it, but I avoided them by skirting along the forest edges. A total of three hours' hard trudging brought me to the river, where a sense of urgency propelled me at a great pace downstream toward the pod. I threw caution to the wind as I raced, to the best of my depleted abilities, toward sanctuary.

I probed for Blade on my back trail, unable to find him. That should have persuaded me that I caught him sleeping with my unexpected move, but it troubled me instead. It is much better to know where the fanger lurks so that you can avoid him.

I came to the tiny glade of purple-black grass where the team had first set forth on Aldenia soil, where the first bot was mysteriously destroyed. Could it have been so few days ago? I fell to my stomach and low-crawled to a point where I peered out of the foliage and across the opening. The river ran black and swift. There was nothing to indicate the pod was submerged there. I wondered how near I had to come before the pod's computers recognized me and sent out the tube. Obviously, I had to go nearer than this.

I listened. I batted falling water from my eyes. I explored with my senses, reluctant to expose myself in the short dash to the river bank. If I was wrong about Blade and he had not been fooled, he was likely already set up with his deadly Gauss and waiting for me to reveal myself.

The way appeared clear.

I took a deep breath and bunched my muscles. I tested my taa reservoir. Perhaps I could get a small boost at least.

Steeling myself to possibly receive a slug through my heart, I jumped up and sprinted across the glade to the edge of the river, already anticipating food and rest and a quick ride the Hell out of this place. I crouched where the water lapped shore, my feet actually in the stream. Rain churned the surface. Debris rode the current, swirling and diving and foaming. I waited for the sunken pod to send up its embarkation/debarkation tube for me. I looked around. Hurry, hurry.

Nothing happened. Maybe I was at the wrong place after all. I stood up and soon found the trunk of a nearby tree where Gorilla had fastened a homing device. This was the right place. Why didn't the pod recognize me?

I returned to the edge of the river. I jumped around like a fool, giving the machine's sensors plenty of opportunity to see and recognize me. Still, nothing happened.

Desperation caused me to consider diving into the river and down to the pod. A foolish thought. Even if I knew how to swim, which I didn't, the current was fierce enough to tear trees off the riverbank, roots and all. Besides, I couldn't get into the pod even if I reached it.

Another thought struck me, freezing my blood. Maybe the pod had ripped free of its anchors and been swept out to sea, stranding me here with Blade and the Presence forever. Common sense soon replaced panic. The pod's systems and backups were designed to withstand unbelievable tidal actions.

No, the pod was still there. It was still functioning. It simply refused to recognize me and open.

That left only one conclusion. The Humans mistrusted me to the point that I hadn't even been entered into the computers. The pod was never going to open for me. But why the lecture from Sergeant Shiva about my being fourth in the chain of command and all that? A pretense, a cruel subterfuge? I felt such helpless anger and frustration that I would surely have gone into lintatai had I sufficient taa to trigger it.

Blade was never concerned about my reaching the pod ahead of him because he must have known all along that he was the ranking live member of the team entered into the pod's computers. He could leave Aldenia anytime he wanted, which he would do as soon as he seized the Indowy case from me. I, in turn, could never leave if all the Humans were dead.

I backed away. The Presence suddenly loomed strong and near. A hideous peal of laughter burst out of the rain.

I turned and ran. The best I could hope for now was that Blade die with me, preferably he first, and that both of us take the secret of the Indowy Hell Box to our unmarked death sites. At least that would delay the genie's release into the galaxy.

C·H·A·P·T·E·R
THIRTY FIVE

I ran hard for an hour, as hard as I could, taking a straight suicidal line to lead Blade as far away from the pod as I could. I crouched by a slow, deep pool in a stream and drank from it like an animal. I saw my reflection rain-dimpled in the surface of the water — the scrap of cammie cloth around my golden hair to cut down the glint, the pointed ears in almost constant spasms, my face scratched and battered and gaunt. In short, to quote an old, old Earth expression, I looked like Hell.

The stream ran between clay banks. I drank, seeing things swimming in the water. Exhausted, I pulled myself back to rest in the bushes. I lay for a minute, using the lindal for a pillow.

Kadar San . . .?

I shot upright.

It wasn't the Presence. There was no feeling of slime to the thought. It had to be the Good Presence warning me not to sleep, warning me that Blade was hunting. So far, he had been so successful in blocking my mind probes that I had no idea where he was. Until he actually fired at me, an event I hoped to delay or prevent, I had only a vague sense of his being near or far.

Kadar San . . . help . . .

What? Help? How could I help? And who was I supposed to help?

The voice was very weak, no more than a whisper. I attempted to extend the contact, but there was no more.

I rested for another few minutes, then forced myself to get up. I sent out feelers for the voice, but it was gone. I was weak from hunger. I had to eat if I hoped to lead Blade to his destiny.

I scooted myself to the pool and easily snagged one of the newt-looking things swimming in it. They were thickly-built slabs about the size of my hand, finned, slimy, and had external gills. Rather than fish, they were more like reptilian larvae. I had noticed little furry mammals eating them previously, so assumed they were edible.

If I could only eat one of them myself.

It wasn't disgust at their appearance that prevented it. Rather, the newt squirming in my hand triggered atavistic cravings I hardly realized existed in my makeup. My taa gland, sensing the coming moment of the kill, was going into pre-orgasmic spasms. A side effect of taa usage other than super power and strength during crisis was the "zombie" switch, which activated a form of lintatai that brought on a condition less spectacular than the lintatai that caused self-combustion or explosions, but no less deadly. It was not an unpleasureable experience. In fact, it could be incredibly seductive. The young Zentadon taa addicts induced the orgasmic "zombie" condition by watching violent shows or simulating violent behavior. Playing chicken with their systems. Wrestling with the taa gland was to wrestle for life itself. Many lost and went into a mindless semi-stupor from which they never recovered. Like Cauri Tan at Mishal's safe house.

The ultimate reason for the taa gland was to aid predator Zentadon ancestors in killing and eating quivering prey. However, circumstances following the Indowy taa camps had made of the Zentadon frustrated predators conditioned away from violence. It was violence itself that could now destroy.

I studied the newt clasped in my hand. I had to eat, had to chance the "zombie" in order to survive. If I failed and "zombie" overcame me, I might well sit here happily by the stream until the sniper came along, finished me off, and took the box. I would neither eat nor drink or perform any other function without specific orders. It was similar to the subservient condition the Indowy Hell Box had induced in its soldier subjects under Indowy control.

My hands shook around the water newt-thing and I drew a deep calming breath. I was half-Human; Humans killed without compunction and serious side effects. I shot the giant snake, hadn't I? I attempted to do Blade. But those were in self-defense and different than this; I didn't intend to kill and then eat them.

I concentrated on my Human side. The mind is a mirror of the soul, the soul a mirror of the mind. The mirror has the stillness of a pond . . .

My mind went blank. Breathing returned to normal. I twisted my hands, killing the little animal. And I ate it. I was becoming more and more Human.

C·H·A·P·T·E·R
THIRTY SIX

The country opened up some, although the sky continued to gush water. Open country allowed me to lead Blade even further away from the pod. The forest turned into numerous meadows where purple-black grass grew taller than my head. Herds of the strange, lumbering beetle-like creatures foraged in the meadows and paid little attention as I skirted the edges, keeping to the trees to remain in cover and concealment. I was more the hunted than they.

At one of these glades I encountered an astonishing and frightful transaction, which underscored how vulnerable to my environment I truly was. As though I needed the underscoring. From my vantage point on a slight wooded incline on the far side of a little park, I spotted a pack of animals the likes of which I had so far only glimpsed from a distance. I immediately hid and watched the lizard-like predators stalk a pod of large gray pill bugs.

I was both intrigued and appalled. With incredible swiftness, slinking low like fanger cats, the lizard-appearing predators broke into three separate groups. One group of three individuals scurried through the edge of the forest to the far side of the clearing and slunk into hiding as a blocking force. A second group of four, the attack element, all but invisible but for their rippling trails in tall grass, silently surrounded the beetles on the near side. Once the two forces were in place, everything went still.

The third group — two lizards larger and more powerful-looking than the others — appeared to be in charge. These two hid in the trees, but in such a manner that they commanded the field of impending carnage. Snake-like tongues tested the air, slithering in and out between sharpened rows of teeth as long as my hand. The tips of long black-green tails twitched with anticipation. Clawed feet dug into the earth as muscles bunched.

The leader of the attack element looked back toward the commanders, as though seeking instructions. These creatures were thinking, reasoning organisms, more than simple bundles of instinct tied to stomachs! I tested my senses on theirs and received such a powerful impression of blood and gore and torn flesh that I withdrew immediately in fear of triggering lintatai.

The leader lizard reared up on its hind legs and gave a

roaring dog-like bark that echoed across the meadow. The pill bugs were agile themselves for beasts of their amazing size, but they were no match at such close range for the intelligence and prowess of the carnivores. The lizards streaked through the grass. The earth trembled. Blood-thirsty cries filled the air. Attackers leapt upon the backs of individual beetles and began ripping and tearing with tooth and claw as the terrified insects bolted, dying on their multi-legs even as they fled.

It was a well-thought-out operation. The main bug herd broke directly into the blocking force, which sprang from hiding and began taking down more quarry. The two big lizards joined the process of finishing off the wounded. They slaughtered more than they could ever eat. They apparently killed as much for pleasure as for food. Dead and dying creatures lay in carnage all over the glade and the grass was trampled almost flat.

The king reptile paused with an enormous chunk of flesh in its jaws. Its triangular head jerked as it looked around. It seemed to peer directly at me through the raveling skeins of rain. My ears twitched. Shivers skittered across my breast like cold raindrops blown by an icy wind. I averted my eyes to avoid looking into his and giving away my position. It occurred to me that the king was sensing me as completely as I sensed him.

"Fu-uck!" snarled an all-too-familiar voice. I gave a start that almost exposed me to the lizards. I felt a surge of taa, but not yet enough to save me from the round that was certain to blow out the back of my skull. I steeled myself for it.

"Fu-uck!"

The epithet came from my battle harness. I crouched and withdrew the small watch-like squad radio.

"Elf?" inquired the voice from the RT receiver I had left stashed in my battle harness. "I know you're over there. Why didn't you leave on the pod?"

He gave that crazy Presence laugh, tormenting me.

"You might as well give it up now," he proposed. "You should be convinced that you can't get away. I can track you wherever you go, and in the end I'll get the case anyhow."

Along with the arrogance, however, I detected a trace of concern in his voice. He might get the case all right, but by then he'd never be able to make it back to the pod before it took off. *Keep on tracking me, big boy.*

"Elf, I've activated your RT because I want you to hear me. Look, there's enough credits for both of us. We'll share. What did you owe the others anyhow? None of them trusted you any more than I did. Why do you think the Captain failed to include you in the rankings for the pod? I did us both a favor by killing them. Hell, I did them a favor. I could have left them out here to be finished off by these monsters."

I had nothing to say to him. Not yet.

"Aren't these fu-ucking lizards magnificent? Perfect killing machines. Now, catch this, elf. Watch! Isn't it beautiful?"

I heard the shot echo from a distance. One of the feeding lizards executed a complete forced somersault off the corpse of the beetle upon which it was feeding. It thrashed about in its terrible death throes while Blade picked off yet another target. Brain shots, both of them. He killed a third as the band raced for the cover of the forest.

"Which of us is the more efficient killing machine?" Blade's radio voice asked. "Elf, look at them. That's what I intend to do to you."

C·H·A·P·T·E·R
THIRTY SEVEN

I had been moving in a straight line for the past few hours. The country was now reasonably flat but rising toward the south. The trees were thinning out into purple-grass meadows. Shimmering rain swept across marshes like the surreal landscapes of a dream. Blade would be delighted. From his point of view, I was moving into good open sniper country in which he could continue to track me until he got a clear shot.

There would, however, be no extreme long-distance shooting because of the rain. Without wind to hurry it along, rain fell as plumb-straight as the strands of a beaded curtain. Its purling streams blurred trees no more than five hundred meters away.

Blade would not want to come within the short range of my Punch Gun. Or within range where I could use taa in order to propel me to his throat.

I felt stronger after eating the newt-thing. Zentadon possess remarkable recuperative powers. I stopped at a pool to fish and eat again. I accepted that I would not be leaving Aldenia, but I still needed to recover as much strength as I could to make sure Blade and the Hell Box did not leave either. The trick was to keep him following me until even a forced march would not return him to the pod. I had to keep enticing his greed with the possibility that he would soon win. Just a little bit further. A little longer.

Squatting by the pool, I sucked on a newt bone. The killing and eating of the little creature hadn't affected me at all this time. I looked into the pool, contemplating snagging another for dessert.

"You realize you are one dead Zentadon?" Blade said from my radio.

He wasn't concerned about attracting the Blobs. First of all, there were no Blobs. Well, maybe one, and that trickster wanted us to return to the Republic with news of the "advance base," which meant he would continue to lay low and not interfere with this duel of wits between Blade and me. Second, communications between the little voice boxes were OPSEC untraceable, another Indowy state-of-the-art development.

I decided to talk to him. Maybe I could use the radio to my advantage for a little psyops, psychological operations.

"Perhaps I will die and perhaps I will not," I responded.

DARK PLANET # 267

"Either way, you will also die."

My senses told me he was somewhere in the vicinity of the higher country to the west.

A shriek of mechanical laughter over the radio, again as much the Presence's as Blade's. If for everything in nature there was an antithesis, where was the Good Presence when I needed it?

"A Zentadon can't kill," Blade taunted. "It's against your carrot-cruncher religion."

I took out my knife and cut off the head of a second newt. I stripped off the flesh and ate it raw in bites. The state of so-called "Zen," what the Humans called it, actually worked.

"Perhaps I am willing to make an exception in your case," I said. "It would not be killing. It would be extermination of a virus."

I felt the hot rise of his rage. It allowed me to pinpoint him. My head snapped toward the source. In the low foothills to my right. Although I was not an outdoorsman, I knew enough to question how he could possibly track me from up there. Even the LF was almost useless at such ranges.

Then he slammed his mind door.

"You are as useless in the woods as tits on a boar hog," Blade mocked, disciplined once again.

"An old, old Earth expression?"

"You're making a track clear enough that I could follow

it blind."

He was lying. He wasn't following my track at all. He was tracing me. How?

Puzzled, I put what was left of the Newt meat into a combat pocket for a later snack and continued to the south, this time making sure I kept forest between me and Blade in the foothills. The route rose steadily out of marshes and grew more dangerously open. Lightning splintered a boulder into pebbles. Ozone filled the wet air.

Our verbal sniping continued over the radio. Psychological warfare worked both ways. Whenever he betrayed strong emotion, I was able to get a fix on his location.

"Zentadon are not Humans," I said. "No Human, even an enhanced one, is as strong as a Zentadon, or as fast."

He laughed. "A Human is if the Zentadon is crippled."

"Aye? I am permitting you to live at the moment because it satisfies my needs."

"Fu-uck. Zentadon are cowards. They have always been, always will be. The Indowy gave you balls when they had you, but now you're eunuchs again."

"Tell yourself that, Human, when I rip your still-beating heart from your chest and eat it while you watch."

That set him aback even as the thought sent a ripple of taa to my brain, a not unpleasant experience. I fought to control it as I climbed into rolling, lightly forested hills. Giant dragonflies darted in and out of the lowering dark clouds, but they ignored me.

"What do you intend doing with the box, elf?" Blade asked.

"Return it to proper authorities. Better yet, destroy it in space where it'll never be recovered."

"Fu-uck." Like he didn't believe anyone could be that foolish. "You want all the credits for yourself, that's what you think you're doing. You can't leave Aldenia without me, elf. I can leave, but I won't without the case. Where does that put us, huh? Fu-uck. You aren't that stupid. We're at a standoff here, boy. It's time to make a deal."

"I do not make deals with killers and thieves."

Again, I picked up his fleeting anger. He was keeping a parallel pace with me, drawing near.

"We can get a billion credits for that box on the black market," he proposed. "I even know a good fence."

"The Homeland terrorists?"

"If they have the funds."

"You have done this before, killed your friends for money?"

"I have no friends. I never liked them much anyhow. Besides, a billion credits . . . Elf, do you have any idea of how you could live with a third of that?"

"A third?"

"I found it, didn't I? Okay. Okay. Fu-uck. Half then."

Rain drummed straight down on me.

"And if I do not 'make a deal?'"

"You think you're just going to turn it in? No reward or anything? What kind of a Zentadon does that make you?"

"The good guy kind?"

I felt his anger and frustration.

"The landing pod takes off without both of us in four more days," he argued. "All right. You drive a hard bargain. Why don't you hide the box or destroy it? Then we can both leave."

I halted in my tracks. It suddenly dawned on me. I sat down on the ground and examined the lindal, running my hands across both sides and the slim ends. I detected a slight bubble at one end where someone, apparently Captain Amalfi, suspicious and cautious, had attached an electronic tracer bug. Blade possessed its monitor. So that was how he managed to stay on my trail so tenaciously.

I beat at the bubble with a stone. I took out my knife and broke off the blade tip prying at it. No use.

I now had some insight into Blade's OpPlan. He was hoping to press me hard enough that I would get rid of the case, and then all he had to do was follow the bug to it. He wouldn't even need the Presence. Now that I knew, I thought I might be able to use it to my advantage. Exactly how, I wasn't sure yet.

Blade snorted over the radio. "Elf? We know how this is going to end. But I got to hand it to you. You're giving me a fine run for my money. You'd make a good Human."

"Bite your tongue."

C·H·A·P·T·E·R
THIRTY EIGHT

DAY SEVEN

The voice came back to me in my sleep. I thought it came from my dreams; the Presence tormenting me while I slept.

Kadar San . . .? Help me, Kadar San . . . Kadar San, I'm dying . . .

The thought voice was weak, but not as weak as last time. It was almost recognizable. I snapped immediately awake. I had crawled down among the roots of a forest giant where they made sort of a cave. It was relatively dry there, if cramped, and I felt safe from any insomniac monster that might come wandering by. I sat there in complete darkness with the rich odor of wet soil in my nostrils and the flash of lightning outside playing silhouette shadow tricks with the entangled roots of my overnight lodging.

I dispatched a thought message of my own: *I am*

listening. Talk to me. Who are you? Where are you?

There was no response now that I was alert and listening. The military sent its ground grunts and SpecOps warriors to various survival schools. We rear echelon types, what the Human soldiers called REMFs, for *rear echelon motherfuckers*, endured minimal combat training. However, I had heard Designated Hitters in the infantry talk about how hallucinations set in after you had been deprived of food and sleep for a few days. One soldier had a conversation with his mother who had died years before. Another sat down to a full three-course meal and started eating his socks and boots and gloves. I wasn't that bad yet.

The rain had slacked to little more than a drizzle pattering gently in the foliage. I crawled out from the roots and stood outside in the forest and gazed toward the distant rocky hills to the southwest. I saw nothing, of course, but the blackness of an Aldenia night.

Pia died in the rocks when Blade's neural grenade went off. I saw her dead, along with the others. The Presence was playing its own little cruel mind games with me, trying to drive me crazy by sending me voices that sounded like hers. But they were so real.

So were my other dreams of being chased by the dead.

I concentrated, listening inside my head. I probed the vicinity of the old campsite where death came for six of my fellow DRT soldiers, including Pia. I silently longed for a whisper of friendly sentient life. I picked up waves from

the bloody lizards, quiet now in slumber. Somewhere closer I found Blade, also quiet and less threatening while he slept. But all I received of Pia were the hollow echoes of empty hopes.

I turned, feeling more alone than before, and crawled back among my roots like a beast somewhere quite low on the evolutionary scale.

C·H·A·P·T·E·R
THIRTY NINE

It didn't seem possible that forest fires could combust in such a drenched land, but the old burn I came to attested to the fact that they happened. I paused at the edge of a woodline and looked out over a wide expanse of dead and barren blackness, the only features being charred stumps and the scorched carapaces of beetles trapped and destroyed by the blaze. I couldn't go back; I couldn't go around to the right without moving into Blade's trap; skirting the burn to the left killed time without leading Blade deeper into the planet away from the pod. That meant I had to go straight ahead, across the burn.

A stream meandered through the middle of the seared plain. Blackened tree skeletons stood along the banks. Further into the opening a herd of Goliath beetles, rather passive creatures in spite of their furious appearance,

browsed on pioneer weeds that were starting to sprout in the wasteland. I girded myself mentally and took to the streambed. The water ran slow and shallow, its surface dimpled by the drizzling rain. The banks were relatively high and afforded some cover.

I tried to pick up the pace, but running for any extended time might cause additional damage to my fractured chest plate. I maintained a steady, slow jog, favoring my right side, sloshing in the stream and bending low to utilize the full benefit of the banks as cover.

I sensed the sniper's frustration and realized with a start that he had spotted me and was trying to get a clear shot. I controlled my taa, refusing to allow it dominance. I was getting better and better at it.

I tasted the Presence and, through it, received a disturbing impression of the sniper. The Republic military always attempted to weed out the "over the edge" types, but no system was fail proof. For Blade, the perfect psychopath, being team sniper was all about power. He was the consummate hunter. He tracked his target, observed it, matched wits with it, waited for the perfect time . . . and then . . . one shot, one kill. Killing became a heady drug to which Blade was obviously addicted.

He was enjoying the hunt. I recognized that in Blade's personality it would be as hard for him to withdraw now as it was to pull out halfway through sex. Good. Maybe I could use that information against him.

I was fairly certain Blade had none of the Hornet sensor rounds remaining, else he would surely have used them by now. That left the dumb rounds. Although they came in faster than the speed of sound, without emissions to give them away, and slammed into a target before the target knew it, they were less formidable than Hornets. Nonetheless, it occurred to me that I might have made a foolish mistake in taking to the open ground for expediency's sake.

I crouched lower and jogged a bit faster to make a flitting target, carrying the Indowy lindal in my left hand, the Punch Gun in my right.

I received from Blade an overwhelming rush of hatred and cruelty and pleasure. At the same instant, I picked up his thoughts. *Elf moving at eight klicks an hour . . . one meter lead . . . bullet half a second in flight . . .*

Calculating a shot.

He "dropped off my scope," disappeared from my senses. I realized he had gone into his "cocoon." Snipers often talked about the state of auto-hypnosis in which all thought and emotion ceased the moment before they squeezed the trigger on a target.

A voice screamed inside my subconscious. Accompanying it came the danger image of a crouching fanger.

Down!

The warning a half instant later would have come too late. Taa kicked in and I dodged.

The bullet sizzled past, only inches in front of my chest.

It thudded, spent, into the opposite stream bank. I heard the distant report of the shot. A wrenching spasm of pain in my chest reminded me that I wasn't yet whole. Ignoring it, I used taa to propel me another hundred meters up the streambed before I flopped to the ground.

Under cover of the near clay bank, I rolled over on my back and let it rain in my face while I took deep breaths to restore my equilibrium. Being half-Human, I supposed, reduced my power of taa to some extent, but at the same time increased my immunity to random lintatai. I didn't think I understood that until just now.

That was close. If it hadn't been for the warning . . . The Good Presence.

Are you there? I asked in thought.

Yes.

Where?

I am here.

I could use some help about now.

We are prohibited from interfering directly. We can only influence.

Who prohibits it?

It is prohibited.

It is the same for the Presence? It can only influence? Is that why it cannot take the lindal from me and cannot directly help the Human destroy me?

Yes.

But the Presence destroyed the robot at the river and the

other one when we found the lindal.

Those were machines only. Their destruction was meant to demonstrate its power and attract evil to it.

That was how the Presence selected Blade? Evil attracting evil?

The sniper responded favorably. He continues to respond favorably.

Blade and the Presence were acquainted from before?

The Presence was acquainted with him.

It was a strange mental conversation.

Who are you? I asked.

I am who I am. That is all you can understand.

Who is the Presence?

It is evil and feeds on evil and grows stronger.

Can you destroy it?

It is stronger than I. The Human is stronger than you.

Great.

But they have their weaknesses. Which you will exploit with my influence. They fear you.

If I fail?

We both fail. We both perish. The lindal you carry will release its evil into the galaxy.

Can you take the box and destroy it?

I can only influence.

Right.

I was stuck with a weak old aunt when it came to a presence. Chalk up another advantage for Blade in his strong, evil Presence. Nonetheless, my Presence had saved my life.

I felt Blade's hate and frustration drop beyond my awareness. He was blocking me again, obviously with the help of his Presence. It was going to be a cat-and-mouse game the rest of the way across the burn. It was time to screw with his mind. I took out the squad radio and calmed my breathing so Blade couldn't tell how seriously I was injured. I had to entice him closer, into range of my Punch.

"As long as you stay at such long range," I radioed chidingly, "I can duck your bullets forever."

"Fu-uck."

"Tut, tut, Sergeant Kilmer. You need to learn the ancient Human art of Zen. Think of calm water, Sergeant Kilmer."

I began taunting him over the radio, pushing the right buttons to get him to relax control.

"If you are going to be a real sniper, Sergeant Kilmer, let me help you. Think: front sight, front sight, breath in, let half of it out, clear your mind, you are in a soap bubble in a gentle breeze . . . squeeze, squeeze . . ."

"Fu-uck you, elf!"

I felt him in the highlands.

A couple of bullets, delivered in exasperation, thudded into the streambed where I had been but was no longer. His anger gave him away before he fired. I knew I had a chance as long as he continued his mind blitz of hatred and pleasure at the instant of his trigger squeeze. Once he learned to control that, however, recognized what he was doing, I would no longer experience an advance warning. Even the Good Presence wouldn't be able to save me.

The twin blasts of Blade's rifle blended into a crack of lightning. The mass of giant beetles, to my rear now, began to move past me in the same direction I was heading. The rifle shots shouldn't have spooked them, accustomed as they were to the pop and banging of lightning. But whatever set them off, I saw my opportunity.

I scurried low along the streambed until I reached the nearest insect. The herd flowed rapidly but was not stampeding, simply moving out of the way of perceived danger. I vaulted out of the little creek and was soon trotting among the beetles, using the masses as cover against Blade's rifle. His fury lashed out at me. He blasted away with the Gauss, hitting the beetles and killing several.

When the burn ended and woodland began, I split from the herd and dropped into bushes to look over my back trail. I soon discovered what had motivated the movement. A pack of the thinking predator lizards was slinking along the edges of the burn. I counted six of them. Because of their number, two of whom were the larger king reptiles, I assumed they were the survivors of Blade's massacre. Obviously, they learned from their experiences, for they stayed in the woodline under cover, circling the burn. I probed their brains. They were cautious, wary. Obviously, since they could actually see me and not Blade because of his chameleons, they associated me with the death that had taken three of their number — and they were seeking revenge.

They were stalking me.

I chilled to the core. Just what I needed. Blade and the lizards all hunting me.

CHAPTER
FORTY

I should have pushed things at the camp after Blade annihilated DRT-213. Had the fight right then and got it over with. But the injury done me by the Hornet round and the ultimate Zentadon prohibition against killing another sentient had stopped me. On the other hand, what ultimate good would it have done, other than raw revenge, to destroy Blade? As it turned out, I wasn't programmed into the pod's computers. I couldn't leave Aldenia on my own anyhow.

What if I captured the sniper? Captured him and forced him to operate the pod?

It could be done. Ironic that the Human who meant to kill me was now my only hope. What a strange turn of events. Whereas I had previously given up hope of personal escape and desired only to rid the galaxy of the dreadful lindal and, perhaps, of Sergeant Kilmer, I now depended upon Blade's survival for my own.

Thinking that I had put some distance between Blade and me, I crawled into the shelter of an outcropping of rock to rest. I sat huddled in the side of the ledge and looked out over a vast expanse of mixed savannah, forest, and burnt plain where bolts of lightning cracked and strobed, sizzling in the rain. I was wet and chilled literally to the bone. I used precious energy warming my body telekinetically, but the loss of energy would be more than compensated for by the restoration it helped accomplish.

I gnawed on the newt I had saved from lunch, barely feeling the taa push that came as the result of consuming what had once been living flesh. So far, in this cat-and-mouse game with Blade, I was managing to maintain control over my taa in spite of how my emotions kept pegging out. Other Zentadon, the taa addicts, pushed the edge of lintatai; I had to push it the same way, but for a different purpose. My survival, my mission, ultimately depended on it. If I went too far, just one time, and succumbed to it . . .

Well, I had seen the Zentadon addicts drifting away, withering into infinity and dying with smiles of bliss on their faces. That seemed an easier way to go than spontaneous combustion. It wasn't comforting to know that I could go either way.

I felt Blade's anger out there somewhere, more dreadful than the storms. I also felt the lizards. Both elements on my trail.

I analyzed the problem logically, as was the Zentadon way. The problem: Only Blade could operate the landing pod. Complication: Blade was going to kill me. Solution: Avoid being killed, take Blade prisoner.

I had this thing half solved already. Everything except the "avoid being killed, take Blade prisoner" part.

I had attempted a booby trap before. It failed. What made me think I could construct one now that would operate more successfully than the first?

I had to play to his greed and to his competitiveness. Make him think he had won. Looking downhill from my rock shelter to a copse of twisted and splintered trees spun into a decaying spider's web gave me an idea. I jumped up immediately, revived by the prospect of taking the offensive, and raced down to the spider's web. I didn't have much time, but I thought I had enough. What a tangled web we weave. An old, old Earth expression. I thought sadly of Pia.

I climbed one of the anchor trees, careful to avoid being trapped and tangled in the web myself. Using my clasp knife with the broken point, I cut all the web's anchor points except the one nearest the bottom of the tree and the one at its topmost. Sticky goo covered the strands. The remnants of a dragonfly long dead with the juice sucked out of it clung near the middle. I climbed the other tree and worked feverishly to prepare that side of the web the same as the first. Above me in the drizzle a giant dragonfly made curious circles. So far, dragonflies had proved no threat. I wondered what they ate.

I attached a thin, pliable vine to each top anchor point and cut both web points half through their junctions with the trees so that a stiff tug would release the top portion of the web. Lastly, I ran a long vine through the grass to a point where I could reach it to give that tug. If everything worked the way I planned, and I saw no reason why it shouldn't, the web would drop silently and swiftly like a net and entangle its prey, Blade, in myriad filaments so gluey that he wouldn't be able to move for the few minutes I needed to complete the capture.

I stood back and regarded the snare with satisfaction. The spider's web, having been long unused and sagging, still looked completely natural even with my modifications. Its bottom lines were at least three meters off the ground, leaving plenty of room for a Human man to walk underneath without feeling unduly threatened. There was a small clearing there so the web could fall without becoming entangled before it served its purpose. The trap vines merged with the foliage so that even an accomplished woodsman like Blade wouldn't suspect anything.

All I needed was the bait.

I radioed Blade.

"What do you want, elf?" he demanded suspiciously. "You've been still and in one place for too long."

The monitor on the lindal would have told him that.

I inserted pain and suffering into my voice. "I am hurt. You have shot me again."

"Well. Is that a fact? My heart bleeds purple piss."

"I will die, Blade. But before I do I will keep going with the Hell Box until you are too far from the pod to make it back in time."

Silence. Blade had apparently considered that possibility. I let him stew over it for a few moments.

"Will you still make a deal?" I asked, forcing myself to plead.

"What kind of deal?" He sounded shrewd and cautious.

"We will have to work out the details so that we each get what we want."

"I'm listening."

"You must dispose of the rifle . . ."

"Fu-uck! Double Fu-uck!"

"That is nonnegotiable."

Like I really expected him to negotiate in good faith. I felt him mulling it over. I felt his deceit brewing.

"Go on," he encouraged presently.

"You keep your Punch," I said. "I will keep mine. That puts us on an equal footing. We select a point and we walk out to meet each other. From that point we can talk."

"You're bringing the box with you, is that right?"

I hesitated to make him think I was wrestling with my decision. "I will bring the box."

Box. That was the only word his greed heard.

"No tricks?" he said. Those who were knavish and treacherous always anticipated those qualities in everyone else, while honest people expected other people to be likewise honest. I would have to be on my guard.

"You want the box," I resumed. "I am hurt. I cannot leave this cursed planet without you. That seems to preclude tricks — as long as each is aware of the other's needs."

My ears flicked. I knew I could not trust Blade. His sole objective was to obtain the box by whatever means, by hook or by crook, as Pia would have put it, and then dispose of me. But then, on this occasion, he couldn't trust me either. It was going to be a tryst built upon mutual deceit; and Blade, I kept warning myself, had much more practice at it than I.

All we needed to do was select a rendezvous site.

"Where are you, elf?" he asked. As though he didn't know already.

I played along, pretending that I hadn't figured out that he was tracing me with Captain Amalfi's monitor bug, not tracking me.

"Do you see the rocky hill to the southwest of the burned plain?" I said. "Near where the dragonfly is circling?"

"Is that where you are? All right. Where do we meet?"

We negotiated. I suggested he come to the ridgeline. He declined it as being too enclosed, which I knew he would. He offered the burn by the muddy stream. I rejected it as too open. Finally, I proposed the copse of trees where my trap awaited. For a moment I thought he was going to reject it outright because the idea came from me.

"It is open enough on either side that we can see each other before we get within Punch range," I said, panting a little in pain for effect, "but it gives me cover in case you decide not to lay down your rifle first."

"Don't you trust me, elf?" he gibed.

"You are an honorable, decent man who has not recently murdered all his comrades. Of course, I trust you."

He laughed over the radio with the unnerving voice of the Presence.

"One other thing," I added. "Turn off your chameleons. I want to be able to see you."

"Done," he agreed. "We meet under the dragonfly. Make sure you're carrying the case or all deals are off."

C·H·A·P·T·E·R
FORTY ONE

He wasn't carrying the rifle. With his cammies turned off, I could see that as he worked his way off the burn and started to climb toward me through the lush grasslands below the trees. I also knew the rifle couldn't be far away. He was exclusive with the thing. He probably conjoined with it.

Rain slashed at his figure. Storms were moving back in. The crash-flash of lightning infused the meeting with all the drama of a state summit. Not so far away now, the six lizards were making their way toward us in the treeline on our side of the burn. The damnable dragonfly flew lower and lower, its membrane wings misting the falling rain and causing the precariously-clinging spider's web to tremble. I waved my arms at it, but that only seemed to whet its curiosity. I watched it uneasily.

I let Blade see me walking down from the ridge carrying the lindal. It was all for show, a deception for which, being basically an honest Zentadon, I felt some guilt. It was necessary to lure Blade directly underneath the web tree while I reached a point where I could trigger the web with my vine arrangement. I walked dragging one foot and hunched around my middle, like I was seriously injured and in great pain. I rested every few steps, encouraging Blade to keep coming toward me.

He stopped short of the trap, a cagey soldier who survived by being perpetually crafty. He scanned every foot of the terrain ahead. His head lifted. I saw him watching the idiot dragonfly now flying so low in circles that it shook water loose from treetops and rustled the uppermost leaves. I thought my heart was going to stop beating from the tension when the dragonfly inevitably turned Blade's gaze to the spider's web. Luckily, rain replaced any big drops that I might have jarred loose from the strands when I was rigging my trap.

Still, a close scrutiny of the type Blade proved capable of might reveal a certain discordance that would tip him off. Thinking quickly, I pretended to stumble and fall, hurling the lindal out in front of me. Blade's eyes snapped immediately to the black case. He started forward again. Cautiously, but he was still coming. That was what mattered.

I gained my feet and picked up the Hell Box, struggling to impress Blade with the extent of my exaggerated wounds.

We were still well out of Punch range when Blade stopped again. He looked all around, including up at the dragonfly. His eyes scanned past the spider's web with hardly a notice this time.

He was short of the trap zone by about ten meters. I had an equal distance to go in order to reach the release that tripped the web. It wouldn't take much to set the sniper off, cause him to go for his gun and rush toward me laying down a wall of fire. For all I knew, that was what he contemplated all along.

"Okay, elf!" he called out.

"We must stop meeting this way," I retorted in an abnormally thin tone.

"What did you say?" he shouted.

I indicated that I could hardly speak and used that as an excuse to proceed even closer. I moved to within leaping distance of my trap trigger. I doubled over in apparent effort to catch my breath from the pain. Humans gave awards called Oscars to actors for roles less dramatic than the one I was playing. While bent over, I examined the trigger hidden in the grass to make sure that nothing had happened to it and that it would still work. I felt vulnerable even thought I was still out of Punch range.

Closer. I had to get Blade closer.

I dropped to my knees and huddled there, breathing hoarsely, clutching my ribs and using the lindal as a security shield. Blade wouldn't want to take a chance of damaging it in the course of ridding the planet of me. He wouldn't know that it was indestructible.

"Here is my offer . . ." I began.

"What? What? Fu-uck."

He took a few more steps to better hear me. Come on! Come on!

"Give me your weapons," I called out in the same thin voice. "Then we can talk."

"Turn over my weapons, you say? Is that it? You must be crazy."

Rain slapped at the trees. Thunder rolled. The dragonfly's wings whirred low over my head. The flyer continued toward Blade. He ducked and waved the creature off. It climbed steeply and circled above the spider's web. It was a gray, wet and noisy world.

"You are the mad one," I said, speaking so Blade could see I was talking but in such a low voice that he couldn't hear me. "You are an evil madman and a suitable vessel for the Presence. Three more steps and I will have your scheming, murdering butt so entangled in spider web that you will go to trial and be executed wrapped up like a cocoon . . ."

He took one of the three steps. I kept muttering. He took two more steps, calling out, "What? What?"

Now!

I lunged for the trigger. In agonizing slow motion I watched the top line of the web begin to crumple. At the same time, the dragonfly soared back around and darted between the two anchor trees above Blade's head and directly below the collapsing net. In stunned disbelief, I saw the winged creature fold into the net. The force of its momentum collapsed the web around its body. Dragonfly encased in a mass of silver silk tumbled out of the sky and crashed into trees further downhill.

Blade roared with anger, suddenly seeing how the web was intended for him. He dashed for cover, firing his Punch over his shoulder. The short round expended itself harmlessly before it reached me.

I fled in the opposite direction, astounded by the way fate and pure dumb luck had saved Blade and defeated me again. The chase was back on. In my wake, the Presence contributed its ghastly peals of humorless laughter. I had no trouble hearing Blade's angry and indignant braying.

"You double-crossing traitorous sonofabitch! There'll be no mercy when I catch you, so don't expect it. Damn you, elf! Damn you to Hell!"

C·H·A·P·T·E·R
FORTY TWO

I remained frustrated over my failure when the longer of the two Aldenia nights fell and I was forced to seek harbor. For the balance of the day I had made a wide circle to bring me near the fatal sight of the DRT massacre, thinking I might be able to scrounge something useful there on my way through, even though Blade was sure to have booby trapped it. It lay in the high country to the west, the same high country to which Blade had stuck after the fiasco with the dragonfly and the spider's web.

I wriggled into a semi-dry fissure in a rock face and decided to put off any further decisions until after I rested.

Kadar San, help . . . Help me . . .

The plea came so strong and clear that I bolted upright, banging my head on the overhead rock. I recognized the texture of the thought-voice inside my head. But it simply couldn't be.

Are you here? I asked the Good Presence.

No answer.

I concentrated. *Pia . . . ?*

Kadar San . . . !

It *was* her! She had read me. She was alive!

I felt the Good Presence. *You no longer need the evil one in order to escape. You need her.*

Why did you not tell me about her?

We are prohibited.

I know. You can only influence.

Yes.

Can I communicate with her telepathically?

Can you?

Then the GP, the Good Presence, was gone. In its place I felt slimy tentacles and the odor of rot as the Presence sought me out. I slammed a mental door against it and found, to my surprise, that it worked. My mind was clear again.

Kadar San . . . ? Kadar San . . . ?

Gun Maid was the living ranking member of the team. The GP was right. The pod would open for her. It wouldn't open for Blade, after all. Did he know that yet?

She couldn't always understand thought words, not yet. Images seemed to work better. I sent her a picture of the river and the pod. *Go!* I sensed her excitement, but she also seemed confused, slightly disoriented, weak, and injured.

I transferred some of myself to her and received a chilling image of her huddled alone in the rain with the dead around her. She remained in the rocks with the others. In shock. Helpless as a frightened, lost child.

I sent her: *Danger!* With an impression of Blade pointing a rifle at her.

I need help, Kadar San.

I cannot come yet, I sent back.

Blade would finish the job if he traced me to her and learned she was still alive. There was no way she could join me on the run in her obviously debilitated condition.

Get away! Hide! I thought-shouted. *Go to the pod. I will try to meet you there.*

Kadar San . . .?

I projected another picture of the river where the pod was and of her running toward it. *Do you understand?*

Kadar Sa . . .?

Then she was gone and I couldn't pick her up again. Which meant she must have lapsed into unconsciousness. Or worse.

CHAPTER
FORTY THREE

DAY EIGHT

Come dawn I knotted another day into my cord. Two Galaxia days remaining before those of us who survived became castaways on the Dark Planet. I was fairly rested, and hungry. Both good signs. I tested for Blade and eventually found him out there, non-localized, but out there. Even when he freshly awakened, his aura was dark and menacing. I wondered what Hells his dreams must concoct.

I sent out energy waves to find the lizards. They were out there also. They were hungry. I wondered about their intelligence. In another thousand millennia, give or take a few hundred, they must likely become sentient beings of some culture and intelligence. They were going to be ugly people with a mean streak.

Discovering Pia still alive changed once more the rules of this deadly game of strategy in which Blade and I were engaged.

It was a game where rules, it seemed, changed minute by minute. Yesterday, I needed Blade alive and captured in order to escape the planet; today, I needed him dead.

As for Blade, he probably failed to realize how the rules had changed; no longer did he have the option of taking off in the pod. Not as long as Pia lived. To the end of keeping him in the dark, I set out in a driving thunderstorm toward the east northeast, drawing him away from Gun Maid and any weapons or equipment that I might have salvaged from the massacre site. I shunned the lower savannahs and kept to the high ground where my own surveillance was better. I hunted along the way, fishing out a couple of newts for breakfast. I would have liked something different, but the newts were nutritious and no longer posed a threat to my taa system. I crouched under a rock ledge out of the rain and tried to contact Pia again while I ate. Earlier, she had been off the air, so to speak. Another old, old Earth expression.

Pia . . . ?

Kadar San . . . A feeling of relief and joy on her part.

I thought of how her nipples had hardened. I must be feeling better.

Kadar San! That's nasty!

She had a Talent. She was getting good at telepathy. My ears twitched with embarrassment.

Pia, where are you now?

She didn't understand. I sent her an image of the massacre site with a question interposed. Still confusion. She sent back a big question mark of her own. I replied with a repeat of the black river, the pod, and her running toward it.

Go to the pod, Pia.

At least she could escape, even if I didn't make it.

Kadar San . . . I'm sorry . . .

About what?

I received a picture message of her turning her back on me, and by it understood she was apologizing for having rejected me in front of the others a few minutes before Blade attacked with the neural grenade.

You are forgiven, Pia.

The connection between us weakened. I sensed she was ill, perhaps injured. I felt her nausea in my own stomach. Its intensity caused me to wretch up newt meat. Pain — her pain — knifed into my skull.

Can you walk, Pia? I gasped.

Walk . . .? Walk where . . .?

In her condition, she made easy prey for predators, even the smallest of them. But, still, reaching the pod was her best and only chance.

Pia . . .?

The Presence suddenly appeared in her place. Its wretched scream of interfering laughter echoed among the drenched hills. Down in one of the clearings, the lizards appeared as watery forms, like creatures seen beneath the gray surface of the sea. They reared to their hind legs and then, as one, darted for cover.

Pia . . .?

She was gone, likely returned to unconsciousness. Chilled by the hideous laughter and what it portended, undecided about my next move, I succumbed to a moment of helplessness and indecision. If I did not go to her, she likely perished from exposure or fell prey to some beast. On the other hand, leading Blade to her was even more certain death. It wasn't so much that the rules of the game kept changing; it was more that there were no rules.

Pia's life depended on me; my ultimate survival and escape now depended on her. Blade needed her dead, although I hoped he didn't know it yet. But perhaps he did if, as I suspected, he and the Presence had become almost as one.

I decided to feel Blade out. I keyed the squad radio.

"Good morning out there in Happyville," I chirped brightly.

He didn't answer. He was still sulking from yesterday.

"Sergeant Kilmer, are we out of sorts this morning?

"Fu-uck."

"Oh. There we are. Sergeant, have we noticed that the lizards you angered are now tracking you, while you track me?"

It was difficult to tell which of us the lizards were in fact stalking, now that Blade's cammies were about to go. When they went completely, we would stand on a more equal footing, predator-wise.

"When they eat you, elf, I'll get the box anyhow."

"But what if they eat you, Sergeant Kilmer?"

"In your dreams, fairy man."

"It is in my dreams, Sergeant."

Psyching each other out, playing mind games.

"Sergeant Kilmer, in two more days the pod will leave without either of us."

"We could have made a deal. You fucked it up."

"A deal with the Devil would be more appealing."

"Give me the case, elf. I'll let you live. Don't be a fool. At least you'll still be alive."

"You sound desperate, Sergeant. Okay. Tell you what I will do. Turn your Gauss over to me. Let me have the weapon."

"Are you crazy, man? Fool me once, shame on you. Fool me twice, shame on me."

"An old, old Earth expression?"

"I'll give you an even better one: Bend over, elf, and kiss your stinking ass goodbye. I'm going to kill you today. I'm going to track you down and waste your sorry ass. Enjoy your last morning on Aldenia, or any other planet."

"Oh, but, Sergeant, the hunted is about to become the hunter."

"Fu-uck. Watch out, elf. I'm coming."

I finished eating, climbed higher, and looked back. The lizards sniffed around in the lowlands. I noticed they kept looking off toward the west. I followed the direction of their gaze and saw a Human form climbing in the rain toward the rocky pinnacle where DRT-213 had started its final camp. Blade's cammies were going on the blink. I saw him for just a few moments before he blended back into the terrain. The lizards returned to looking for me.

The rules that were not rules changed again. Blade must have gotten near enough the scene of his crime to pick up Pia on his LF tracker. He was heading her direction. To eliminate all survivors, all obstacles.

C·H·A·P·T·E·R
FORTY FOUR

Playing with lintatai was playing with the dark side. Taa reacted to hatred, fear and aggression, all the demons that lurked in the Zentadon soul. I released a trickle of it, carefully, experimenting, as I threw caution to the wind and hastened from the high ground and back onto the savannah, a straight line being the shortest distance between two points. I counted on Blade's being so preoccupied with whoever had survived his ambush that he would overlook me for a little while. His LF would not tell him who the survivor was. Whoever it was had to die. Especially if the survivor outranked him and therefore controlled access to the pod.

I also counted on Blade's being unaware that I also knew about the survivor. As long as that ignorance continued, he would not expect his prey to turn and become the predator.

Rain slashed at my face, painfully at the speed I was going under taa, and stabs of quicksilver lightning strobed overcasting grayness into alternating instants of blinding brilliance. It was a little disorienting. I drew my Punch Gun in one hand while carrying the case in the other. I hurried to break a straight path through the purple grass that grew taller than my head. Water and mud sucked at my boots. The strain drew on the frailty of my injured ribs. Someone observing from a high point would have seen the path I made through the grass, like a line drawn on a child's etch-a-sketch toy. Overtness was a chance I had to take to reach Pia in time.

I intended to kill the sniper if I could. I was on the trail of my first kill of a sentient. That thought alone caused a taa feedback, threatening lintatai. The evil genie in the Indowy box was not the only genie attempting to break free. I cleared my thoughts of the killing itself and thought only of Pia. I bulldozed through the grass with deadly purpose.

My thoughts called out to her desperately. *Pia . . .! Pia . . .?* Without an answer.

Looking up to the high ground, I estimated Blade's position relative to mine. He was going to beat me to her, unless I used a significant burst of taa. But if I used it now, it would leave me weakened and there would be little left for the confrontation.

I explored for Blade's emotions, finding them at last. They tasted fierce with determination and violent intent.

The Presence was with him. At the same time, however, I sensed something else. Uncertainty. Like he knew a survivor was there, but wasn't exactly sure where he hid. That could mean his LF was starting to fail. Perhaps Pia and I still had a chance.

Hurry! said the Good Presence.

What do you think I'm doing?

Quickly!

You could help.

No.

Can you at least tell me, is she alive?

She is alive. But hurry.

I crashed recklessly through the weeds, heedless of the big lizards nearby, having forgotten all about them in my desperation to reach Pia Gunduli. They had not forgotten me. They reminded me of their proximity in a most startling manner. One of them sprang into the air and rode the slash of rain to a landing directly in my path. It towered head and gleaming teeth and unsheathed front claws above me, eyes like black holes punched into leathery skin. A thin screech of triumph hissed from its cavernous gullet.

Peripherally, I spotted a couple of the others leaping up and down in the grass like hunting terriers in order to get a look at me. They seemed overly cautious as a result of their previous encounter with Blade's bullets. Their wariness and hesitation gave me a slight edge.

I exterminated the first beast, blasting him into a pink

mist of body parts. Taa kicked in like a Starfighter's afterburner to help me escape from the others. An observer of the savannah etch-a-sketch would have seen a straight line appear in the grass as if by magic. I was almost all the way across the meadow during the time it took a bolt of lightning to jag from one edge of the sky to the other.

Taa ran out abruptly. I felt what I assumed to be the beginning stages of lintatai. I stumbled, returning to normal time, and fell exhausted to my hands and knees. My head dropped between my arms into an inch or so of collected water. I breathed heavily, trying to regain control, feeling my body heat up like a stove. Heating up rapidly.

Wait!

Easy enough for you to say.

Look, said the GP, the Good Presence. A vision appeared. A peaceful Ganesh evening when the sky blazed with stars and planets and there was a breeze across a silver lake. The breeze was cool and it touched my face. *Feel it? Let it take away the heat. Look for the peace.*

There can be no peace.

Peace is inside us. That is where we must look.

Who are you? I asked again.

I am who I am and who you are.

That tells me shit.

Later.

I felt the heat dissipating.

Thank you, whoever you are.

It was your doing.

After some more deep breathing, I managed to stagger to my feet and look back on the trail I had made through the grass. The lizards were out of sight. I called out thought-wise to the GP, but it was gone. I wondered what assistance the evil Presence provided Blade, if it were in fact stronger than my Presence.

I struggled out of the meadow and into the rocks and twisted electric-wrecked jungle below the old campsite and still some two or three kilometers to the south of it. I had made up some time with the taa, but now my feet were leaden weights and it was all I could do to put one foot before the other as I began to climb. Blade must still be ahead of me. He would reach the camp first.

Kadar San . . .?

Pia! You must run! Run for your life!

I lurched forward, attempting to run toward her plea. I tripped and fell hard. I hadn't the strength to get up. Pushing the Indowy box ahead of me, still holding the Punch Gun, I crawled on hands and knees. I couldn't make it to her in time. I had failed her.

Kadar San . . .?

I collapsed in the mud and dank forest growth. Water ran off the hillside and over me. My muscles refused to work. All I had left, at least temporarily, was my Talent. I reached out with it and felt Pia, frightened and alone but not as ill as she had been before. I had to get across to her the urgency of her situation. Whether Blade's LF was fully functional or not, he would find her if she remained near the old camp.

I pushed with my mind, pushed hard to overcome any inadvertent resistance on her part.

Pia, I will show you the way. Can you walk?

Kadar San . . .?

Yes. Move it. Now! Look, I am showing you where to go.

If Blade's LF was losing power, its range would be considerably reduced. That was our only hope, her only hope.

I formed a route in my mind and transmitted it to her. I showed her how the hill was a waterslide that she could use — that I had used before — to escape into the forest below.

I don't understand. You want me to slide . . .?

Go! Go!

Images were coming back from her now. I felt terror and saw through her eyes Blade toiling up my side of the slope toward her, disappearing in and out of the rocks and trees. His chameleons were off and he carried his rifle. His head looked huge and otherworldly in his battle helmet. He glared up the hill toward her. He moved with caution.

I screamed at her through my thoughts. I showed her the waterslide.

She started crawling on her belly, slithering. I saw through her eyes Atlas' body sprawled before his half-erected pop-up bivvie. He seemed to have shrunk over the past few days. Pia gasped and looked away from him, and I saw through her how the camp was torn apart. Destroyed items were scattered about everywhere among the corpses of the dead former DRT-bags.

She tobogganed downhill with the runoff water. She cried out from the pain of slamming into rocks and other obstacles. I was afraid she would pass out again, which meant her end and the end of all hopes for my own escape.

She made it to the thicker forest on the lee of the slope opposite me, still conscious and retaining some energy.

There is a game trail. See it? I showed it to her. She reflected it back to me.

Follow it.

It was raining hard and the rain would wash out her tracks before Blade followed them.

It was almost dark in the forest where she was. Her breath came in quick, fearful gasps. Creepers and finger-like vines snatched at her clothing. Shadows lurked in dangerous places. I felt her poor heart thudding in her chest, pounding out a rhythm of sheer terror. She kept tripping, falling down, getting up, and falling down again.

He's coming! He's coming!

Keep going, Pia. There is a little waterfall over a ledge . . .

My head spun and I blacked out for an instant. When I revived, Pia was still there, anxious because I had disappeared for awhile.

The waterfall? she prompted.

She revealed it back to me.

Good.

I showed her how to get through the fall and into the little cave underneath where it was reasonably dry and all but concealed. Within a minute or two, I saw the underside of the waterfall through her eyes. I felt her nausea again, her weakness coupled with mine.

Do you have anything to eat? I asked her.

It didn't come through. I played a scene of her eating so she would understand.

Food? she said.

Yes. You need to eat if you have food.

An energy bar?

Yes. Something.

That was all I could do for her now. Hopefully, Blade's LF would not be able to find her. I used my remaining strength to pull myself deeper into thick brush. I rested my head on crossed arms. Tired, so tired . . .

Pia . . .?

There was no answer. I felt myself slipping into oblivion.

CHAPTER
FORTY FIVE

The shorter of the two nights came while I lay passed out with the Indowy lindal eavesdropping on me, sending out its message: *Here he is! Here he is!* When I regained consciousness, I assumed Blade went looking for Pia. Either he had found her or he had not. Whichever, he must surely have noticed that my signal on the box went stationary. He would approach me now, more cautiously this time, suspecting a trap, locking up his thought and emotion the way he did so I couldn't locate him. He must be near, I thought, waiting for first light.

I probed for Pia. Off the air. That meant she was unconscious again, sleeping — or dead, a possibility that filled me with sadness. It was a risk going to the cave, but one I must assume for my own sake as well as hers. We needed each other.

I moved one hand, then the other. Finally, my legs. I gingerly sat up. I felt much stronger and somewhat recovered, although my body ached all over and pain carved through my chest with each indrawn breath. I must have re-injured my chest plate during the taa burn to escape the lizards.

I was one beat-up elf. These Humans played a rough game.

It was a relatively short distance over the crest of the ridge and down the other side to the cave where I hid the first night after Blade's neural grenade. It was rough going in the darkness, but soon I experienced a sense of deja-vu as I came near, like a replay of an old VR. Been here, done that, got the T-shirt, doing it again. Some things, I thought wryly, shouldn't be done more than once.

I couldn't see shit in the dark, to coin an old, old Earth expression. I found the vicinity of the cave only through intuition and the lay of the land. I squatted and listened, hearing nothing but the dripping of the forest and, off in the distance, the shriek of some creature disturbed by bad dreams or injured by a lightning strike. I sent Pia a thought message so concentrated and forceful that it must surely wake her if she slept. I kept sending it for long minutes. I felt my body temperature rising with the effort.

No answer.

I tried again.

No answer. Blade must have found her.

Then: *Kadar San . . .*

A wave of relief swept over me. I could have almost cried.

Are you alone?

It would be like Blade to capture her and hold her for bait, but there was no way he could control her thoughts.

I'm in the cave, Kadar San.

Guide me. It is too dark out to see.

How?

Just keep thinking about yourself. I will follow the brain wave.

She must be feeling better as well. With a hint of mischief, she showed me how she looked when she was getting into the time couch, wearing only her panties. They were blue. I bumped into trees and other obstacles following the delightful image. I soon heard the waterfall. A minute later, I ducked through the liquid curtain. She hugged me mightily and smothered my face with kisses.

"I knew if you were like most men," she explained happily, "that your penis would guide you when everything else failed."

"Females follow their intuition. Men follow their member. Is that the way the old, old Earth expression goes?"

She laughed her wonderful laugh that I thought never to have heard again. Tears mixed with the laughter. She shuddered. I warmed her with my campfire hands. She snuggled into my arms. I endured the pain in my chest in order to hold her.

After a moment, whispering, she brought me up to date. She survived the neural grenade when it went off, she said, only because she was sitting with her back shielded against a rock. When she regained consciousness — hours later? Days later? — she lay in mud face up. She could not move. Neural grenades affected the central nervous system. The only thing she saw was somebody's lifeless body nearby sticking out from behind a boulder.

"I . . . I kept lapsing in and out of awareness. I didn't know what happened. I thought maybe the Blobs . . . I didn't know. I thought everyone was dead. I had some nutrition bars in my cammie pockets. Finally, I moved my hands and I ate the bars to stay alive and drank the rain. They gave me strength enough to sit up and look around, but I still couldn't walk. I was too weak. I . . .They . . . Captain Amalfi, Sergeant Shiva . . . Atlas . . . All of them lay dead and I couldn't get away from that place of death. I had to sit in the middle of that . . . graveyard and watch their bodies . . . Once, the dragonflies came like vultures and I had to watch them . . . They ate Gorilla first. They sucked out his bodily fluids and . . ."

Her voice caught.

I squeezed her. "Do not think about it, Pia."

"I'll have to think about it later."

"But not now. Later."

She touched my cheek. "I called for you, Kadar San. I kept calling for you in my mind the way you said I could."

"I was not listening for awhile. I thought you were . . . with the others."

"But then you heard!"

"I heard."

She sighed. "It was Blade, wasn't it? Everything in the camp was destroyed when I woke up, like someone had gone through taking what he wanted and wrecking everything else. The only bodies I didn't see were Blade's and . . . yours."

"You thought I had done it?

She squeezed me hard.

"Not once did I think that, Kadar San," she cried. "In my heart I knew you were the most loyal among us. It was just that sometimes . . . sometimes . . . I can't explain it. Something came over us as a team, something evil that caused us to turn on each other. Do you understand?"

"The Presence," I whispered.

I felt her shiver because it had a name.

"I am not certain I understand either," I admitted. "I call it the Presence for lack of a better term. It first appeared in the pod when we water landed. Remember?"

"How could anyone forget that awful laugh! I said it was evil then. Remember? It destroyed the robots, didn't it?"

"The robots got too near the energy source and it blew them up as a demonstration and a warning. I think whatever it is, it is not entirely sane. Apparently, however, it cannot affect sentients the same way. They can only influence.

They cannot exert actual control or cause physical harm."

"They?" Pia asked, sounding alarmed. "There's more of them?"

The running waterfall and the rain hissing in the little stream covered our voices, as they also might cover the approach of an enemy. I drew my Punch Gun and lay it across my lap. *Stick your head in here, Blade, and it will end now.*

"We talked about opposites once, Pia. Darkness and lightness, right and wrong . . ."

"Good and evil . . ."

"Good and evil. There is a Good Presence to counter the other. I think the bad Presence was testing us at first to determine which of us it could use."

"It chose Blade."

"Or Blade chose it. Not this time, but the time before when he was here. It has patience. It used his greed and his basic cussedness against him and against us. Now, it is hard to tell where he leaves off and the Presence takes up."

"What does it want . . .?" She caught herself. I felt her hand reach across me to the Indowy case. "Pandora's box," she said in a wavering voice.

"Pia, this lindal is one of the machines the Indowy developed to control the Zentadon through taa. To one extent or another, it can do the same thing to other races and intelligent species. The Revolution assumed all such machines had been destroyed, but this one must have survived. The best I can determine, the Presence has only one motive — to release its evil on the galaxy once again. It is using Blade as its vessel."

"Destroy it, Kadar San! Destroy it now!" Pia cried.

"I have tried. I thought of shooting it with my Punch, but I am sure the Indowy thought of that and built in protections. There must be ways of destroying it, but we don't have them here."

"Get rid of it, then!"

"We cannot leave it here. Even if Blade does not find it, the Blobs might. Imagine what could happen if the Blobs came into its possession. There is also the likelihood that one day this planet will be colonized, Dark Planet or not. After all, Humans and most other intelligent races and species have a strong urge to go out and conquer. I have a feeling that the Presence is a spirit that lasts for eternity. If not this Blade, then some day the Presence will find another Blade. We cannot take a chance that the genie will ever be loosed upon civilization again. We must take it with us and lose it in the vastness of space where the Presence cannot follow."

She was silent for a long fearful moment. "Where does that leave us?" she asked. "Blade will keep chasing us until he gets it."

"Even if I give him the lindal, which I will not, he still has to kill you before he can get off the planet," I said. "You are the ranking living member of the team, the only one who can activate the pod. He will have examined the bodies by now and know it is you."

"Life is just one damned thing after another," she murmured.

"An old, old Earth expression."

She giggled in spite of the situation. "Here's another one for you: Out of the frying pan and into the fire. How far are we from the pod?"

"We could be there tomorrow except . . ."

"Except . . ." She sighed. "Except it took everything out of me to drag myself this far. I heard you calling me in my thoughts, Kadar San. I tried to do what you said, but I kept passing out." She paused. "Did you say there was an opposite to the evil Presence? A good presence?"

"It saved my life."

She squeezed my hand. "It selected you to fight the evil because you were the best and strongest among us."

"If this is good versus evil, then I am losing the fight," I said wearily.

I leaned forward and stuck my head outside through the waterfall. It was still pitch black out, but daylight would be coming soon. The chase must resume. Only this time I was burdened with a handicap who happened to also be the key to our escape.

"How can Blade track us in this rain?" Pia asked. "The LF has to be running out of power, like everything else. Can't we beat him to the pod?"

I explained about the tracker bug Captain Amalfi

placed on the box. It didn't require much energy to monitor it and keep on our trail.

"It will be easy for him to block us from reaching the pod," I said.

Blocked at every turn.

Pia put something into my hand. "It's an energy bar. I've been saving it. This is as good a time as any for a celebration."

I checked outside again. It was either my imagination or I saw trees dimly emerging from the darkness.

"We will have to go soon," I said. "Eat up, Pia. The odds are about to even up some," I added encouragingly. "I actually saw Blade when he came up the hill. His chameleons are failing, and there are some really pissed off lizards back there aching to get even."

C·H·A·P·T·E·R
FORTY SIX

Exhausted and unwell from her ordeal before, during, and after the neural grenade, Pia dozed with her head on my chest and her arms wrapped around me and mine around her. I stroked the short crop of her hair with one hand, luxuriating in the contact. My Human mother had hair like that, thick and soft and dark. It was one of the few things I remembered about her. I always told everyone she was dead, that she died of heartbreak when she saw that I was born, minus the tail, more Zentadon than Human. I told it so often that I believed it myself. In fact, I didn't know whether she was alive or dead. She abandoned me when I was five-years old to a Zentadon orphanage.

"Who is my mother?" I asked the Keepers when I was ten-years old.

"A Human whore."

"Who is my father?"

"A Zentadon fool."

"Did he have a beautiful tail?"

"It was thin and mangy."

"Was my mother beautiful?"

"No Human is beautiful."

"Do I look like my father?"

"You father had a tail."

That was all I knew about them. My mother was a whore and my father a fool with a thin tail. As I grew older, I discovered that my parents were criminals because cross-breeding, then as now, was an act forbidden by law on both sides. I was born in a detention center. My mother was ridiculed and scorned by peoples on both sides. Segregated and alone, my mother and I lived in the prolie slums of the Galaxia Capital after we got out of prison. Until I went to the orphanage, I thought I must be the only cross-breed freak in the galaxy. It was in the orphanage that I first saw other outcasts like myself.

"Your mothers, if they were Human," said the Keepers, "were ashamed of your ears and tails, for those of you born with them. If your mothers were Zentadon, they were equally ashamed of taillessness and nakedness of hair. Your mothers covered up your heads and would not let you be seen in public. You were all ugly and are still ugly. You simply cannot be half this and half that."

"But what are we to do if we cannot be half this and

half that but *are* half this and half that?" I asked when I was older.

"Some day there will be laws to euthanize babies who are born half this and half that."

"Kill us!"

"It is the merciful thing to do. You can never fit into either world. You are despised and mistrusted on the one side because you are half the other side, and you are equally mistrusted and despised on the other side for the same reason."

My hand paused in its stroking of Pia's hair. In the dark or with your eyes closed, it was difficult to tell the difference between Pia and, for example, Mina Li, except, of course, for Mina Li's hyperactive tail. Pussy, Ferret crudely remarked once, is all the same in the dark.

What Pia and I were doing was illegal because of my Zentadon blood. By the same token, Mina Li and I, should we conjoin, were equally felonious due to my Human side, even though the Zentadon were more tolerant of mixed-breeds than Humans. One drop of Zentadon blood, it was assumed among the Earthlings, made a Dirty Zentadon out of you. You and your offspring into all future generations were tainted.

When I was old enough to leave the orphanage, I went in search of my genetic roots. The pursuit led me to Prolie Town and a Human by the name of Bobo Wilkest.

"My sister might have been the bitch that whelped you,"

he said, "but you are no blood of mine, no tail or not."

"Please," I begged. "Tell me about her. I need to know."

"She screwed a Zentadon."

"Was she exclusive?"

Bobo Wilkest laughed lewdly. "Your mother was exclusive to lots of men . . . and to some animals."

"But she was only sixteen-years old when I was born."

"She had a snatch a lot older than that."

"Where is she now? Can you tell me?"

"She was transported back to Earth to live with the mutants as punishment for her lifestyle. That's the last we've heard of her. She could be dead now for all we know or care."

There was little glamour in my Human ancestral origins unless you somehow considered slum prolie whores charming. I was left with one Bobo phrase to sum up my mother's sordid existence. *She could suck the brass off a brass door knob.* It was a hell of a legacy. It was many years before I knew what that meant.

So I wasn't a lost prince, at least not on my Human side. I expected my Zentadon genealogy to be composed of finer, more noble stuff.

My mother's name was Alicianana Wilkest. My father was a hustler and part-time revolutionary called Kadar San Be. My mother had named me after him! Why would she do that if there were so many males conjoining her that she couldn't remember their names?

"Oh, she remembered his name all right," I was assured by my father's aunt, a dwarf-like ancient whose tail looked as scaly and worn as that of a space-dock rat. In fact, she could have passed for a rat if she were any smaller. "She attempted to murder him out of frustration. She conjoined the fluid out of him for nine days, day and night, and then the breeding season ended. She was screaming and pulling her hair out by the roots, saying how much she loved him. He could do nothing about it. The season of conjoining was over and your father went back to the Revolution. Your mother shot him with a cheap gun she obtained on the black market. He survived, but never saw her again. I do not think he ever saw you."

"My father fought in the Revolution? Impossible. That was centuries ago."

"Not the Great Revolution. He and that bunch of taa addict heads he ran with were always talking about a revolution of their own that would free Zentadon and return Ganesh solely to us. Your father, if he is your father, was a dreamer. Radical, charming, and a good orator, but a more worthless Zentadon being you could not imagine. His only outstanding quality was the Talent."

"He was a Sen?" I cried, pleased.

"They did not call them Sens then. But he could read minds. He made credits that way."

"Where is he? I need to see him."

The scaly-tailed aunt mined her nose with her little

finger. "He went to prison for conceiving you. He liked it so much that he went back for trying to blow up a Republic military space port. As far as I know, he is still in a penal colony somewhere on Ganesh. If you are finished asking your foolish questions, I would rather my neighbors not see me conversing with you. Reputation, you understand?"

"I am sure your reputation is sterling and should not be soiled. Just two more questions."

She pulled her finger out of her nose and examined what she had caught.

"Was my father's tail skinny?" I asked.

"Not as skinny as yours." And she laughed uproariously.

I crossed my fingers for luck.

"Question number two: did he share a family resemblance with you?"

That produced even more laughter. "No, no, no. He was the ugly member of the clan."

No lost prince on this side either. The Keepers were right. I was descended from a whore in one lineage and an ugly fool in the other. The only beneficial qualities I inherited were the Talent from my father and intelligence from somewhere else back there. I used both to forge a career in military academia. Fear of invasion by the Blobs, who communicated telepathically, was producing a demand for Zentadon Sens. There was even talk of making us officers.

I began stroking Pia's hair again, very tenderly, and out of a deep sadness. In falling in romance with this beautiful

Human female, might I not be promulgating the sins of my father? It was not fair to her, much less legal. Sooner or later, if we survived, it was something we had to deal with.

C·H·A·P·T·E·R
FORTY SEVEN

E lf?"

Blade's voice on the radio sounded a little too strained, a bit stretched. Pia gave a little jump. I pulled her closer to reassure her. I noted the growing desperation in the tone of the sniper's voice.

"Time is running out, elf."

It wasn't yet light enough to move. I checked through the waterfall, then popped back inside, shaking water off the dirty makeshift head rag that covered my hair.

"Is it still raining?" Pia asked.

I looked at her.

"Foolish question," she acknowledged.

"Elf, maybe we can still pull a deal. You'll never make it with the cunt. She'll hold you back."

"The deal," I radioed in reply, "is the same as before;

you give up your weapons and submit to being our prisoner. We all go aboard the pod. We all survive."

"For what? So I can be charged with killing this bunch of self-righteous cowards who were supposed to be a DRT team? Do you think I'm crazy?"

"I do."

"I'm not crazy enough for that."

"You are being used by a force stronger than you, Sergeant Kilmer."

"There is no force that strong on this planet."

"I can prove it if you will allow me."

He hesitated. His steel door opened a crack and I felt his uncertainty. I hurried to get in before he blocked it again. I crammed images through the temporarily-opened door of his mind. I reminded him of the insane laughter, the destruction of the bots, how team members went at each other's throats when the Presence appeared, how we were led to the Indowy box.

"You are a soldier, Sergeant Kilmer. You are tough, mean as sin, to coin an old, old Earth expression, you are bigoted, nasty and greedy, and you were used the last time you were here as well as this time."

Maybe I was stretching things a bit, but I had to give him a way out by not specifically mentioning murder.

"Remember how everything was just before you threw the neural grenade? Gorilla and Ferret were fighting. They were the best of friends. They never fought like that. Atlas was wanting to lynch Sergeant Gunduli and me. Does that sound like the DRT-bags under normal circumstances? Under normal circumstances, would you have thrown a grenade among them?"

For a billion credits or so he would have thrown one at his own mother. That was why the Presence selected him.

Voices through the squad radios sounded tinny and amplified. I worked to make mine come out controlled and reasonable.

"What is this force you're talking about?" Blade asked, as though wavering.

Pia squeezed my hand.

"I do not know the full story," I admitted. "It is a Presence and it is evil. Its goal is to release the Indowy curse in the box into the galaxy. Of that I am certain. It will use any means possible."

Blade remained silent, but I still felt him, less malevolent, up there in the rocks among the dead team members. That was a positive sign.

"Blade, you were here before. What happened?"

"Nothing happened," he snapped, too quickly.

"You were the only survivor," I reminded him.

"I was very young." Defensively. "It was my first expedition away from Galaxia."

Blade may not have been ready for the Presence the first time; this time he was.

"What happened to your other team, Sergeant Kilmer?"

There was a long silence over the radio. Through the static I heard a hoarse whisper, like it came from deep inside an inflamed throat. I cringed in spite of myself. Pia stiffened next to me in the cave.

Begone!

Begone?

"Fu-uck," Blade said suddenly. I was losing him. I felt him hardening.

"I didn't kill them all, if that's what you're implying," Blade growled. "They . . . they killed each other."

The horror that ran through his body echoed in mine.

"Then . . . then the critters got the others," he added. "All except me."

"What about Stanto?" I pressed.

I felt him narrowing. "What about Stanto?"

"You dumped his body off a cliff."

"He was already dead. But so what if I killed him? So what if I killed them all? What difference does it make now?"

"It makes a difference because you are back, Blade. The Presence has patience to wait. The same thing happened this time, the same way as before. It is using you again."

Blade mulled that over. "How did you find out about Stanto?" he asked suspiciously.

I was getting to him, making him unsure of himself. I could feel it. If there was one thing Blade was certain to resent, it was the idea that he wasn't always in control of himself and his environment.

Begone!

"Sergeant Kilmer, Gun Maid and myself will both testify on your behalf if you give yourself up . . ."

Begone! Begone! Begone!

I felt the coiling of something slimy inside Blade's soul. His mind slammed shut. The little radio in my hand began to sizzle. I flung it out of the cave, through the curtain of the waterfall. Just in time. It exploded with a sharp bang.

Hideous laughter snuffled and snorted in the darkness outside.

C·H·A·P·T·E·R
FORTY EIGHT

It never lets up," Pia complained weakly, meaning the rain. "He never lets up. Kadar San, I'm holding you back. Go on without me."

"Where would I go? Only you can open the pod."

That should have ended the discussion.

"Sergeant Shiva said no one alive was to be left behind," I continued, helping her negotiate a small stream running around tree roots. Rather, we helped each other, for both of us were about done for. "Besides," I added in a lighter tone, "it is almost the Zentadon breeding season."

That almost made her giggle, but she didn't have the strength for it. She made only a single small sound. How I would like to hear her giggle again.

"If we were exclusive," she asked when we reached the top of an incline and looked back through the rain, "would we make love only once a year for nine days?"

"Of course not," I exclaimed. "I am half-Human. Eighteen days."

"Once a year for eighteen days?"

"Ten times a day for eighteen days."

"Kadar San, are you pulling my leg?"

I looked puzzled. Then I got it. "An old, old Earth expression?"

"Jerking my chain. Floating my bucket." She was on a roll.

"You need rest," I noticed, easing her to sit on a large moss-covered stone.

"So do you, Kadar San."

"I was so happy when I heard you in my mind, Pia. I could have almost kissed you in my mind."

"It isn't as good in your mind as the real thing."

She leaned toward me, her brown face streaming rain from her cropped black hair. Her blue eyes melted into mine. She closed her eyes and gave me a long and tender kiss. My ears twitched. She put her hands over them and giggled softly into my mouth.

"Does this mean you are putting your tail over my shoulder?" I asked.

"The left shoulder," she said. "When do the eighteen days begin?"

"When we reach the landing pod," I replied. That sobered us. She stiffened.

I felt her stiffen an instant before she cried out. "Kadar San!"

I looked in the direction she indicated. A wide basin savannah opened toward the northeast. Several scattered herds of the Goliath beetles browsed in the tall purple grass while dragonflies soared above, scavenging. Halfway across the clearing moved Blade, purposefully bent on inserting himself between us and the black river — and succeeding. His chameleons were either malfunctioning or he had turned them off to conserve energy for when he really needed concealment. At this range, he held no fear of me and my Punch Gun.

A bolt of lightning blasted from horizon to horizon, all the way across the gray-black dome of sky. Blade halted. His helmet looked like a bubble attached to his shoulders. He stared directly at us on the incline. Then he turned and looked to his left.

There were the lizards, moving in and out of the trees, stalking Blade, five yard intervals between them in good military style. Feeling Blade's eyes on them, somehow sensing his intent, they instantly melted into the terrain. These were intelligent beasts; I would not like being on a recon and surveillance team returning to Aldenia if the lizards were provided a few hundred more generations of evolution.

"They never let up either," Pia said, her voice thin with fear but trying to cover it. "All we need to have a real party are the Blobs. Did you forget to invite them, honey?"

"I am afraid they may be invited to another party -- on Galaxia," I said.

"And we have no way of warning people until . . ." She caught herself. "Until we get to the pod, or until the pod leaves without us."

Down on the grasslands, Blade disappeared into his activated chameleons. That answered my question. He was conserving energy. Confused, the lizards stepped cautiously into the opening, walking on their hind legs, cocking their heavy heads from side to side, testing the air, snapping their mighty teeth-laden jaws. The chameleons masked scent as well as sight. To the lizards, it must have seemed their intended prey simply vanished.

They looked in our direction. We were still visible and present. Disregarding the now-disappeared Human, the pack of reptiles dropped to all fours and made etch-a-sketch lines in the tall dark grass as they headed across the meadow directly at us.

"We have to run!" Pia screamed, lurching to her feet in near-panic, pulling on my sleeve.

"We cannot outrun them," I said, not meaning to be fatalistic, only realistic. "They are not looking for food. They seek revenge. But they are smart. They will not charge us head on. They will attempt to ambush us from hiding."

Pia's eyes widened so it was almost like she disappeared into them. In the open, we became easy targets for Blade's reach-out-and-touch-someone Gauss rifle. In the forest, we fell prey to the avenging lizards. That left what? The sky?

Where the grasslands ended and rainforest began, the lizards split off toward the north. It was almost like they knew our route of march as well as Blade did and intended to cut us off. Pia grasped my arm with both hands, breathing hard. I drew my Punch Gun and checked its supply of ammunition. There were five lizards left and one Human sniper. I had four firing rounds remaining. I looked at Pia. She read my mind.

"Blade took all our weapons when he thought we were dead," she apologized. "I don't even have ammunition. Kadar San, are we going to die?"

"All things die; but not in this Dark Place."

I don't believe you.

You must believe if you would survive.

Pia gave a start. "What was that?"

"You heard it!" I exclaimed. "That's the GP, the Good Presence."

"Oh, Lord. This place is populated with things both seen and unseen."

You have described life, said the GP.

The fanger appeared in my mind, the warning sign of danger. Almost instantaneously, I felt the elation and cruel excitement Blade always projected just before he squeezed the trigger. I dived for Pia and brought her down. A bullet seized the air where we had been standing. Thunder muted the report of the distant rifle.

"That was close," I said into Pia's ear as we lay in the wet grass. "We were careless. Now we both owe our lives to the Good Presence."

We were in big trouble if Blade ever learned to control his emotions at his kill moment. I rose to a half-crouch and pulled Pia with me into the cover of the trees, both of us injured and weak and dragging each other. It was just as well that the Presence had destroyed my radio. There was no further benefit in Blade and I psyching each other out. I might have thought earlier to appeal to Blade's better side, but the better side, if he even had one, was now dominated by the Presence.

One of us, either he or I, was going to win. But if I were a betting Zentadon, I would put my credits on neither. My credits would go on the lizards.

C·H·A·P·T·E·R
FORTY NINE

The lizards boxed us in after midday. Blade continued to pop in and out of vision as his chameleons gradually lost their camouflage properties, but he kept his distance. Obviously, he had us cut off from the pod and intended to work on our desperation to win the strange and deadly game in which the three of us and the lizards were engaged. The reptiles possessed no such subtlety.

Blade's coming in and out of their senses the way he did continued to confuse them. They soon ignored him altogether and concentrated on us. Lucky us. They posed the most serious immediate threat. It was terrifying the way, unseen but felt, they dogged our trail and then ranged out on either side and in front, occasionally barking signals at each other. Pia hyperventilated from fear at living this waking nightmare and almost passed out. I supported her and we supported each other. Our lives were reduced to simple repetitive motions of placing our feet one in front of the other.

"There," I said, pointing from an opening on a wooded ridgeline.

Pia batted her lashes against slashing sheets of rain which fortunately reduced the sniper's effective shooting range. She seemed disinterested. She clung to me, weaving on her feet.

"It is the black river," I said.

"We'll never reach it, Kadar San."

She was crying. I knew it by the snuffling sounds she made. Her tears were invisible in the rain washing her brown cheeks. The nearby lizards had to know their quarry was about done for and susceptible to attack with little risk on their part. Like most predators, they sought as first choice the aged, the weak, the debilitated, and the injured.

The only category Pia and I did not match was that of being old. I *felt* old, however. The Dark Planet had aged me.

"The river is right there, Pia," I said, sounding irritable even to myself. Couldn't she see it?

"Don't you see, Kadar San?" she snapped back, pausing in between words to gasp for air. "All Blade has to do is wait for us in ambush at the clearing."

"You cannot count us out so readily," I flared. "You Humans are so fatalistic."

"And you Zentadon have such chips . . ."

We both froze at the sound of the guttural chuckle, the not so subtle odor of ozone and rot. The Presence was still able to pit us one against the other.

I am here, I am with you, said a kind voice in my head. I recognized the GP.

The Presence snarled, like a hot gust of scorched wind through the rain. Then it was gone.

What are we to do? I asked the GP.

You are to do.

What the . . . What does that mean?

I placed my hands on Pia's cheeks and neck and used some of my remaining energy to allay her suffering. I looked below to the black river. Once again so near, yet so far away.

Helping each other, we labored along a rocky ridgeline off which water ran in thin, shimmering sheets. There were caves in the rocks. I felt tempted to call a long rest halt to rejuvenate our strength and replenish my taa supply for one final assault on Blade at the pod. In my present state, the use of taa was out of the question; lintatai was inevitable. I couldn't even get enough air to fuel my body's engine because of my injured chest plate.

In light of all this, I was still *to do?*

The second, the longer, of the two Aldenia nights was approaching. That gave us tomorrow when I would tie the last knot in my cord. One last chance.

I was thinking of the river, fixated on it, when the

intelligent lizards sprang their trap. I was too far gone and dulled by fatigue to heed the fanger warning even if it had been sent. The first animal appeared as an ominous black-gray hardening of the rain, a product of it, like a block of cloud gone vicious. It was suddenly upon us with slashing teeth capable of ripping off our heads with one bite.

Instinctively, for it is within Zentadon as within Humans to protect females and children, I flung myself at Pia. We both sprawled on the spongy ground. At the same instant, sharp teeth ripped into my thigh with such excruciating pain that I thought I would pass out.

The next moment I felt myself lifted head down and being shaken so savagely that my teeth almost rattled loose. I glimpsed Pia below me cowering in terror. A second lizard leaped forward with the intention of dispatching the defenseless female.

The lindal flew from my hand. I held onto the Punch Gun with the other. I thrust it at the lizard's body and squeezed the trigger. The resulting explosion ripped the lizard's body apart. The head with me still in its jaws slammed against the other reptile with enough force to knock it over. It scrambled to its feet while I struggled to extricate myself from dead razor teeth.

I pointed the Punch. It refused to fire since it required at least a second and a half to recycle. The lizard recognized the gun as a weapon. It sprang back away from Pia. The king lizards waiting under cover barked commands.

Another lizard appeared behind me. I rolled out of the dead jaws to confront this new challenge. This attacker held up its charge, intelligent enough to understand that the little piece of steel in my fist was capable of immense destruction. After all, it had shredded the first attacker into bloody pieces which now ornamented every tree within a fifty-meter radius.

The scene of five surrounding beasts blurred and swam in front of my eyes. I verged on lintatai. I still lay on the ground, sweeping my gun back and forth at the surrounding enemy.

Kadar San?

Go away. Let me die untormented.

She will also die.

Pia crawled on her belly toward me, her breath making funny little catching sounds of fear in her throat. I stood up gingerly, using willpower I wasn't sure I possessed. I swept the gun back and forth, keeping the lizards temporarily at bay. They barked and snarled and gnashed their teeth, but I had earned their respect.

I copped a glance at my leg. The sight of it roiled my stomach. It was mangled almost beyond recognition from the knee up. The flesh was torn and bloody. I was bleeding to death.

I had three shots remaining and four lizards. Wonderful! Any way you looked at it, Pia and I were bound to come up with a lizard too many. One lizard and one sniper too many.

The lizards didn't know that, did they?

"All right!" I shouted at them. "Which one will it be next? Who will sacrifice himself?"

I jabbed the weapon at the nearest beast. It twisted its snout and bellowed, but it took a step back. I pulled Pia to her feet. She looked so pale I feared she was about to faint.

"Get back!" I shouted at the nearest lizard. It rose on its hind legs. Its long, thick tail lashed back and forth. I advanced on it step by step. It retreated step by step. The lizard behind us moved with us but kept an interval. I whirled and covered it with the Punch. It halted.

"Grab the case," I ordered Pia. It didn't get through the haze of her near-shock. "Get the case," I repeated more sternly. I squeezed her hand and shook it to snap her into awareness.

"The case?" she murmured. Then she understood. She bent down and picked it up, but never took her eyes off the terrible reptiles. I never took the gun off them. I was thankful they were intelligent enough to understand the situation.

"Pia, we are backing out now. Remember the ledges? They are not far. There were small caves."

She nodded and kept nodding. A crack of thunder made her cringe. I took her hand.

We backed slowly. The lizards gave way, but they followed, barking and slavering. We passed two caves. Their entrances were too large to keep the lizards out. We came to a third whose doorway in the rocks appeared as a mere slot. Maybe it wasn't a cave at all, perhaps only a mere shallow crack in the rocks. We would have to chance it.

"Do you see it, Pia?"

She nodded when I shook her hand to get her attention.

"These guys are psyching themselves up for another attack. I can get one, but the other three . . ."

The trembling of her hand told me she understood.

"When I give you the word and release your hand, run for your life. Get to the cave."

"What about you, Kadar San?"

"I will be right behind you."

"But, your leg . . ."

The lizards crouched in front of us, tongues like quick, liquid black ropes, lapping out to test us. Perhaps it was through their tongues that they tasted the essence and demeanor of their intended victims. If so, I realized what they sensed in us would not hold them back much longer.

I released Pia's hand. "Run!"

I made threatening gestures with the gun to keep the lizards off-balance for another moment. Then I turned and ran after Pia, dragging my leg and clutching my ribs. The lizards saw what we were doing, but by then Pia had disappeared into the cliff. I dived in after her. Heavy jaws snapped at the air where I had been.

I rolled into what appeared to be a fairly large room filled with dry dust and animal smell. I pulled myself away from the entranceway where enraged lizards were snapping and barking and trying futilely to force their teeth inside.

Then I passed out.

When I revived, my leg felt stiff and heavy but the bleeding seemed to have stopped. Pia had ripped up part of her uniform to make pressure bandages. It was too dark to see in the cave, but Pia felt me move. She delivered a barrage of kisses to my face.

"Kadar San, I was afraid you were dying."

She sounded better. Part of her old toughness returning.

My mouth felt dry from fever. Pia put her canteen to my lips. I drank.

"Are you feeling better, Kadar San?"

"It is a good thing I do not have a Zentadon tail, or I would not have it now."

"You almost didn't have a leg."

"How long was I out?"

"It's dark outside."

"And our friends?"

"Still waiting."

I edged up to rest my back against the wall of the cave. I moaned.

"Kadar . . .?"

"It is over," I sighed. "The lizards have trapped us. Blade will be here at dawn to finish us off."

"Yes," she agreed, equally resigned to our inevitable fate.

Blade had already demonstrated what he could do to the lizards with his rifle. Once he killed them or drove them off, there we were, complete with the Indowy case, the prize. Trapped inside a hole in the side of a hill.

I was too weak and beaten to care anymore. I hadn't enough taa left for lintatai. Maybe at dawn, but not now. Pia curled up at my side, shivering from the cold. I closed my eyes.

Kadar San?

I can no longer "to do," I protested.

"I can hear him too," Pia whispered in awe.

I wish you both to hear.

Go away. I have done all that is in me. Can you not see the condition we are in?

You would give up without a fight?

We have been fighting. We have lost.

You haven't lost until your spirit is gone. Do you want such evil as before to be released into the galaxy through that wretched genie in the case?

Leave me alone. Who are you?

I think you know.

It had occurred to me before. *You are from the Zenta-don who were prisoners and died here,* I guessed, and I knew I was at least partly correct.

I am their combined spirits.

And who is the Presence? The combined spirits of the ancient Indowy?

It is a simplification, but that is all as true as you would understand it. You see, Kadar San and Pia Gunduli, there really are two poles in the universe. Opposites, as you would say. Evil and good.

Why is evil allowed to exist? Pia asked in her thought-voice, clearly amazed that she could communicate in this realm and with an entity that existed only in our minds and souls.

Because it is necessary to have opposite poles for us to appreciate the best there is in the universe. The only way we who are at the poles can direct events is through our influence. Otherwise, we are powerless and good and evil are equal and the same.

You said the Presence was stronger, I pointed out. *Does that mean evil dominates?*

It depends.

On what?

On whom we influence. Sometimes evil prevails. Sometimes it does not.

I sighed.

You bet on the wrong horse race. I looked to Pia to see if I had got the old, old Earth expression right.

You are half-Human and half-Zentadon, said the Good Presence. *Both suffered from the Indowy and their wicked inventions. You have the opportunity to prevent further evil from those times, to make amends for what was done to both peoples. You can be the right horse.*

I scoffed. *I see. I am the son of a Human whore and a Zentadon fool . . . and I can save the world?*

We have to use what is available.

Exasperated, I attempted to shut the GP out of my head. I felt it waiting, waiting.

Start a fire, it said.

What?

Start a fire.

How is that going to help? We will suffocate. The smoke has nowhere to go.

I cannot help. I can only influence. Start a fire.

If that will satisfy you . . .

It will satisfy you.

I felt around on the cave floor until I found a nest of dry twigs built by some small mammal. Using an energy stick left in Pia's battle harness, I soon had a fire going. The light from it revealed a rather large chamber. Instead of the smoke clotting in the chamber, it sucked into the back of the cave and down a small corridor. The cave had a back door!

That gave me an idea. But first I had to rest, regain strength.

We have made a wise choice in horses, said the Good Presence, sounding satisfied.

C·H·A·P·T·E·R
FIFTY ONE

DAY NINE, THE LAST DAY

Blade's only choices, if he would leave the planet, were to either kill Pia or leave with her. That meant he had to follow the signal given off by the Indowy artifact. He had thirty two hours — one Galaxia day, two Aldenia days if you counted each of the short nights — to accomplish his treacherous mission. We had the same thirty-two hours to accomplish ours.

I felt somewhat recovered, my ebbing spirits and courage restored, after sleeping three of the four hours of the longer night. I roused with a renewed sense of purpose and mission. It was up to me to make sure the Indowy box of evil vanished. Sen, warrior, and savior of the known world. Commander Mott would be stroking that useless tail of his furiously if he knew of my predicament. Even if I succeeded, however, no one must ever know about it, else scores of other adventurers, opportunists, pirates, and assorted riffraff, with or without tails, would descend upon the Dark Planet looking for other boxes that might have survived to make them rich.

Pia awoke and was solicitous of my injuries. Zentadon have amazing recuperative powers. My leg was stiff and painful, my chest plate beyond tender, I was hungry, I lacked sleep, the taa hormone was kicking in a little again and acting up under stress . . . Other than all that, I was five-by, good to go. I felt fully capable of kicking the ass of any one-hundred-year old deaf and blind paraplegic Human on Galaxia.

I didn't tell Pia that, though. I didn't want her to think of me as a braggart.

"It is a bit stiff," I said of my leg. "Wait here, lovely Human female. I will be right back."

I kicked up the fire again, adding another mammal nest of twigs, dried grass, and other stuff that stank worse than a lizard's breath. The lizards waiting outside barked sleepily. There was still some night to go.

Aided by the firelight, I followed smoke into the natural chimney. The cleft narrowed and squeezed around me so that soon I had to drop to my belly like a legless, blind reptile. I pulled myself forward and ever upward with the tips of my fingers and progress was measured in inches. I heard Pia coughing back in the chamber from the buildup of smoke. I was clogging the flue with my body.

I thought I tasted fresh air soaked with the incessant rain, but there was not even a trickle of water oozing down on me. That concerned me. An opening on top of the ridge would surely collect water, unless the chimney came out into another protected chamber or something. I had to hope for that.

I rested frequently, a necessity of my enfeebled condition. During one rest break, I probed with my mind and touched Blade in that unguarded moment of his first awakening. He was nearby, I could tell that. I sensed his desperate awareness that time was running out. Then he slammed the door on me, accompanied by a peal of thunder that crashed and rolled across the sky like pins in that silly alley game of Human prolies.

I breathed deeply for a few minutes, still tasting fresh air. I felt my way forward, unable to see so much as the backs of my eyelids. I came to a small opening that even my slender elfin body could not negotiate. I attempted to force myself through but without success. I touched around it. Nothing but rock and it apparently solid. Outside air circulating beyond mocked me with its inaccessibility.

I dropped my head on my arms. Moisture in my nostrils and in my eyes collected dry dust, making it difficult both to breathe and blink my eyes. Frustrated and all but defeated, I lay still for a few minutes and simply breathed.

It would soon be daylight. Blade would be coming to drive off the lizards with his rifle. Good for Sergeant

Kilmer. Then all he had to do was lob a grenade into the cave, fire a round from his Punch gun . . .

Goodbye cruel world, hello eternity. Rich Blade. Poor enslaved world once more ravished by the savage heirs of the recently pacified Indowy.

I had to keep fighting. If not for myself, then for Pia. And for the ultimate destruction of Pandora's box and the salvation of the galaxy. A lot of weight on one lowly Zentadon's shoulders.

I tested the small opening again, reaching through where the chamber widened once more. I felt some moisture in the dust. I ran my hand around the opening on the other side. There. A small rift in the rock, a tiny fracture. I pried my fingertips into it and worked and pulled until the moisture was my own blood and not rainwater.

I thought I detected a slight give in the rock. I concentrated my entire strength into it. Nothing. My muscles must surely snap from the effort, like a rubber band stretched too tautly.

Suddenly, the rock gave. A little pile of rubble came out with it. Elated, I shouldered my way through, using both hands to pull.

Another fifty feet of easy going and I saw the flash of lightning. Smoke boiled out behind me. The flue suddenly opened as I dropped from the chamber into another small cave. It was protected by a ledge with water pouring over its mouth like a curtain. I looked outside. It was still dark. Flashes of lightning revealed a forested valley twisting around to the east and paralleling the black river.

I gave smoke time to clear out of the chimney before I returned to where Pia waited. I explained my plan to her.

"Rest," I told her. "I will draw Blade and the lizards away from the cave. When I give you the word, head due north. You should make the black river within six hours or less."

"I can't leave without you, Kadar San!" she protested.

"You will not be leaving without me, Pia. We Zentadon believe we are eternal and that we become a part of the essences of those to whom we are closest. At least one of us must return to carry the intelligence about the Blobs."

"Kadar San. Let me come with you . . ."

"Hush." I placed my fingertips to her lips. "It is better this way. Besides, I will be back."

"I love you, Kadar San."

I thought of my father and mother and the bastard they produced who belonged comfortably in neither of their worlds. Now was not the time to confront it, however. There was a better than even chance that neither Blade nor I would be accompanying Pia on the pod shuttle when it took off. I had to keep our final minutes together light. For her sake, and for mine.

"Does this mean we are exclusive?" I asked.

That brought up another worry instead.

"Where will we go?" she asked. "We're against the law

within the Galaxia Republic."

"There has to be a place. Maybe we could go to Earth."

"Earth . . ." she whispered longingly. "I have heard there are places on Earth free of the mutants. Perhaps we really could go there."

"We will go," I promised.

"Do you think the Blobs are on Earth?"

"We will deal with the Blobs, then go to Earth."

That seemed to satisfy her.

We raided her combat harness for anything that might be useful to my scheme. Its pouch contained a clasp knife, some personal items, and a roll of what DRTs called "thousand-mile-a-minute" tape. It stuck like cement glue to anything it touched. Blade had taken everything else when he ransacked bodies after the killings.

"Perfect," I said, taking the tape.

The dying firelight reflected in the incredible blue pools of her eyes. She ran her hand through her black crop of hair, the way she did whenever she was upset or nervous. My ears twitched. She placed both hands over them. She kissed me tenderly.

There was nothing else to say. I rose quickly, picked up the black box, and headed for the chimney. It was the day of reckoning.

"Kadar San?"

I paused.

"I'll keep the light burning for you."

C·H·A·P·T·E·R
FIFTY TWO

The rules of the game were now under my control. I intended changing them. Since my plan called for leading the sniper into a trap, it was vital that I make new contact both with him and with the lizards, then break it again at the appropriate time after luring them away from Pia's cave. I derived considerable satisfaction in knowing that Pia had a chance, even if I didn't make it. Love was a strange Human condition. The word was applied emotionally to everything from "greasy Big Burgers" and fast hovercraft to pet terriers and each other. Zentadon had a single word, unpronounceable by Humans, which applied — and then only rarely — to the bonding of exclusives. Only death broke such a bond, not courts of divorce or a sweaty tryst with a non-mate on a long interstellar flight.

I felt that unpronounceable word for Pia Gunduli as

I squirmed back into the chimney and emerged into the open beneath the rain-veiled ledges on the ridge above. I permitted myself a moment of sadness as I waited for enough light to travel by. Then I shut it out. A hero did what a hero had to do and never looked back.

I plunged into a strengthening downpour and circled around to where I attracted the attention of the lizards. I took a chance on inciting another shot from Blade, whom I sensed vaguely in the vicinity, but it was a risk I had to take. If I didn't draw them away, the lizards seemed tenacious enough and one-tracked enough to lay siege to the cave for days. I needed to give Pia every possible advantage to make it safely to the pod.

"Hey!"

The big king of the reptiles jumped up and looked puzzled, inasmuch as a beast could look puzzled. He began barking surprised commands to the three survivors of his dwindling patrol. Although the lizards were intellectually evolved tooth and claw, so to speak, above the other inhabitants of this wet and dreary planet, they were still stupid. But not stupid enough to try to take me on face to face again. At least not right away. I was counting on their following me while they screwed up their courage and devised another pattern for my takedown.

It worked well enough. They fell in behind me at a distance, like a troupe of trained Hrimfaxi zantels the Humans captured and trained to entertain and pacify the prolies in their circuses. I counted on Blade following the signal from the Indowy Hell Box; that was his only choice.

Whenever the lizards got too close, became too froggy, to coin one of Pia's old, old Earth expressions, I turned and pointed the Punch Gun at them. They backed off, barking and grumbling among themselves.

I first angled toward the pod to make Blade think Pia and I were making a desperate run for it. Along the way, I captured a couple of the newt-things for breakfast. I had to have energy. I closed my eyes, put a damper on my returning taa and broke the backs of the little organisms, skinned them with my clasp knife, and ate the flesh raw. It immediately renewed my strength.

In spite of my injuries, I willed myself to function at some level above what I might have otherwise been capable by releasing minute traces of taa into my system. It reduced the pain of my leg wound and gave a modest sensation of well being. With it, I could do this job, accomplish what I and the GP expected of me.

I sensed Blade's bewilderment when I unexpectedly changed directions and headed as rapidly as I could for the large burn I had discovered a few days earlier. I expected him to be slightly ahead and to the northwest between me and the pod, where he would attempt to establish a hide from which he could launch a long-range ambush. My sudden change of directions to the hard east had to confuse him while it momentarily gave me the advantage of increasing the distance between us. He took the bait and followed. What other choice did he have?

Kadar San?

I am fit as your fiddle, Pia. What is a fiddle?

An instrument for making music.

I can hear the music. I will contact you telepathically from now on. Do not contact me unless it is an emergency. I must keep my mind clear. When I am thinking of you, it is not clear.

That is a compliment? She sounded pleased.

Yes.

Please take care.

It was a good feeling to have someone treasure me. It gave me strength and courage. I liked my Human side for perhaps the first time.

I counted on the burn being populated with herds of the giant Goliath beetles, as it had been the first time. They seemed to relish the new growths of pioneer weeds that sprouted in the wet char. I was not disappointed. Their dark forms dotted the burn, smudged and eerily ghost-like through the layered gray membranes of rain.

I made my way into the streambed with the high concealing banks that transfixed the burn. The water in it, relatively shallow before, now ran waist deep and slowed my progress. I was in the middle of a terrific storm, several of them, or so it seemed. Daylight was not much lighter than darkness, only a deep gray instead of black. Lightning furiously attacked the forest, splintering trees with a crashing bombardment that sounded like a nuclear cannon barrage delivered by Star War systems. A bolt of it lit up one of the beetles, detonating it, and splashing guts and blood and parts in a wide radius. His herd mates ignored him and kept on browsing in the rain.

I felt like the elements had turned against me. I listened for the Presence's hideous laughter.

The lizards followed me to where I entered the streambed at the edge of the burn. They hesitated, clearly undecided about venturing into the open. I yelled insults at them and waved. Agitated, they jumped about until anger overcame their inhibitions and they also took to the stream. They kept their distance. The beetles sensed their presence and began to bunch and move away and ahead.

Good. Exactly what my plan needed. I wanted the Goliaths on the move. Not stampeding, just moving. I hoped the lizards had fed recently and would not be distracted by so much food on legs.

I selected one of the "herd bulls," a huge six-legged creature with an enormous purple-black forward carapace. To support that bulk required an exoskeleton of a material far stronger than chitin. Although it would be an easy kill at near range with a Punch, I had discovered earlier that even Blade's Gauss would not always take down one of the creatures easily. That was important in the event he prematurely discovered what I was doing.

I backed the lindal with tape. I crouched as the herd

bull approached. Then I scrambled out of the stream and darted at the insect, trying to do this fast to reduce Blade's chances of discovering what I was doing. Always before, the beetles ignored Humans and Zentadon, as we were not in the local food chain, unless we appeared to be a direct threat.

The Goliath apparently perceived me as a threat. It whirled and caught me with an antenna that felt like a whip lash and knocked me rolling. I instantly sprang to my feet and circled the creature. It wheeled back to the left, but by then I was ready. I dashed in and leaped, slamming the sticky side of the lindal high on the giant's carapace.

It stuck. I fell back and scrambled to my feet and dashed for cover into a small copse of charred tree stumps. I hid there as the big insect, now carrying the case on its east side, continued south with its west side exposed toward Blade's approach. Later, I would have to recover the case, but it now served a more useful purpose.

I used taa and the masking herds to disappear out of the burn. I dropped exhausted into shrubbage near the treeline, leaving the lizards dumbfounded. I lay on my belly, panting to prevent lintatai, and watched as Blade entered the burn from the far northwest corner. He cut directly across, following the signal from the lindal and obviously assuming Pia and I were using the beetle herds as cover and concealment. His chameleons had apparently gone completely out by now, but he had nothing to fear from my short-range

Punch. Nor did he fear the predators. After all, wasn't he in his own mind the most efficient killing machine on the Dark Planet?

It was working.

The lizards made the beetles nervous and kept them moving. Blade followed the signal attached to the big bull Goliath. Having lost me, the lizards took up Blade's track at a respectful distance. The beetles, Blade, and the lizards moved across the burn and toward the tree-studded savannahs beyond.

Humans told an old Earth story with a moral. About how little creatures called lemmings periodically followed each other to die in the sea.

CHAPTER
FIFTY THREE

Over the generations and centuries and millennia of interstellar sentient evolution, we "intelligent" and "civilized" life forms developed technology to increasingly isolate ourselves from our environments. We broke or bent or changed all the natural laws to meet our demands for comfort, convenience, safety, and wealth. We wrenched control from nature and assumed it for ourselves. Nature was put at bay while we created, or so we thought, artificial habitats that met our own selfish requirements. There were many people — Human, Zentadon, Indowy, Kutaran, Terran — who lived their entire lives catered to by technology. They ate processed food the origin of which few knew, they worked through the media of artificial intelligence, which even fewer understood, they traveled by means almost none comprehended. They lived, worked, procreated, were entertained and pampered by artificial means. Some among us, the most wealthy, even managed to cheat death through the rejuv process, at least to some extent. Many individuals died without ever being truly alone with themselves and with nature. No wonder God had been wrenched from his throne.

But nature had her own little ways of snickering up her sleeve. The Kutaran generations lost their teeth, no longer needed for eating soft processed foods. We Zentadon were gradually giving up our tails, as the balance they provided for speed across open plains and savannahs proved unneeded in an age when most complained of sitting on their tails. Young among the Indowy were reared in colonies by the government; few females possessed teats for nursing infants and even sex was being done in test tubes. Humans were flabby, soft creatures, except for those like Gorilla, Sergeant Shiva, Atlas and Blade, who were provided with certain enhancements to facilitate their function as soldiers. Heaven only knew what the Blobs had given up as they became shapeless, sexless forms virtually indistinguishable one from the other and bent on a single collective goal; conquering the universe.

Within the few days since our landing on Aldenia, the members of DRT-213 had been thrust back into raw nature. Technology failed us piecemeal. The sensors, communications, monitors, robots, chameleons, processed foods, all environmental controls . . . gone. Death and the threat of death returned as a reality. I, a reformed predator, caught my food with my own hands, tearing it apart and eating it while it was still alive. Any dominance Blade or I professed over other creatures on the Dark Planet would vanish the moment we used our last bullet from weapons created worlds away. The lizards, the scorpion-things, the giant snakes, they understood nothing of our sovereignty, would not understand it even as they tore our flesh from our bones and ate it, as I tore flesh from the newts.

How much more irony could nature deal out than to drop two "civilized" beings into a savage world and pit them against each other *mano a mano*, as the humans put it? Without our weapons, Blade and I would be thrown back to fighting tooth and claw. How much indeed had we advanced when stripped of artificial accouterments? I pictured God back on his throne while the Presence and the Good Presence acted as referees, each partial to its own champion and eager to bestow upon him any advantage. Nature might be impartial, destroying equally the good and the bad, the smart and the stupid, but the forces within natures were anything but.

Sens were amateur philosophers. How could it be otherwise for those of us whose profession encouraged the exploration and reading of others' thoughts and emotions?

I restlessly sifted for mood and tone coming from either Blade or the lizards. The lizards were easy to read, being fairly uncomplicated beasts of revenge attached to stomachs. Blade proved more of a challenge. He kept his mind locked down for the most part, knowing that I located him through his cognitive waves, much in the same way that he positioned me with the sensor bug on the Indowy Hell Box. He was about to find out, however, that technology could be deceptive and manipulated.

My ears twitched in anticipation as I broke off the trail and took to the high country. I cut a path to intercept ahead of the one being inscribed by the beetles, Blade, and the lizards. Hunter instincts previously dormant surfaced so that my wounds, aches, and pains were relegated to some locked room in my brain. Commander Mott of the broken tail always said that a Zentadon was physically capable of much more than he ever realized. He only had to be tested under real life circumstances. It was all in the mind, he lectured. The mind was the engine that powered the machine. The machine kept going as long as the mind continued to function.

Thank you, Commander Mott. I wondered if he had ever been tested beyond the breaking of his tail.

It was more satisfying being the hunter than the hunted.

The herds of lumbering beetles, mere monstrous gray forms through the swirling clouds and shimmer of rain, illuminated into frequent brief highlights by the pop of lightning, were being funneled into a boulder-strewn narrows between the descending apexes of two mossy hills. There the burn ended. I squatted under cover on one of the hills and scanned below, watching as Blade darted and dodged, maneuvering in an attempt to catch a sight picture of either Pia or me among the Goliaths. He was bare headed after finally discarding his malfunctioning helmet. The beetles appeared jittery, either because of the activity among them or the increasing ferocity of the storms, maybe both. They milled, circling and kind of rearing up on their back sets of legs to test with their antennae before continuing their forced march toward the narrows.

Blade seemed so focused and intent running across the burn among the bugs, trying to locate his prey, that he paid no attention to the remaining four lizards in the pack. The lizards were as centered upon him as he was upon what he thought was me and the treasure. Time was running out. For him. For all of us. I tasted his desperation when he relaxed enough at moments to let out traces of himself.

The lizards cautiously kept to the cover of the streambed. The stream twined toward the narrows. All forces were converging there. I pulled myself up by my shoe laces, an old, old Earth expression, sucked it in, and hobbled as fast as I could toward the collision point. The element of surprise should get me close enough to neutralize Blade's advantage with the Gauss and place us into dueling range with Punch Guns.

It was going to be shootout time in the rocks. It required extreme extra effort to control my taa output. Even if I won, I could also lose.

Life is a choice and a chance, said the GP.

It wouldn't be long now before Blade discovered the hoax. I figured he would catch on about the time he reached the narrows. I thought I heard fiendish chuckles coming muffled through the fury of the storms. I thought the Presence sounded less self-assured than before.

C·H·A·P·T·E·R
FIFTY FOUR

By an effort of which I thought myself incapable under the circumstances, without using taa, I made it to the narrows ahead of most of the Goliath beetles, Blade, and the trailing lizard pack. I selected a knotted slab of limestone and black volcanic rock overlooking the narrows and burrowed into a slot among mossy boulders and bushes. From this vantage point I overlooked the stream as it came out of the burn and passed through into savannah and forest beyond. The ground lay open on either bank of the creek, although it was strewn with glacial rock and boulders, some of which were as large as dwellings on Galaxia.

A few of the lead beetles moved past, pushed by those behind, who in turn were being pressed by the predator reptiles. I squinted into the storm deluge, wiping at the rain driven into my face, blinking against the almost-constant flicker, flash, and pop of lightning. Even with the fireworks, my view was limited because of the heavy rain. Water filled the stream and swept off the hill around me in a solid liquid veneer.

My home planet of Ganesh was an arid place in which rain was virtually worshipped. Zentadon had more than one hundred words for rain. Until now, I never thought I could dislike rain.

The giant beetle insects appeared in dark spots of one or two or in dark clumps of several. They gradually took shape as they approached, brought on and off into relief by the lightning. They passed like silent monarchs in a fog. I was suddenly afraid I would not see Blade before he made it through the pass, or that he would detect me first.

That wasn't going to happen, I reassured myself. There was too much sky activity to light up the terrain. As for his spotting me, I had to believe his LF had gone completely on the blink. Otherwise, he would not be chasing the box on the Goliath and assuming it was Pia and me.

Thinking of my enemy and my designs on his well-being loosed a slight reservoir of taa into my system. I began to get light-headed. It was good to know I still had a cache left. I needed to preserve it for the showdown. I deliberately thought of other things.

Pia?

Because of her Talent, so easily developed, we were reaching the point where we no longer had to differentiate

372 # CHARLES W. SASSER

between modes of communications; thoughts and words were becoming one. She was waiting for me on the edge of her consciousness.

I am here, Kadar San. Are you all right?

I am good.

Can you show me where you are, what you are doing? she asked.

I relayed a clip of the storm in the pass and the beetles lumbering past like giant specters. I masked the fact that I lay in wait to kill the Human when he approached, after which, if I were able, I would reclaim the Hell Box.

The shorter night will soon come, I told her. *As soon as it is light again, go to the pod as quickly as you can. Are you rested? Can you make it?*

I can if you promise you will be there.

Keep the light burning for me.

I blocked her out for my own sanity. Still no sight of Blade. I readjusted my head rag to cover any glint of golden hair. I checked the makeshift bandage on my thigh. It was wet and muddy. Lichen or mold or something equally disgusting seemed to be growing on it. Undoubtedly it also grew on the wound itself. After this was over, if I pulled through, I was going to require a great deal of physical therapy. Perhaps psychological therapy as well. No current Zentadon had ever killed another sentient and survived it.

But I was half-Human, wasn't I?

I lay on my belly on the slab of rock to make of myself a

smaller target. Runoff water laked behind the dam I formed. I drew my Punch. I had to make the three remaining shots count. I used an upcropping of rock as a weapon rest. The gun was stubby in a flat black color. Considering what I had to do, it seemed almost too heavy for me to lift. I heard my heart thudding against the rock underneath. I closed my eyes and concentrated to stop the release of taa to bring on that state of Zen in which it was almost like you and your body became two separate entities. The body functioned while you, the real you, hovered somewhere aloof from it and watched. Snipers called it "getting into the bubble." I never understood what that meant until now.

I got into my bubble. I opened my eyes. Weapon in hand, ready, I waited for Blade to come to me.

C·H·A·P·T·E·R
FIFTY FIVE

He came, only not the way I expected. I had him in my sights, following him with the Punch barrel in the frenzied stutter flash of lightning and waiting for him to come within range. I was coping with taa too. Big bugs crept all over the landscape, splashing. There was Blade, darting about among them like a mother who had just lost her only child in a crowd of perverts. I kept losing him and finding him again.

Then I had him. He was near enough that I saw the intense look on his face as, puzzled, he tried to discern me out of the insect horde. I had heard that it was easier to kill in the heat of battle than it was to look a man in the eyes at close distance and drop the hammer on him. That made it personal, you and him. It was almost like murder.

A trained sniper would not have hesitated. Not only

was I not a trained sniper, I possessed within my Zentadon side generations of compunction against killing. I hated the Human for what he had done. I wanted to see him dead for Pia's sake, for my sake, for the sake of the Galaxia forces who waited for word about the Blobs, and for the sake of future civilizations that would be destroyed if the genie was not exterminated. But I hesitated, and in that hesitation lost the opportunity to end things quickly.

I clearly saw, even through the rain, the expression on his face when he spotted the lindal taped to the side of the big herd beetle. It was a combination of elation turning to dismay and then rage when he realized he had been duped. While he might have the treasure, he had no way of getting off the planet with it. His eyes shifted in the direction of the pod, which he clearly expected to see blasting off without him aboard it.

This time my trap had not failed.

Suddenly, a howl so primordial that certainly no mortal throat emitted it. Only something disembodied from flesh and its constraints could have expelled such a raw note of emotion. It came from Blade, yet it was more than Blade. It was Blade and the Presence conjoined. Their unleashed rage stabbed into my brain like a bolt of electricity. I dropped my Punch and grabbed my head with both hands.

Blade went on a sudden rampage, throwing a tantrum. His Punch slapped, recycled, and slapped again. He was shooting up the herd in his mindless fury. He shot two or three as they ran across the little creek. Green-pink blood slime mixed with the water and was quickly washed away.

He lost sight of the "herd bull" wearing the lindal. He looked for it again, found it, and shot it. The Goliath crashed to the ground and rolled onto its back. All six legs thrummed the air like trees in a hurricane. I saw the black box still stuck to its side.

Blade ran for the case, carrying his Punch in one hand and the Gauss rifle in the other. Another beetle got in his way and he disintegrated the front half of it with his Punch. He screamed in his fury, but it was only his voice this time. The Presence had abandoned him, as though sensing it was time to fold on this losing hand.

My head cleared. I snatched up my Punch and pointed it at the darting figure. Although a Punch delivered tremendous kill power, it was not an area weapon like a grenade. Getting close didn't always count.

Wind shrieked through the pass as though the storms chose that opportune moment to let loose. Blade staggered, almost lost his footing. A gust snatched off my head rag and flung it through the air like a crippled bird.

I glimpsed Blade along the line of my barrel.

C·H·A·P·T·E·R
FIFTY SIX

It was time to cut bait or fish, as Pia might have put it. With Blade looming in my gun sights, I took a deep breath and squeezed the trigger.

Too quickly. I knew even as I fired that my subconscious prohibition against killing had kicked in and diverted my aim. The projectile struck the already dead bull beetle instead. It exploded in a shower of guts and exoskeleton, legs, and antenna parts. The lindal from its demolished side flew into the clouds. At first, I thought it would land on my bank of the creek. It hit on Blade's side instead.

Fanger! Fanger! Fanger! the GP warned shrilly in my head.

My last little cache of taa kicked in, allowing me to instantly propel myself from the slab of limestone. I landed in a cluster of boulders in the pass by the stream. The slab where I had lain disappeared in a shower of rock and vegetative debris as Blade opened fire.

Blade's war cry cut through the tempest. "Fu-uck! Fu-uck!"

I felt light-headed as I peered around my stone shield. I caught a fleeting glimpse of Blade darting among the moving beetles, using them for cover as he maneuvered on my position. I also tasted the return of the Presence. It hadn't deserted Blade after all. Apparently, it decided to stay in for one more hand.

Blade's blazing eyes located me. His Punch came up with unnerving speed. I ducked and lunged for other boulders nearby. My previous hide exploded behind me. I rolled and came up for my own shot.

Blade had disappeared. My eyes frantically searched the boulder fields on the other side of the stream. Beetles lumbered about everywhere like eerie tanker ships in the rain.

I dared not stay in the same position too long. I dropped to my belly and low-crawled to new cover. It was a trick I had learned from Blade when he massacred the team: disappear in one location, reappear in another.

"Elf?"

Blade's disembodied voice came from the boulder field. I peered around my own cover rock, attempting to locate him. The beetles were in the way. Driven by the lizards, they kept coming to cross the creek.

"Elf, I'm talking to you."

The voice came from a different direction. I didn't dare reply. That was what he wanted.

"You thought you had won, huh? Fu-uck. You ain't got the balls to win. You Zentadon can't kill. Don't you know that by now?"

He switched locations again. He was closer the next time he spoke. He sounded somewhere off to my right.

"Let me tell you how this scenario is going to play out," he taunted. "You had your chance at me and fucked it up. You made it easy. See that box? It's already as good as mine. I got plenty of time to take care of you and the cunt and make it back to the pod."

He changed locations again. Even nearer.

"I'm coming now to wax your ass. After which I'll take care of the cunt. Maybe I'll fuck her first. What do you think about that? If she screws you, she'll screw anything."

Wind howled. Rain drove in horizontal slants against me with such force that it stung. I clutched my gun in both trembling hands and peeped cautiously out of hiding. I saw nothing out there except the watery outlines of boulders and giant beetles, with the muddy swollen stream flowing between us. The beetles remained oblivious of the little drama being played out between Blade and me.

I looked up and down the stream. I thought I glimpsed the lizards downstream, but I couldn't be sure. The Hell Box, the cause of all this, lay on Blade's side of the creek where it had fallen. Blade was still nowhere in sight.

Where was he?

I fell back in exhaustion from the use of taa. Light-headedness was making me dizzy. I had never experienced lintatai. Few had and survived. Judging from the symptoms, however, I surmised I was in lintatai's beginning stages. Light-headedness, a growing sense of disorientation and disconnection, dreaminess... I shook my head. I didn't have much time left before I either exploded or went zombie.

For all my braggadocio and internal posturing about killing that human out there, I simply couldn't do it when the time came. My resolve and my hand wavered. The taboo against Zentadon killing ran too deeply. I missed my chance and now Blade was going to do exactly what he said he was going to do.

"I'm coming!" Blade yelled. His howl came punctuated with thunder and lightning, wind and driving rain.

Killing is not the same as murder, the GP argued inside my head.

I am trying.

Try.

You can only influence, not help? Even now?

Even now, said the Good Presence.

You are a weak old aunt.

Am I?

I collected my senses and sent them out exploring. After his initial rage, Blade shut down again and I couldn't find him.

"Elf? You were right. I killed everyone before just as I killed everyone this time."

Why was he telling me this?

"You know what? I enjoyed it. I want you to know I enjoyed it because I'm going to enjoy killing you. Are you ready, Freddy?"

Humans were strange creatures.

I fought off lintatai. If I could only squeeze out a few more minutes. I looked out again and this time I caught Blade as he jumped out from behind a rock and used a fording beetle as cover to cross the creek to my side. My hands were still consumed by uncontrollable trembling.

I winged a shot at him. I couldn't be sure this time why I missed, whether because of the taboo or my shaking hands. The bullet streaked out to the limit of its short range and simply vanished without an explosion or anything.

"Here I come!" Blade called out.

I rolled over onto my back and looked up into the rain. Light-headedness was fast turning to a sense of well-being and contentment. It was very pleasurable. All my cares dissipated, as though turning to mist and being swept away by the storms. In the distance I heard the triumphant shriek of the Presence.

I laughed back at it, truly happy for one of the few times in my life. It was the moment that counted, and nothing beyond.

C·H·A·P·T·E·R
FIFTY SEVEN

Lintatai was always fatal. The victim tranced out into another world until he slowly died; he blew up from the heat and energy; or, in my case, his enemy walked up on him while he was transfixed and shot him into little bitty pieces. Carefully, as though placing a treasured item into safekeeping, I lay the Punch Gun with its two remaining energy bullets on the ground by my side. I rolled over and pulled myself up to lean my back against the boulder. The wet chill deep in my bones went away as my body began to heat up.

Deep inside somewhere where there was some Human left, I realized I was entering a state of lintatai. I had fooled around with taa once too often and had now lost control. Drug-induced euphoria was setting in. My limbs felt dipped in warm cement. I couldn't move. What's more, I didn't want to move.

I was going to sit right here and enjoy. I smiled up into the storm, not realizing until now how beautiful lightning really was, or how much I liked the feel of the rain and the wind on my face.

I felt warm and as comfortable as though I were back on Galaxia in my own quarters, about to go to sleep in that safe stage before unconsciousness.

"I'm coming, elf."

Blade's voice sounded near, very near, but why should I care? I was going to make do. I laughed happily and reached out with one finger to nudge wonderful black clouds racing past my head. I lounged in the monsoon and played with the scuttling clouds. Everything but the clouds was out of my hands. All my choices were being made for me. Rules kept changing. Thing is, I didn't really care.

Annoying thought-voices banged and shouted in my head. The GP, who was only supposed to influence, was influencing in such a loud voice that my teeth rattled.

Go away, go away, I resisted. *Can you not see how happy I am?*

It's an illusion, cried the GP.

Oh, I do like the illusion. Bring me another cocktail of it.

Another voice came in, summoned by the GP. It pleaded and begged in mounting distress.

Please, Kadar San . . . Tearful. *Kadar San, please get control!*

We are never in control.

Kadar San, he's going to kill you. Please listen. It's me. Pia. I don't want to leave without you.

Go with your God, Pia. There are not two opposites after all. Everything is the same.

The GP gave up arguing. Instead, it showed me what was happening. In my mounting lintatai state, I witnessed a scene as through a VR or as one of the old-fashioned movies still viewed by the Human prolies.

Crouched and so strung out with tension that he almost hopped across the ground, Blade advanced on my position. He had slung the Gauss and gripped his Punch Gun with both hands, arms thrust straight out in front of him, sweeping, like an Enforcer arresting a dangerous criminal. Water ran from his brutal crew cut and veiled the dark hollows of his cave-like eyes. This Human man would not hesitate.

His heavy face remained on point, but his eyes flicked toward the Indowy lindal lying in the weeds. Greed and triumph flecked into them and he permitted himself a grim, humorless smile.

He was winning after all, or so he thought, and with plenty of time left to make the pod's schedule.

"Gun Maid? Listen, cunt. You and the elf give up this shit. It's over."

He still thought Pia was with me here. I smiled dreamily. She was going to be safe.

Water streamed from his cammies. Cautious and taut, he was the consummate predator aware of every small changing nuance of his environment. The GP must have been playing the same scene for Pia. Her voice inside my head grew thin and strident as Blade advanced on me.

Oh, God, Kadar San! Can't you hear me? Wake up. He's coming. Kadar San, he's coming!

He is coming? Who is coming?

Don't you remember, Kadar San. Blade. He's coming.

Oh. Blade. The ugly Human? The mean Human? Does he have fleas?

I thought that funny and sat there chuckling to myself.

Blade halted at the unexpected sound. A scowl transformed his face into something hideous, an old Frankenstein monster face irradiated by a sky charged with electricity. Suspicious, he pressed forward slowly, ready to fire at the first movement.

He is part Human, the GP babbled desperately to Pia.

Inch by war inch, Blade neared where I sat happily waiting for him to finish me off. In another few steps he would have me in sight.

I still didn't care.

He is part Human, the GP declared.

What was that supposed to mean? I felt a jolt as recognition swept through Pia's mind. Suddenly, the tone of her thought-voice changed from pleading and tears to chiding and harsh.

Sergeant Kadar San, get your cowardly ass off the ground. Are you willing to sit there like your Zentadon ancestors and play victim? Think about the taa camps. None of you had the gonads to do anything about it till the Humans made a revolution. You're part Human. Kadar San, damn you, act like it!"

Go away! I retorted.

That's right, she shot back. *Get mad. Do something about it instead of sitting there like a knot on a log or a wart on a frog . . .*

Old, old Earth expression?

One more step. Blade craned his neck to look around the boulder.

Kadar San, he's going to shoot your fraidy-cat elf ass. Desperation and horror returned to her voice.

The sense of well-being was leaving. I didn't want it to leave.

Pick up the gun, Kadar San!

I hated the rain in my face. I never wanted to see rain again. I reached for the Punch Gun as though awaking from a dream. I picked it up.

Blade's mask of a face appeared. I looked up directly into the muzzle of his Punch Gun.

Shoot him, Kadar San!

Blade laughed, but it was not him; it came, deep and hellish, from the rotted soul of the Presence.

I attempted to roll away and get a shot at the same time, knowing even as I thought it that it was too late. The sniper had the drop on me. My one consolation was knowing Pia had made it.

"You're wasted, elf," Blade snarled.

The trigger squeeze never came. A savage part of the clouds fell on Blade. The lizard snatched him off the ground and tossed him high into the air, like a baby fanger toying with its live prey.

Blade was too mean to give up without a fight. Even as he was being flung from one animal to the jaws of the next, he got off a shot that exploded the first creature.

The second reptile, one of the big kings, caught him in the air and snapped off Blade's leg. A hideous scream of pain and terror. The sniper fell helpless at the animal's feet.

The lizards were coming for me next!

I shot the king into all his component parts. Seeing the leader disintegrated took the fight out of the remaining two. They barked and leapt back into the woods from which they had emerged in ambush. I heard them crashing through the forest in retreat.

There followed an eerie quiet. Even the storm slackened. I labored to my feet, swaying a little, not fully recovered from lintatai and all the other hardships of past days. I kept my eyes on Blade as I slowly approached. He blinked up at me.

"My leg . . .?" he murmured.

I retrieved his Punch from where it had fallen alongside and shoved it into my belt. I relieved him of the Gauss and slung it over my own shoulder. I stood over him and aimed my weapon at his head. My hand did not waver this time.

Blade stopped blinking and glared at me. "Fu-uck," he growled. "You haven't the balls."

"You forget," I said. "I am half-Human."

I felt absolutely nothing. No taa, no emotion. I was empty. Killing was not so difficult if you were Human.

No.

It was the GP.

Killing is not always murder, but murder is always murder. You cannot destroy evil by the use of evil. You take part of the evil with you.

I cannot take him with me to the pod. There is not time. I haven't the strength.

We have prevailed, counseled the GP. *But I can only influence.*

After a moment, I dropped the Punch and let it hang from my hand at the end of my arm. I looked down upon

Blade and he glared back with his baleful, unrepentant caves.

"I knew you didn't have the balls," he said. "Now, patch me up before I bleed to death."

Blood oozed out the stub of his right leg. The lizard's teeth had cauterized the main artery. Nonetheless, untreated, he would still bleed to death before the coming of light after the approaching shorter night. He remained a threat to me, and to the galaxy, every minute he remained alive.

I knelt at his side and applied a tourniquet fashioned from a piece of his own dirty uniform. That would see him through for awhile longer. I gave an ear flick as I stood up again. Blade seemed to suddenly realize my intentions.

"You aren't going to leave me here alone!" he exclaimed.

"No," I agreed.

He still looked dubious.

"I'm going to leave this with you."

I placed my Punch Gun on the ground about ten meters away. I kept his, and I kept the Gauss. I might need them. The Presence seemed uncharacteristically chastened during all this.

"By the time you reach the weapon," I said conversationally, "I will be out of range and well on my way to catching the pod with Sergeant Gunduli. The Punch Gun has one energy bullet remaining. Sergeant Shiva said I was not to leave a live trooper behind. I would suggest you use the bullet before the lizards regain their courage and return."

AFTERWORD

The Dark Planet appeared on the view screen of the orbiting Stealth, its boils of lightning burbling on its crust. A destroyer sent from the dreadnought *Tsutsumi* flickered into sight on the screen and launched a wave of small-yield kinetic energy strikes against the Blob coordinates supplied by Sergeant Gunduli. She shuddered, reached, and took my hand. Ground-based missiles and beams from the Tslek decoy camp on Aldenia blazed to intercept, providing a spectacularly brief fireworks show that was, as Pia put it, mostly sound and fury without substance. After all, there was no real power in the Blob camp. Only a single soldier with a bunch of holograms and a few weapons to put on a show and make the Republic think it was an advance base.

The destroyer's systems tracked in on the fake base and hammered it into mushroom clouds. Meanwhile, I knew, the main Galaxia fleet was elsewhere preparing for a great war. DRT-213 — what was left of it, two of us — had reported back in time to prevent significant forces being lured off the line to Aldenia. The fate of the Galaxia Republic, as Pia put it, might have been decided by a Zentadon.

I smiled thinly. "Half-Human, half Zentadon," I said.

Extraction of the Stealth from the Dark Planet's gravity began. The ship accelerated out of its orbit and whipped back around Aldenia's two moons and onto a trajectory for redocking with the *Tsutsumi*. As soon as the ship slipped from gravity's pull and the G-forces bled off, I prepared to eject the lindal from the garbage port.

"There'll be an investigation," Pia pointed out. "The loss of the team does not have a good explanation without the box to confirm it."

"I choose not to give Humans or any other race or species the ability to artificially control one another," I said with a determined ear flick. "Pandora's box will vanish forever into a black hole, like a grain of sand on the desert. Higher-higher will just have to believe us that the soldiers of DRT-213, including Sergeant Blade Kilmer, died bravely battling our way back to the pod."

The lindal propelled free of the craft. Pia and I stood together before the view screen and watched it tumble away until it became less than another speck of sand on the vast beach that was space. It would induce no more evil. Perhaps it was my imagination, but I thought I heard the

Presence shriek with disappointment.

"We may have seen the last of it," Pia said, "but we have not seen the last of evil."

I looked at her. She smiled, suddenly shy.

"I do not think I have the Human part of me accomplished yet," I said.

Oh? What on Earth could you mean?

I am speaking particularly of the kiss.

"We have two whole Galaxia days before we redock with the *Tsutsumi*," Pia pointed out demurely. "Practice makes perfect."

An old, old Earth expression?

Hush! How can you kiss with your mind going like that?

I was thinking that if you had a tail . . .

THE END

LORDS OF DARKNESS
VOL: I
THE SOULLESS

L.G. BURBANK

AN UNLIKELY HERO . . .

Mordred Soulis is the chosen one, the man
ancient legends claim will save the world from
great evil. There's only one problem. Before
Mordred can become the hero of mankind, he
must first learn to embrace the vampyre within.

A FORGOTTEN RACE . . .

With the help of a mysterious order, a king of
immortals and a shape-shifting companion,
Mordred is set on a dangerous course that will
either save the human race or destroy it.

A TIMELESS STRUGGLE . . .

Journeying across the sands of the Byzantine Empire; in
the time of the Second Crusade, to the great Pyramids
of Egypt and then on to the Highlands of Scotland,
Mordred will face the Dark One. This evil entity is both
Mordred's creator and the Soul Stealer he has become.
As champion of mortals, Mordred must accept his
vampyre-self . . . something he has vowed never to do.

ISBN#0974363960
$6.99
Available Now
www.lgburbank.com

For more information

about other great titles from

Medallion Press, visit

www.medallionpress.com